Anne Marsh writes sex romances because the‿‿‿‿‿‿ more happy ending. Sh‿‿‿‿‿‿ getting laid off from he.‿‿‿ quickly decided happily-ever-afters trumped software manuals. She lives in North Carolina with her two kids and three cats.

Discover more at afterglowbooks.co.uk

THE CODE FOR LOVE

ANNE MARSH

All rights reserved including the right of reproduction in whole or in part in any form. This edition is published by arrangement with Harlequin Enterprises ULC.

This is a work of fiction. Names, characters, places, locations and incidents are purely fictional and bear no relationship to any real life individuals, living or dead, or to any actual places, business establishments, locations, events or incidents. Any resemblance is entirely coincidental.

Without limiting the author's and publisher's exclusive rights, any unauthorised use of this publication to train generative artificial intelligence (AI) technologies is expressly prohibited. HarperCollins also exercise their rights under Article 4(3) of the Digital Single Market Directive 2019/790 and expressly reserve this publication from the text and data mining exception.

® and ™ are trademarks owned and used by the trademark owner and/or its licensee. Trademarks marked with ® are registered with the United Kingdom Patent Office and/or the Office for Harmonisation in the Internal Market and in other countries.

First Published in Great Britain 2025 by
Afterglow Books by Mills & Boon, an imprint of HarperCollins*Publishers* Ltd
1 London Bridge Street, London, SE1 9GF

www.harpercollins.co.uk

HarperCollins*Publishers*
Macken House, 39/40 Mayor Street Upper,
Dublin 1, D01 C9W8, Ireland

The Code for Love © 2025 Anne Marsh

ISBN: 978-0-263-39755-0

0725

This book contains FSC™ certified paper and other controlled sources to ensure responsible forest management.

For more information visit: www.harpercollins.co.uk/green

Printed and Bound in the UK using 100% Renewable Electricity at CPI Group (UK) Ltd, Croydon, CR0 4YY

This book is for all my fellow armchair travelers
who plot imaginary journeys on Pinterest.
Where shall we go next?

One

The asteroid floats in space like a rocky hedgehog. It's a tiny hippo filling the viewport of my spacecraft. A baby moonlet hugging a larger asteroid, a speck of infant rock wrapped in glowing ribbons of nebulae. This is my happy place. This is my *jam*.

I shift my gaze from the viewport to the controller in my hand, tapping the minus button beneath the sticker that reads EARTH TO PANDORA to bring up my galaxy map. The data scrolling over my screen has me relaxing, the kinks in my spine popping. Numbers make sense. Numbers are easy to understand.

Space mining is part treasure hunt, part science. Beneath the asteroid's crusty, untouched surface runs a sparkling vein of pink geode, and I'm the only miner for a light-year. No one visits this galaxy. They refuse and mutter predictably bad excuses. *The cost of fuel is prohibitive. Who wants to dodge asteroids the size of battleships?*

I do. A girl needs a hobby, after all.

Since I travel alone and have no one to tell me this is a terrible idea, I guide my spacecraft down onto the rubble-strewn surface, dodging house-sized boulders to perch gingerly on loose rock. When I don't sink, I congratulate myself. *Well done, me!*

A series of calculations flicker across my screen. Even though I've meticulously planned each minute of my trip, I steal two seconds to snap a photograph of the milky band of cosmic dust floating overhead. Starlight turns the soot-like bits of dying stars a dusky red. I'll post it on an online forum, where it will get no views or likes.

There is no one to talk me through this, no mission control center, no recovery convoy. I'd just irritate them anyhow. People make things complicated.

I suit up. Geodes don't collect themselves. The air lock depressurizes, then hisses and pops.

Something surges outside the viewport. I glance over, startled out of the space simulator I'm playing on my game console and back into IRL by this unfamiliar deviation. My breathing picks up as my body releases adrenaline. *No.* This is my world, my safe space. I'm here for rocks, not *human contact*.

The man rushing toward me through the near darkness is muscled, a broad-shouldered package wrapped in black neoprene. Wet hair falls around the chiseled lines of his face in glorious, riotous waves. He could be the star of a shampoo commercial, and that's before he shoves a hand through the waves, carelessly, effortlessly lasering in on…me? He's the most beautiful thing I've ever seen, balancing with feline grace on top of his hovercraft.

No. Not a hovercraft. A surfboard.

"Hellooooo," he hollers.

He adds an arm wave.

As if I'd overlook someone the size of a lumberjack (not that I've actually met one) with muscles on his muscles. He's an unexpected invitation to stare.

So, I do. Blatantly.

He's not a stranger, I realize. I've previously ogled him—on the down-low and entirely surreptitiously—on multiple prior occasions. Strictly for work-related reasons, of course. He stars in the YouTube videos the marketing team for Miles to Go has assembled to promote our software. Marketing determined a sexy, shirtless surfer would get more clicks, eyeballs, hits, and other body parts to pay attention to our new app. This is a successful strategy.

Fun fact: Ozzy Wylder has tremendous appeal. This makes him the perfect smoke screen to draw attention away from the tsunami of bugs my engineering team has yet to squash. No one cares if the product doesn't work when Ozzy smiles at them.

Sometimes, even *I* don't care. The man is downright lethal to productivity.

For some reason—a reason that absolutely does not concern me at all—he's in the ocean rather than up on the pier at the company launch party.

I. Don't. Care.

I drag my gaze back to my screen. I have gcodes to mine. Space rocks to add to my collection. Unexplored planets in the Crystal Cluster Cosmos to explore. Ozzy Wylder's thoughtless surfing is *ruining* my self-care time.

He's still talking to me. *At* me. Why?

"I'm coming in hot!" he yells. His loud voice booms off the pilings of the pier I'm hiding beneath.

I glare at him as I switch off my video game console and zip it into my tote bag, but he's oblivious to his interruption. He punctuates his noise with waving and pointing, expansive gestures that I can't be bothered to interpret. Mostly because I'm now concentrating on the impressive muscles flexing beneath his wetsuit. He is mesmerizing.

"Incoming!" He glides toward shore on a nineteen-inch-wide piece of wood as if he's strolling along a sidewalk. He's such a show-off. Fortunately, a roar of sound from the party drowns out whatever he says next.

I'm supposed to be at that party, a boardwalk-themed launch for the hotel booking application I've worked on ninety hours a week for the majority of my adult life. Ironically, I've devoted my professional hours to selling vacations to other people when I hate traveling myself. I'm Camp Stay Home.

When I'm not mining virtual space rocks for my collection, I'm a software programmer. This means I spend 10 percent of my time coding and 90 percent in team meetings where we argue over a never-ending list of bugs and changing specs from the executive management team that has an average age of twenty-one. At twenty-nine, I am ancient and will spontaneously combust like a vampire in sunlight the day I turn thirty.

Up until this morning, it was unclear if we would have a product to launch today, so the party overhead is merited. The feat of coding that I pulled off after three consecutive all-nighters deserves fireworks. Possibly a confetti cannon. I casually completed the big bug fix yesterday. *Ho hum, no need to thank me but I just rewrote your entire product and made it work.* I'm sleep-deprived and underappreciated, but it's worth it, right?

Ozzy glides the remaining feet to shore, all muscled and coordinated. He bestows a grin on me and jumps off the board into the knee-deep water, splashing about and doing mysterious things to his surfboard. Crooning sweet nothings to it. It is a *good boy* and an *awesome ride*. It is THE BEST BOARD EVER! I try and fail to imagine someone saying these things to me, about my code.

I'm no longer certain that the law of time is immutable. A quick check of my smartwatch confirms that fifty-seven endless minutes remain before I can awkwardly excuse myself to go home to hide in my cozy loft. It will take an hour to get there thanks to the nightmare that is San Francisco traffic.

Watching Ozzy, however, I grudgingly add a check mark in the plus column of partying. Is this why people go out and interact with other people? He unzips his wetsuit to his waist, uncovering a Viking-worthy chest. I ignore the words coming out of his mouth—they're polite, hi-how-are-ya syllables and therefore unimportant—in favor of admiring my view.

No wonder beach vacations are so popular.

God, he's gorgeous.

I'm a weak person, because I'm disappointed that he settles for shrugging out of the top half of the wetsuit.

Even though he's not technically a coworker, ogling him is more complicated than the simple social calculus that declares him a popular extrovert and me an introverted hermit. I work for the software company that hired him to be the public face of their new product—or at least to say good things about it on his social media. I am boss-adjacent. He also has approximately a million social media followers, give or take a few. They likely share my interest in his tattoos.

The wetsuit descends to his waist, revealing a delightful collection of ridges, grooves, and stomach muscles. I am in no way prepared for spotting this six-pack in the wild.

Even though it's darker than a black hole under this stupid pier, I can still tell that he's sun-bronzed and glowing, a veritable golden boy. He could do shampoo or self-tanner commercials. He probably has. Right now, though, he blithely finishes peeling his arms out of his sleeves. The empty neoprene flaps around him like the discarded skin of a snake. A... butterfly chrysalis?

I'm no expert in living creatures.

Or living.

Perhaps I should reconsider my life choices? Attempt voluntary people contact? I frown. Try to categorize Ozzy. Blink sand out of my eyes. Conversation is not in my skillset, but I give it a stab in the interests of self-reinvention.

"Are you aware that juvenile great white sharks tend to be active in this area after dark? They're not just beyond the surf break." He's still knee-deep in water, so oblivious to the potential danger posed by five-foot-long baby sharks that I half expect to see a fin splitting the water behind him.

He flicks a semi-cautious glance at the surf surrounding him. *Yes, pretty boy, you could be delicious people sushi*. I spare a wistful nanosecond at the thought of the *deliciousness* of tasting Ozzy—I'm human, even if I prefer to live mentally in space—while he beams a confident grin my way. His biceps flex. He could arm wrestle a shark if his charm ever failed.

"I like to live dangerously." He pulls his board out of the water, punctuating his grandiose claim by stabbing the wooden slab into the night air. I'm riveted by the interplay of shadows and moonlight on the muscled expanse of his bare, wet skin. The last time I touched someone was when the train car came to an abrupt halt, and I slammed into a fellow commuter.

I desperately try not to look like I'm imagining touching Ozzy. "I don't have time to apply a tourniquet to what's left of your leg."

From the smile tugging at his sinfully soft lips, that was the socially incorrect thing to say.

Still, I work up an answering smile, the better to sell the lie that I'm happy conversing with a near stranger and not wishing I were home. Making eye contact with him, however, is a rookie mistake. Eye contact says, *Talk to me, baby*.

"You're direct." Now he's laughing at me, although I'm sure he'd argue that the correct preposition is *with*.

I shrug. "And you're still standing in shark-infested water. I'm not the one who's risking amputation, Ozzy."

The skin between his eyebrows crinkles as he wades to shore. I've confused him. His eyes roam over my face. "Do we know each other?"

He's met me, but he's not the first to forget me. He is, however, the most recent. Ozzy was trotted around our workplace like a passed app on a platter. He met the entire staff in the space of an hour, and my muttered greeting was not unique. There was insufficient time for him to have been struck by my good looks or my wit. I should help him out here, but I don't.

"Maybe it will come to you." Despite our admittedly brief personal history, I'm still a little testy, because this isn't the first time tonight that I've had to remind someone *I work with* of my name, occupation, and reason for being at tonight's company event. The lead on my team forgot my name, and the assistant director of engineering called me Doreene, which correlates to my sulking down here in the shadows like Gollum 2.0.

Ozzy grins some more. No one has forgotten his name tonight. He's Mr. Popularity, so fun and likeable that he gets paid for it.

"The silent disco in Ibiza? That night is way too fuzzy." He winks at me. Maybe he's got sea water in his eye. He's certainly got it everywhere else—little drops snake down his amazing chest. "Wait. I know! The escape room I did last week—were you the murderer?"

I know my next line in this weird script. "You have a good night now."

And...exit stage right.

Except that before I can leave, Ozzy stomps toward me, kicking up dead seaweed and sand. He discards his board in front of me as if he's a medieval caber-tossing Scotsman.

"Don't go," he begs. His accent is disappointingly Scots-free.

His eyes twinkle, and while I do actually possess a (well-hidden) sense of humor and (sometimes) enjoy a good joke as much as the next person, I'm still not convinced that he's not laughing at me. He's the social media star, the famous surfer who competes in exotic locations like Tahiti and Australia. He gets paid to spend the day at the beach and can do whatever he wants, unlike us mere cubicle-dwelling mortals.

Proving that life isn't fair, he seems to be a disgustingly, genuinely nice guy—he's laid-back, full of smiles and far too pretty. Worse, he's *smart*. He has a brain and he uses it. Surfing is highly mathematical, all dependent on working out Newton's equations about mass times the acceleration of the surfer, plus he's built a successful business out of being himself.

Everyone likes Ozzy Wylder. After he won a few big surf competitions, people waved money in his face to say nice things about them and their products. Currently, he's whispering sweet nothings about a cardboard-tasting protein bar, which I know because he had boxes of the new chocolate and strawberry flavors sent to us for free. The day he toured our offices, he took endless photos and signed ball caps for the engineering team.

We shook hands, and I stared into his beautiful, beautiful eyes.

Now he's standing in front of me, half-undressed, bare feet planted on the sand, smiling away as if we're friends—if only he could remember my name.

"I'd like to use my lifeline." He takes a step toward me. I have no idea what he's talking about, so I stare into his hazel eyes some more. "Can I buy a hint?"

He's looking over my shoulder and up the beach as he says this, which is why he doesn't notice the large wave that barrels out of the darkness toward us. I'm too busy calculating acceleration and distance traveled to remember my words. In fact, I'm still doing the math when the wall of water slams into his broad, bare back, pushing him up, up, up the beach.

As Ozzy flies into the air, off balance, I learn that I am a decent person after all. I'm also unusually coordinated because I plant my tote bag up above the waterline with the skill and speed of a professional shot-putter before I reach for Ozzy. I'm *rescuing* him, I realize with no small amount of glee, as his forward momentum halts abruptly, the soles of his feet sinking into the wet sand. He's going down like the biggest pine in a Christmas tree forest.

I hold my arms out, and the universe tosses him into my embrace.

My Christmas wish list is complete.

As dropping him would be rude and I've worked hard on my manners, I cling to him, trying to hold him upright.

I lose to gravity and Newton's first law of motion.

We crash-land gracelessly—and loudly—on the sand. I sprawl like a beached starfish, my back rubbing against the wet, gritty stretch of broken shells, rocks, and general detritus. Since this is California, not paradise, there's trash, too. Ocean water sinks through the back of my black dress.

Ozzy braces himself above me on an impressive pair of forearms. He's laughing, but his lower half is pressed against mine. My brain short-circuits.

I replay the last ten seconds and am strongly tempted to lie here forever. The sun will come up and I'll still be clutching Ozzy Wylder.

Ozzy is warm. His massive body radiates heat. Despite the skunk-weed stink of wet neoprene, I wriggle closer until our bodies touch from waist to toe. As there's still too much space between us, I push up on my elbows.

Neoprene funk aside, he smells good. Salty and masculine,

apples and mint. I want to bottle him. Drink him up. Devour him down to his bare toes.

He's impossibly big, his mouth out of reach, an observation that makes me realize I've shifted gears from well-intentioned rescuer to something more personal. An unanticipated heat unfurls in me, starting in my cheeks and fleeing south.

He grins down at me. "Is this all right with you?"

Yes. Yes, it is.

I surprise myself sometimes.

We're two almost-strangers who met briefly for a minute. Lying on top of each other on a beach.

The surf rushes in. My heart beats harder, my cheeks heating up. I'm not a random kisser, but I'm also not the same person I was ten seconds ago when I didn't know what it felt like to have Ozzy lying on top of me. I study him for another second and come to the conclusion that tonight is not going to plan.

And I'm fine with that.

"Yes." *Please accept my enthusiastic consent and continue down this carnal path.*

Now would be great. Yes, yes, YESSSSSSSS, my body shouts. My mouth stutters some more affirmative monosyllables. If he wants Shakespearean sonnets, he should have crash-landed on some other girl.

He stares contemplatively down at me. He might be thinking. Or maybe he's memorizing my face, coming up with his own plan. Because he curves one big, warm hand around my jaw, his thumb stroking over my cheek. He's looking.

At *me*.

My insides warm. My reserve melts like an icicle in July, feelings drip-drip-dripping down my throat, from my heart, rushing southward.

"You're something else." He memorizes me with his thumb.

"You... What?"

"May I?" His eyes hold mine as his thumb investigates the corner of my mouth. "Kiss you?"

The logical answer is no.

I abandon logic. "Yes."

Consent confirmed, he closes the distance between us fast, spearing his hands in my hair as he angles my face up. There's some rolling around because the ocean's cold and kissing in the surf is an advanced level in the kissing game, but somehow we end up on the sand where it's dry, and then his mouth is devouring mine. I'm on top, riding him like my very own sea cowboy, and he's sprawled beneath me, warm and hard, his hands keeping my mouth on his and...

Ozzy Wylder is an amazing kisser. It's better than any book kiss I've read, better than anything I've ever imagined, let alone participated in.

Because of how he cups my face gently but firmly, as if he'd let me go if that was what I wanted but he really can't bear to do so.

Because of his hair, tousled on the sand and spread out around his face, clinging to my fingers where I hang on to him.

Because I'm not alone. Because he's right here with me.

He's my new favorite flavor, my new best thing. A day past shaving, his jaw is stubble-roughened beneath my fingertips. There's nothing soft about him now, which is perfectly, amazingly, wonderfully clear from my perch on top of him.

We kiss and kiss, familiarizing ourselves with each other. Touching, lightly at first, then harder. His lips part, sharing a breath. I open, take it in, give back. Our kiss achieves lift off, punching through the atmosphere. Our tongues tangle. He grunts, a male sound that punches through my shields. I'm more of a silent kisser but this...this...

"You..." I start to say when his mouth lifts off mine for a nanosecond, but then he's kissing me again and complete sentences are overrated.

"Yes?" His mouth detours, kissing eastward up my cheek, toward my ear, as if I'm every direction he wants to go.

"More." I demonstrate by wrapping myself around him. Personal space is overrated.

Ozzy is hard. His wetsuit does nothing to hide his enthusiasm for our kiss. He's unashamedly openly turned on, and that makes me burn faster for him. My hands head south, burrowing beneath him, exploring his back, mapping the man dimples at the base of his spine, groping his amazing, amazing ass.

"You're amazing," he groans against my skin, stealing the words from my mind. Of course, he possesses superhuman powers. "This is—"

"Yeah." I might whimper. I follow this with more incoherent sounds, seconds and seconds of noises that I will never, ever admit to making, as we kiss and kiss and I realize that I might not want to slow things down or do anything other than stay here all night with Ozzy.

The universe has other plans for us. There's a horrible noise like a thousand seagulls shrieking or nails on a chalkboard. We're not alone. An invasion of talking people spills over the sand dunes. *Keep kissing,* I tell myself. *He's used to having an audience, and you can learn to ignore it.*

Sadly, Ozzy jackknifes upright. Since he brings me with him, I decide our new position is acceptable. It lets me wrap my legs around his waist and hold on tight, and he's...he's...

Sliding me gently off his lap and onto the sand.

It's over?

He certainly seems to think so, popping to his feet with an impressive flex of his abs.

When he extends a hand to me, I take it automatically. This is not an outcome I predicted.

"That was *AMAZING*!" he whoops, pulling me upright. His hand slips out of mine.

Did I think tonight was amazing? Because it's not. It's a disaster. An epic, total, colossal, insert-your-adjective-here calamity of a night.

Ozzy grins back at me. *Back* is the operative word. Because he's already padding up the beach away from me, waving and calling at the group of people spilling over the dunes toward us. And then it gets worse.

"You coming, babe?" He tosses the endearment over his muscled shoulder.

He doesn't know my name.

Could I be any more invisible?

The universe accepts my dare. My phone blares the incoming transmission sound effect that plays when my boss texts. He's up there on the pier, so I don't know what's so urgent that it can't wait until he sees me. Perhaps he's in the crowd wading through the sand and wondering why I'm kissing the company mascot? I slog over to my bag and fish my phone out.

We're cutting the team. Sorry, Doreene. You're terminated, effective immediately.

Ozzy disappears over the sand dune. There are whoops, laughter, and likely a video of our kiss winging its way onto the internet. I can't help but wonder if he'll bother to find out my name. It's time somebody noticed me for me.

It's time to rewrite my life.

Two

Self-reinvention is trickier than getting autocorrect to stop changing my profanity to "ducking."

Six months after the ignominy of my wrong-name, under-the-pier termination, I'm floundering. I flirt with possible jobs on Monster.com like working is the new hookup. You look good, yes, I'd like to meet up—no need to bother with "get to know you" chitchat. I've connected with multiple workplaces, but TripFriendz, my current place of temporary employment, is starting to look like a long-term relationship.

We've made it past the coffee meetup.

The dinner bang.

The awkward morning-after texts and performance review.

TripFriendz likes me and I love having a job again.

I know what to do next. I have a *plan*. I'll make work friends, lead a team, effortlessly scale up the project, and shake out more bugs than Moses in Egypt. I'll be the go-to person San Francisco's hottest tech firm wants, begs for, can't do without, and they'll like me back.

They'll *KNOW WHO I AM.*

Yes, I've printed this out in 124-point font and stuck it on my fridge.

It'll be a walk in the (technology) park.

It says wonderful things about my ability to focus that when Noah and Enzo race by my desk with wall-shattering speed on their scooters, I barely look up. I do, however, press Command+S and wrap a protective arm around my laptop. It's great that my team members have taken to heart the American Heart Association's exhortations to get up and stretch every hour, but it adversely affects our productivity that they've broken two laptops, unplugged a critical server, and forced me to pull backup tapes not once but twice this week.

"Outside!" I bark before I catch myself. Then I remind myself to smile, even if it's more of a grimace that looks like gas. *Don't sound critical. Be friendly! One of the guys!* I (somewhat, mostly) love my newest team, but it's crystal clear that I'll never be the fun parent. That role has been permanently awarded to Margie, the woman I am temporarily replacing as chief play officer. She oversees a team of software engineers, providing creative vision and direction for new features. She's God or Mother Nature, picking and choosing which DNA molecules make it into the app that TripFriendz is gestating. TripFriendz is her baby and it will look like her.

Except that now it's starting to seem like it might, quite possibly, be mine. Margie is cruising around the world and/or writing the book of her heart in a Blue Ridge Mountains cabin with a lumberjack. Yoga might be involved. She's been vague about the specifics, which has sent the office rumor mill into overdrive, but she's deeply missed by everyone who's met her. They hate her blatant hints at retirement.

I, on the other hand, am thrilled.

Hello, Opportunity. So pleased to meet you.

"Do you want a turn?" Noah pops a wheelie on his scooter, making another pass by me.

I don't have a death wish. "Let me check on the status of my insurance first."

He tries again. "Tomorrow?"

Noah is a perpetual oxford-shirt-wearing optimist. He pairs his positive outlook with blue jeans and flip-flops. Noah hasn't believed in socks since he was a teenager in Buffalo, New York, and the balmier weather of Northern California is a blessing. He tells me this frequently, usually while asking for (our unlimited) time off to jet off to even balmier, more tropical locations for vacation. The only traveling I do is between the office and my loft condo.

I relocate my laptop to the back of my desk and stand up. *Today's your day! Smile*, the sticky note stuck to my screen exhorts me. I smile. "What's up?"

"Hot lead on a new travel partner. Big commission dollars." Noah stabs a thumb at Enzo, who is disappearing through the doors that lead to the elevator and the outside world. *Go, Enzo, go.* The software app we're building is no good if no one agrees to sell their hotel rooms on our site.

TripFriendz's office space was formerly a tobacco warehouse in a grittier-than-is-desirable part of San Francisco. The exposed brickwork in our open floor plan workspace is pretty, but walls and cell phone reception are nonexistent. Since our NASA-worthy landline phones require a Mensa-level IQ to operate, Enzo took sales calls in the days of Margie while hanging out the window (where Spider-Man-worthy athletics equate to a meager bar of cell phone service). Since coming on board, I've successfully argued that plummeting two stories down onto the sidewalk is a financial liability our startup cannot afford. Ergo, Enzo now races outside whenever he needs an uninterrupted phone call.

"Good luck!" I chirp at Enzo's back. I am such a team player. *Smile! Be positive!* New lines bracket my mouth, carving themselves into my skin. I have no idea what I'll do if they fire me.

Neither Noah nor Enzo acknowledge my supportive attitude. Enzo disappears to take his very important call and Noah scoots off toward the free chocolate that is couriered over to our community kitchen each afternoon from the organic hippy grocery store our CEO patronizes. We have an endless supply of flavors, like lavender blueberry sunshine smiles and hemp quinoa fiber-filled chocolate pistachio.

I'd follow him—free chocolate is excellent team-bonding material—but picking quinoa out of my teeth will not instill confidence in my professional skills.

Rosie, our intern, pokes her head around the corner. "Oh, good. You're awake."

Margie was a big fan of nap time. Essential, appetitive, fulfillment, caffeine, power, siesta—she took and endorsed them all.

Miraculously, we're only eleven months behind on the Trip-Friendz launch.

"Please tell me we're making the code release in eight weeks." Rosie wanders around my desk like a lost puppy and slumps down onto the exercise ball jammed in next to my ergonomic office chair.

Fun fact: I am the only adult who sits in an actual chair here.

We have fifty-four days, seven hours, and twenty-nine minutes until release, but who's counting?

I opt for brevity. "Yes."

It's not lying—it's optimistic thinking. Manifestation. A desperate prayer to the universe. When I checked twenty minutes ago, there were 741 open tickets in our bug tracking software. They *need* me here too much to get rid of me.

Rosie makes puppy dog eyes at me, flashing heart hands.

"Would you lie to me?" She tries to laser inside my brain with her eyes. "Because we were supposed to code freeze three months ago, and I have more bugs than a squirrel does fleas. Are we feature complete?"

She's so naive. "We don't have a product spec."

Like unicorns, warp drives, and the zero-bug state, an actual product spec—the list of stuff that's supposed to be in the finished TripFriendz app—does not exist.

She shrugs, rolling effortlessly on the ball thanks to her youthful obliques. "So we have creative license?"

What we have is an epic disaster. I am not a creative person. Or even a traveler. As a perpetually single person, I don't have someone to go anywhere with in real life. Vacation packages are terra incognita. Still, as I desperately covet Margie's job (or any job), I'm singlehandedly rewriting most of the app, making it up as I go along. "This is a software start-up, not a fanfic forum."

"We could make a fortune writing Reylo fan fiction! We could go out for tacos and brainstorm?" Rosie is now doing crunches on the exercise ball. Space lasers from my laptop announce another bug joining its companions in my queue.

I suspect we've missed the opportunity to monetize the dubious relationship between Rey and Kylo Ren, but staying open-minded is important, particularly when it comes to employment opportunities. I had to grovel my way into this temp job because it's hard to make "terminated" sound like "was not my fault" and/or "really talented programmer, available immediately."

"I can't today. We have the product demo for the VCs and the director of engineering in two weeks," I remind her.

We're supposed to showcase TripFriendz's features. Worse: those features are supposed to be fully functional. To psych myself up, I review the company website while Rosie brainstorms inappropriate sexual fantasies about Rey out loud. My name is not listed on the site. Margie's is. As is Rosie's ("Happiness Engineer-in-Training") and Noah's ("Innovation Engineer").

Pandora Fyffe, Chief Play Officer. That will be me. I'll rock it. I'll be on one of those thirty-under-thirty lists that I screenshot in *Cosmo* magazine and pin on my digital inspiration board. It's a vague but heartfelt plan.

Oblivious to my career goals, Rosie sits upright. She's all joints and bendy bits. There's not a bone in her body. "What features are in the demo? Do they have to work?"

Her questions confirm why I will be leading the demo.

"All of them. Yes. Search engine, booking engine, AI-driven recommendations based on the user's history," I tell her. Not for the first time. "The goal being that you and your friends can book an itinerary that has been customized just for you."

"Like a dating app." Rosie bounces gently in place. "But for group sex? But maybe without sex and with a preplanned perfect date. Like…masturbation? So not like a dating app at all."

She scrunches her face up, lost in her workplace-inappropriate metaphor.

"For travel," I say firmly. "Just travel. Places, not people. Companions are not included."

The space lasers sound again. Our launch draws further and further out of reach.

Rosie planks, still musing, "Do you think the VCs are going to pull our funding?"

Not if I have anything to say about it.

"I'm bringing this app to market," I vow.

Rosie serves the conversational ball back to me. "What would your perfect trip look like?"

"I hate traveling."

There are no hotels in the Crystal Cluster Cosmos. There are no airports, no single supplements, and no sympathetic looks when I request a table for one. My virtual spaceship has just one seat, all mine.

Rosie is oblivious. "Where would you go if you could go anywhere?"

My beloved spaceship beckons. There are so many galaxies I could explore if I only had more time.

"Nowhere." I shut down the conversation. "I'm staying right here. At home."

Or at work, rather. I work at home and sleep at work when I'm pulling an all-nighter, and the boundaries blurred ages ago.

"You don't want to travel?" Now Rosie sounds horrified. I have maligned our baby, rejected TripFriendz's reason for being. I have singlehandedly jinxed our launch. "Shonda would say yes to travel."

I am almost certain there is no one by the name of Shonda employed at TripFriendz. "Who?"

"Shonda Rhimes," Rosie says. She mimes ecstatic excitement. Shonda is her hero. Heroine?

"You should say yes more," Rosie urges. She texts me a link to an illegal download of Shonda's book. "Let's do the Shonda method! You say yes to everything for a year!"

Has she met me?

The answer to that is a Shonda-approved yes, because she promptly amends her previous statement. "Or maybe just try to be more like Shonda? But without the creative vision and the whole I'm-a-household-name thing? It'll be fun."

I'm the least impulsive person ever. "Can you make me a slide deck? Pitch it to me next week?"

"Just try it." She mouths YES. Then points to me. "Would you like to take a trip?"

I give agreement a shot. "Okay, yes. I'd like a vacation."

It's a weak answer.

Rosie pulls a face. She wants adjectives. Florid descriptions. An entire novel of a conversation. "With your boyfriend? Sister? Mom?"

She means: *don't you have any friends?*

Try harder, I urge myself. *You're not being likeable.* "Maybe you and I can travel around Asia together?"

Rosie nods. She's willing for us to travel tag team style.

In my fantasy world, I indulge in travel documentaries rather than actual travel. I lurk on Pinterest rather than in hotel rooms and take contactless take-out delivery rather than urban food tours. Also acceptable: a housekeeper who zips in unnoticed and a moat for keeping out intruders.

Perhaps I should buy a fixer-upper castle in England?

I assign the newest bug to Rosie and excuse myself to go hide in the restroom.

Three

The very toned half-naked man climbing up the wall of my building is a violation of the condo covenants, conditions, and restrictions.

Even at three in the morning, I'm fundamentally incapable of letting an infraction slide. This Spider Man imitator is breaking the law.

And while I should be worried about my physical safety, I'm delirious from lack of sleep.

Grabbing my phone, I scan the sidewalk three stories below. It's all concrete and shadows, punctuated by pools of light from the streetlights. The coveted street-side parking is bumper-to-bumper cars, but traffic is still nonexistent. A siren wails in some more distant part of San Francisco. Things don't get lively on weekdays until my fellow building residents stage a mass exodus at five and six o'clock.

Yes, in the morning.

It takes forever to traverse the city, so everyone rushes out before the sun rises. It is one of life's many ironies that San Francisco rentals cost a fortune, requiring you to work insane numbers of hours and therefore never having any free time to enjoy the city.

The tsunami of software bugs filling my TripFriendz testing queue runs through my brain like a badly nested for loop of code. In my out-of-office hours, I wear pajamas and subsist on Sour Patch Kids, the food of choice for important deadlines and existential crises. I'm on top of things. Integral to my team. About to make the magic happen.

Liar.

Tonight, I allowed myself an hour to work on my cozy space-mining game and somehow it became two hours. Then six. Now I have to be up in three hours. The sugar crash hitting me is why I stare morosely at the man climbing the wall rather than take defensive action. My brain spirals listlessly through options.

```
for (burglar count > 0; burglar count <=10) {
System.out.println(Panic later!);
}
```

I debate calling down to the doorman, but the nightshift guy has indicated that I'm not to bother him again unless something dire happens. Since he's provided multiple examples of said direness (earthquake registering greater than an 8.9 on the Richter scale, catastrophic ceiling or water damage involving an antediluvian flood, photographic evidence of the Four Horsemen of the Apocalypse riding down our San Francisco street), I'm aware that he does not actually want to hear from me. The words *when hell freezes over* may have come out of his mouth. As a building resident whose monthly rent partially funds the man's salary, I pointed out that it's his job to be on call. We ended by failing to negotiate the maximum number of times per week I can bring my late-night concerns to his attention. He argued for none, which did not work for me.

Tomorrow is another day.

Unless, you know, Mr. Wall down there turns out to be a serial killer. It's an inefficient way to go about a crime spree, although he's definitely getting his workout in.

Given his slow upward progress, I have time to plan. Since my brain is beyond tired, however, it spins, going nowhere. Bits and pieces of the most recent book I've read suggest themselves as a possible solution. What *would* my favorite alien barbarian hero do in this kind of situation?

I give it a quick thought, but I'm fresh out of wooden spears. Rock-studded, leather-wrapped snowballs are also infeasible. The only logical option is calling the police.

Is this a TikTok video gone awry? A drunken prank? The climber's hand slips, but there's no need to despair. The impressive musculature of his bare shoulders bunches and flexes, saving the day. A husky chuckle floats up to where I crouch out of sight on my half of the balcony I share with the next-door unit. It's fortunate for me—and unfortunate for the intruder—that I decided to bring my laptop outside to work.

My phone buzzes with an incoming text, and I look down automatically. **Can you plz review my code ASAP? THX!**

Who… Oh. My late-night texter is Jayson, a coworker from my former place of employment. Naturally, no one at TripFriendz is working this late. My coworkers have personal lives and excellent sleep hygiene. This is why we're so behind on our product launch.

Equally naturally, Jayson assumes that I'm a) working in the middle of the night on a weekend and b) willing to drop everything to help him out.

He's 98 percent right.

And yet, as a former employee of Miles to Go (and damn

them for ruining my favorite Robert Frost poem), reviewing Jayson's code is not my responsibility.

The problem is, *he* doesn't seem to have noticed that I was terminated six months ago. Nor have any of the other engineers on my former software team. While my access to all things corporate ended during the time it took me to trudge from the beach to my car in the overflow parking lot, my former coworkers continued to randomly message me throughout the remainder of the week. And not to offer sympathy or to network—no, they'd wanted me to review their code before they committed. Brainstorm solutions for a particularly knotty piece of Java. Forward me bugs so horrible that they were the office hot potato, bouncing from one developer's queue to the next.

Despite the ubiquitous open floor plan at Miles to Go and eighteen months of non-adversarial working together (or at least adjacent), they haven't connected my empty cubicle with my permanent absence.

I was just a nameless, faceless robot blessing their code with the green light or fixing their blocker bugs.

Hi, my name is Pandora Fyffe and my secret power is invisibility.

Things will be different this time. TripFriendz is my redemption tour.

The burglar makes it to the second floor and pauses. Presumably he's searching for handholds. Or maybe his impressive biceps require a rest break. Since I've never climbed a vertical surface, I am unfamiliar with the appropriate process. Maybe it's like diving, and without regular stops, your lungs explode.

While the burglar hangs in there, I make a quick call to the cops (who advise me to go inside and lock my door while promising to send someone out just as soon as they've finished handling all the serious crimes in the city) and then hold my phone through the decorative railings of the balcony to snap a picture of the intruder. I've watched enough true crime documentaries to know the power of photographic evidence. Never underestimate the power of a good cell phone tower and its ability to sniff out exactly where you were with creepy certitude. This guy won't get away with breaking and entering. Not on my watch.

I wait.

Impatiently.

He's the world's slowest climber.

Eventually, I lean over cautiously. The balcony's railing appears made to code, so the likelihood of my tumbling over it and down onto the street is acceptably low.

"Psst!" I whisper-shout like a lurker librarian.

I must be louder than I think—sound does carry at night, which is why the condo has a noise ordinance that starts at nine o'clock—because the burglar's head snaps up. *Gotcha.* I take a new picture, this time with my flash on. The unexpectedly bright pop of light kills any chance of subtlety on my part, but I'm not the person caught in the middle of a felony.

Burglar Boy curses, a low, rough sound, followed by an even lower, huskier laugh. His happiness at his exposure sounds like a lion chuffing. Hmm. I'm not sure if they do that right before they pounce on their prey or not. My knowledge of lions is deficient.

I make a note to google the predatory habits of *Panthera leo*.

He tips his head back and yells up at me, unconcerned about sleeping neighbors. "You've blinded me, darling."

I revise my animal identification. He's not a lion. He's a patronizing ass.

Despite my tank top riding up, thanks to my Sour-Patch-Kids-influenced belly, my yoga pants more than cover my lower half and my ancient cardigan is toga-sized. I'm not the person who's in danger of being arrested for public indecency.

Squinting downward, I try to memorize his face. Since my glasses are inside the condo, he'd need to be less than two feet away for me to appreciate his details.

Still, from what I can see, he is, objectively speaking, gorgeous. Those good looks will get him exonerated by sex-starved, lonely juries. And wasn't there a romance I read where the hot burglar broke into a house and then showed his appreciation for the housewife's blind eye while he cleaned out the family jewels? There are way too many puns in there.

He laughs while I try and fail to remember the book title, pulling himself up another foot and closing the distance between us. Wait. Is he coming *here*?

"You want to throw down a rope, Rapunzel?"

"This is private property."

I double-check the time on my phone. Five minutes since my call—not enough time for the cops to make it here. I'm not sure what the etiquette of the situation is. Do you make small talk with a burglar? Drop things on his head?

He sighs. It's a loud, gusty, very put-upon sound. I've spoiled his night.

"I've called the cops," I inform him. "And I've got your picture."

He grunts, unconcerned, and shifts upward. *Game on.*

My phone buzzes urgently. Jayson again. Can you code review me?

I feel an unexpected moment of camaraderie. Jayson's Saturday night plans are as unsexy as mine. Software engineers tend to be nocturnal. We're the bats of the corporate world, coming out at dusk and generally misunderstood by the rest of the world who believe that we coders are all the same (geeks and nerds), nuisances that get tangled up in your hair (we certainly can mess with your deadlines) and are blind to all but our laptop screens, banging out lines of unintelligible gibberish that run the world.

I'm brainstorming polite ways to ask Jayson if he knows that I'm no longer employed by Miles to Go and am therefore an inappropriate choice for his after-work-hours request when my phone buzzes with a follow-up text of a big-eyed puppy dog. PLZ?

I was a sure thing at Miles to Go. I worked eighteen hours a day and was always online. I never refused when someone asked me to review their code because I never said no.

Sometimes, Shonda, a *no* is harder than a *yes*.

I fire an opening salvo. Do you know who I am?

Jayson does not respond. I hope he's having an existential crisis or suffering horrible pangs of embarrassment.

"A little help here?" This comes from the shirtless cat burglar, who has even less right to be asking me for my help than Jayson does. Fortunately for them both, I'm good at multitasking. Unfortunately, I've reached my limit.

I march over to my door, flick on the balcony light, and then spin around to assess his progress. Sun-bronzed fingers with knuckle tattoos wrap around the bottom of the railings; I'm certain the rest of the man will shortly follow. My options dwindle. I should go back inside, lock the door, and either retrieve my aluminum baseball bat or, more prudently, retreat downstairs to wait for the police. This is a job for a trained professional, not a software engineer.

I lean forward for one last look at the intruder, the better to identify him in a police lineup later, and his face comes into focus.

A jolt of recognition travels from my eyes down my body, making heady pit stops in my chest, heart, and stomach on the way. Possibly, that jolt keeps right on going, too, down to more southern regions. Delicious curls of sexual awareness sprout in my belly like Jack's bean stalk seeds, shooting tendrils up toward the sky.

This is impossible.

Like perfect random number generation or an infinite loop that does not consume all available resources like a ravenous code locust, Ozzy Wylder cannot possibly be scaling my condo. He kissed me, he bounced away with his pack of admirers, and he never, not once, reached out to indicate that he might welcome a repeat appearance in my life.

To sum up: screw Ozzy Wylder.

Nevertheless, I double-check and confirm that it's him. I've been unable to forget him, having fiendishly googled him after our midnight kiss. Pictures of his beautiful, laser-focused face filled my browser history for weeks.

Maybe it's his doppelgänger? Does he have an evil(er) twin? I just want to go inside, throw myself down on my bed, and sleep for a month. I'm delirious from lack of sleep. I don't have the bandwidth for this level of embarrassment.

There's also anger. Social paralysis. Lots and *LOTS* of confusion.

Ozzy Wylder should be riding house-sized waves in Maui and collecting gold trophies, not climbing buildings in the dead of night.

And he really, really has no business climbing *my* building.

We don't have that kind of relationship. I'm not Rapunzel, and he's not my prince.

Ozzy pulls himself up, bracing his bare feet on the outermost edge of the balcony, arms folded on the top of the railing as he winks at me. It's déjà vu. "Good evening."

For a brief second, I hope he recognizes me.

I *expect* him to recognize me.

My body certainly recognizes him. He's imprinted himself on me with his beach kiss and his big, wet body. I'm going up in flames—flames that are one part humiliated embarrassment and one part lust—and yet here he stands, unbothered and mellow, calm and unflappable. My evil, thoughtless brain that can't remember the day of the week or even the month has no problem recalling his half-naked, sea-drenched self. I have memorized each and every second of him sauntering up the beach, water droplets trickling down his body like he was in some sexy photo shoot, neoprene wetsuit cupping his goodies.

He's broken me. Replaced my logic with lusty chaos.

My eyes inventory his sculpted shoulders, the tousled, sun-kissed hair that is neither brown nor blond but a delicious shade halfway in between. Powerful arms, lots of muscles, and the man's chest...well, it's an outright miracle, a miracle that descends straight to a sexy V-cut that I have been unable to forget since our brief beach encounter. Unlike last time, he wears a pair of faded blue jeans, a grin, and nothing else. *Sweet baby Jesus.*

He pauses while I stare, as if he could care less that he's mostly undressed and about to be visited by cops. Or maybe he just recognizes the effect he has on me (even if he doesn't recognize *me*).

Ozzy Wylder.

My kryptonite and my crush.

"I'm your new neighbor," he declares.

"No way."

"Yes way," he retorts, as if we're five and arguing on the playground.

I can feel my eyes narrowing as he swings himself up over the railing. The physics are suspect. One second, he's poised on the other side, the next, he's vaulting over the railing to land lightly on his feet. He's probably an Olympic-caliber hurdler in his spare time, my brain suggests. Or a pirate. He'd board a vessel with panache.

He sticks his hand out in my direction. "Let's start over. Ozzy Wylder. And you are?"

Mad. Very, very mad. Does he not remember me? Am *I* the asshole here for remembering *him*? I should play this off, act nonchalant. *We kissed? That was you I rolled around on the beach with? Four out of ten for execution, but bonus points for style.* I should say these things. But I don't.

"Uninterested," I lie, instead.

In a rookie mistake, I stare down at his palm while he mulls over my response. Ozzy's hands are big and callused, sun-bronzed and powerful. They make me shiver. I squint, trying to make sense of the ink decorating his knuckles. He chuckles and holds his hands up, backs toward me so that I can better admire his artwork. He's the helpful sort of burglar.

"I lost my key." He flashes an easy grin at me, willing me to trust him. For a period of three sandy moments, I thought his interest in me was genuine. I look at him now, relaxed and open, and I want to make him want me back. I want revenge. To push him off the balcony and out of my life.

I restrain myself. "And your shoes and shirt."

He shrugs as if to say, *details*. "They're with my things. Inside."

I counter with the obvious. "You don't live here."

According to Google, he has a house in Maui. It's an award-winning contemporary design that blends natural and tropical elements. Whatever that means.

A frown creases his perfect forehead. "You're not very welcoming."

"I'm on the building board," I inform him, "and no new residents have been brought to my attention."

"Is there an application process? Are you taking applications for friendship?" His eyebrows draw up in mock surprise.

A police car pulls up below, double-parking in the street. Reinforcements have arrived.

I ignore his questions and go with the truth. "You are not a middle-aged dentist."

When I met my dentist-neighbor, he explained at great length how you could tell someone's stress levels by examining their smile. He followed this up with pointing out several very stressed people on a house-flipping show he'd been watching on Netflix. It was both informative and memorable.

"Thank Christ, no. That would be boring." Ozzy leans back on the balcony railing. He and gravity are best friends, and gravity has his back. "My dad would love it, though. Thumbs-up."

I ignore his FOO issues and focus on the relevant data point here.

"My neighbor is a middle-aged dentist. He's in South America at the moment, providing free root canals and dental implants in rural communities."

"Very charitable." Ozzy sounds unimpressed. The only thing he gives away are kisses.

"You don't belong here. Get off my balcony."

I stab a helpful finger in the direction of the street. He ignores me, folding his arms over his muscled, bare chest and planting his feet firmly on the dentist's half of the balcony. A ridiculous waist-high wall divides the two parts of the balcony, a his-and-her solution that makes a fine boundary line on a map but that affords me with zero privacy. Fortunately, the dentist travels frequently.

"No," he says. "Also, it's only half your balcony."

I exhale. Inhale. Count to three. Go back inside and let the cops into my unit and provide them with a brief rundown of the intruder climbing the wall of my building to trespass on my balcony.

When I step outside with my new police friends, Ozzy blinks. I swallow down a triumphant laugh. See? I'm not a pushover.

"The cops?"

"Trespassing." I raise a finger. "Breaking and entering." I add two more fingers to the count.

"But I am your neighbor," he says.

I don't believe that, but I do believe he has no business climbing the wall of my building—and I'm *not* feeling like the bigger person.

"I don't know you," I lie sweetly. "And I just witnessed you climb up the wall of my building. Have a nice night now."

Then I turn and go inside.

Four

A loud palm slaps against my door, interrupting my unpleasant discovery that someone on my engineering team has blithely checked his code in, wiping out my prior commit and introducing more bugs than a locust swarm in Egypt. *The rubber chicken of shame is coming for you, Noah. It will be on your desk tomorrow, announcing to the whole TripFriendz world: I broke the build.*

Slap.

Slap, SLAP SLAP.

From time to time, annoying sounds invade the cozy space of my loft. Jackhammers, for instance, when the city decided to replace an entire sewer line at six in the morning. The whine of the drone owned by the creeper from the penthouse suite. The couple that enjoyed noisy sex, the more public, the better.

On a scale of overheard sex to rampant pneumatic tools, this, however, is a nine in terms of irritating. It sounds like there's a battering ram working on my door, possibly an entire drum set that's gone AWOL and is now banging out a percussive rhythm.

It morphs into an SOS, a pattern, three short taps, three

long, and then three more short, the rhythm shifting smoothly into the shave-and-a-haircut earworm.

Ugh. I'll have to reprogram my brain. Listen to some advertising jingles. If this is someone come to convince me that the end times are near and I need to repent, that someone and I are having *words*.

I stride to the door, mentally rehearsing ways to convey this sentiment. *No, I do not need your salvation, thank you very much. Jesus and I have a prior understanding.*

When I look out the peephole, an eye stares back at me. One beautiful, hazel eye with long, long lashes. OMG. I yelp, scrambling backward.

"Sorry!" someone—a *male* someone—shouts cheerfully. He backs up with outlandish thumping noises and then freaking waves at my door.

Ozzy Wylder is standing on—or at least adjacent to—my doorstep.

What the hell is wrong with him? Suggestions bubble up in my brain. He's here for revenge. He wants to present me with the bill for his legal fees. He's filming a stupid TikTok video.

I glare even though he can't see me. It's my default mode. I have resting grumpy face. "Go away."

"Can we talk? I think we should talk! Can you come out? I'm not busy."

This is irritating. And also, inconceivable.

I walk away. He doesn't need my words—he has enough of them for both of us.

Point in case: he keeps on monologuing at my door. At the top of his lungs. "We need to improve our communication skills! This relationship isn't working for me, and I feel like we should address my concerns. We should talk about this."

He assumes I care about how he feels.

He's *so* mistaken.

I throw myself back down on my couch. Remove my glasses. Refocus on the screen of the laptop that I've been glued to so long that it has become an extension of my body. Feet thud across the floor in the next-door loft. The walls are made of brick, but somehow fail to mute the sounds coming from next door. I need to introduce the topic of better soundproofing at the next condo association meeting.

More noise. Thumping interspersed with banging. Whistling. Ozzy lives life at full volume and likes singing about wieners. He's deluded if he thinks I won't complain. I slide back into my code and lose myself in the messy strands of Java.

Inked knuckles knock on the slider that leads to my balcony.

I know they're inked because the brisk rat-a-tat-tat startles me out of my work and I inadvertently look up. Plus: memories. So much for me pretending that Ozzy Wylder does not exist.

The laptop threatens to slide off my thighs. I make a grab for it, assessing my options. I am curled up in a nest of pillows on my sofa, my spine bent in an S-curve that I'll regret when I'm forty. My live-work space is a baby loft, a tiny studio only slightly bigger than my TripFriendz cubicle, because San Francisco is expensive and it turns out that you cannot sell a kidney on the black market for rent money.

An Ozzy-shaped blob shouts enthusiastically at me through the slider. "I come in peace!"

Perhaps he would also like to sell me a nice bridge or his sea-view property in landlocked Missouri.

He takes a step back from the door, hunching his shoulders inward. It dawns on me that he is trying to look nonthreatening and small. The lion wants me to think he's a harmless gazelle. A fuzzy kitten. A cute little bunny.

FYI: I was not born yesterday.

"What do you want?" I growl.

He waves enthusiastically. "To reintroduce myself!"

I narrow my gaze. I am a clumsy puffer fish, inflating into a spikey ball to deter a determined predator. "Go away."

"Ozzy Wylder." He rocks on his bare feet, grinning at me. "I just moved in yesterday."

He fishes something out of his back pocket and holds it up to my slider door. I put my glasses back on and determine the object is his driver's license. As the seconds tick by, I learn that he is six feet three inches tall. He has blond hair and hazel eyes. He *does* belong to the fine state of Hawaii and if he dies, I have permission to harvest his organs. It's tempting to make good on that promise right now.

"You're standing on my balcony," I point out. "Get off my lawn."

He blinks. My user input has startled him.

Is he nervous? Experiencing a nanosecond of vulnerability? *Impossible.* It's just a system glitch.

"I live here, too." He clears his throat. Resumes smiling because of course he does.

My laptop dings, announcing the birth of another software bug. I don't have time for emotional connections. I have work to do before I head into the office. "No, you don't. I believe we went over that earlier with the nice policemen."

"Do, too!" He rocks back on his bare heels. Light blond hair dusts his feet. Apparently, I have a thing for feet. Ozzy's feet, specifically. I stare and he wiggles his toes. He's one big grinning sexual fishing lure.

I jerk my gaze away from his beautiful feet. Drag my eyes up his body because I will make eye contact if it kills me.

He's fully clothed (disappointing) except for shoes. A tear in one knee of his faded blue jeans frames inches of sun-kissed skin. I want to lick him. The denim hugs his legs, his crotch, his whale of a surfer dick. I may need a better sexual vocabulary, but I do not need a better imagination. *Do not sexualize thy neighbor.* He is a pain in my ass, an interruption, a problem to be dealt with.

He holds up a sheaf of papers in his other hand. "I have a lease!" He is nice when he should be gloating. Or ignoring me. "Can I slide a copy under your door?"

He bends without waiting for permission, then frowns as the bottom of my slider door thwarts his stupid plan. My door is well-sealed against his intrusion. And also: ants. "Can we talk? I'll buy you coffee!"

I glare some more. He beams back, brighter than a lighthouse. We are at an impasse.

My Roomba chugs obliviously between us, on a mission to eradicate dust and dirt.

Ozzy taps his chin thoughtfully. His driver's license lies discarded on my patio table.

Whatever. Perhaps I can bore him into leaving. I return my attention to my laptop. Type a few lines. I'm so productive.

"We're neighbors!" He points at his papers again.

Neighbor implies a degree of friendliness that I refuse to entertain. We merely share a border constructed from drywall, wood, and hostile intentions.

I look at him over the edge of my glasses. It is my patented irritated librarian look.

He grins. "We should hang out! Get to know each other!"

He speaks in exclamation points. Imagine being that positive. How would it feel to be so confident that everyone you meet wants to speak with you? If I *were* magically transformed into Ozzy for a day, I'd spend the first hour running up and down the beach like one of those nineties TV shows, effortlessly churning through the sand and flicking droplets of water from my chest. Then I'd randomly walk up to people—in the coffee shop, the produce aisle at the grocery, on the sidewalk—

and chat them up. Perhaps my mission to be a nicer, better person is misguided and people aren't worth the effort and I can slink back into my ogre lair to live alone forever?

A girl can hope.

I shift my glare back to my laptop. Then I move two new bugs into my queue. I've resolved more tickets than my teammates this week and it's still the weekend. There are zero boundaries between my work life and my (nonexistent) personal life, which is fine. I'm nothing without my job.

I whisper to my screen, "Remember my name." Everyone else on my team uses cute nicknames like BugHugger and ByteFixer. I have spelled mine out. *Pandora Fyffe fixed this.*

Ozzy raps on the slider door again.

He's persistent. He knows that I know that he knows he's there. There's a one-way electric connection between his eyes and my belly. I stare at the screen until he drops his hand. Do I look as messy and disorganized as I feel? My bun slides from its precarious perch on top of my head. I haven't showered in forty-eight hours and I can't remember the last time I applied deodorant or brushed my teeth. The door between us is as much for his sake as it is for mine.

I open up my text editor. I don't need fancy software to do my job. *What would Shonda do?*

Shonda vowed to say yes for an entire year. My favorite word, on the other hand, is no. No, you cannot hard code values into the code. No, you may not sit there. No, you should not copy and paste from your last gig into our codebase because I do not endorse plagiarism.

"Can you come out to play?" Ozzy's voice carries through the glass. I'm not sure I locked it, and my fingers twitch to check.

He waits. I wait. We're attempting to out-wait each other and I am losing.

I unfurl myself from my sofa nest. It takes an embarrassing number of seconds to straighten up because my back is kinked into a curve and my foot prickles, protesting my weight. I need an exercise regimen. Or a lobotomy.

Instead, I stagger over to the slide door, unlock it, and shove it open halfway. "Why are you still here?"

I wish for a trebuchet, the better to lob him back to Maui.

"I live here." He lobs me an easy one. "Let's be friends!"

"No!" No is such a versatile word. It can be an adjective, an adverb, or a noun. Those two letters adapt themselves to so many situations.

Hazel eyes regard me. He's turned down the wattage, so that he looks almost—

Lonely?

No. It must be a trick. He's luring me in with his charisma, and *then* he'll do something awful like, say, kiss me and walk away. He's singlehandedly (mouthedly?) responsible for my cynicism. I lean into it.

"But we're neighbors," he says, not for the first time.

He's overestimated the importance of our proximity. We have a hostile détente at best.

"Are you worth the investment of my friendship? How long will you be living next door?"

Spoiler: this is a trick question. The answer is no. I won't be friends with someone who kissed me and then *forgot about it*.

He gifts me with a one-shouldered shrug. "Dunno."

I revise my earlier estimate of his intelligence. "How long is your lease for?"

He peruses his papers. He's either never seen it before or signed it without reading.

"Six months," he says triumphantly.

That's doable. I can survive six months. I can stop using the elevator, shun the parking garage, lurk on the sidewalk until the coast is clear. I will cede the shared balcony to him, although I will never, ever tell him that. I am the best at avoiding human contact.

The Roomba nudges my ankles, off course. Its love tap sends me stumbling toward Ozzy.

Ozzy steadies me briefly, his big hand wrapping around my upper arm. His fingers are warm, callused, and gone faster than I would like. "Careful," he croons to my tiny robot cleaner friend.

He bends down and swipes it up before it can careen off the balcony and dash its itty-bitty robot brains to smithereens on the unforgiving San Francisco streets. He lifts it to eye level. It whines and whirs in his big hands.

He rumbles, "Cute," in his deep voice and sets it inside my loft.

The Roomba swoons.

I feel the need to point out the obvious. "It's not sentient."

"So," he begins. Pauses. Backs up to put some space between us.

The irritatingly cheerful Ozzy Wylder isn't quite sure what to say next. He's lost his place in the script. He might be... off balance?

I wait for his internal software to reboot. It's safer not to fill in the space.

Hazel eyes laugh at me. He's reset to a clean state. "You got me arrested last night. All my dad's worst fears came true. I'm officially the family black sheep."

He looks neither repentant nor ovine.

"In point of fact, I did not get you arrested." True story—and yes, I'm still disappointed. I know that the cops took him downstairs and put him in the cop car. After that, my spying skills failed me, but presumably someone called someone else and then Ozzy was sprung from his temporary captivity and the entire penis party reconvened in the loft next door. Laughter filtered through the wall. Jokes were told. I assume Ozzy showed them his driver's license and the lease. Checked with my doorman nemesis. Pulled up his YouTube videos. Bribed them with free surfing lessons. However he managed it, I do know that when the cops pulled away, they did not take Ozzy with them. Their loss is my unfortunate gain.

"You tried," he accuses.

"And you climbed up my wall in the middle of the night." My eyes drill into his face. Laughter has carved delicious crinkles into the delicate skin around his eyes. These lines are a feature and not a bug. His default mode is laughter and happiness. He's an absolute ray of sunshine. I have overlooked an important specification: he doesn't know how to be mad.

I don't think he's dwelling on the ignominy of last night at all, whereas I can imagine all too well how it would feel, being kicked out, told he didn't belong, that no one knew his name. If I don't explode from internalized rage, it'll be a miracle.

"Can we please talk?" he asks.

I concede the battle and step outside. *Take that, Shonda! I said YES!*

Well, not out loud. But…details.

"I locked myself out." He shrugs. The cotton of his T-shirt stretches over an immense expanse of muscles. "I needed to get back in."

Are these the same blue jeans he wore last night? Bracelets wind around his wrist. A string one that reads Free. One with turquoise-colored beads. A metal band that seems more like a keepsake, simple and silver.

"My spare key is right there."

Just as I think we might have a rational conversation, he points to a key frog on his otherwise empty half of the balcony. There is a flaw in his plan.

His illogicalness pains me.

"Spare keys should be by the door. The idea is to be able to reach it. Plus, the slider doors just have a simple latch. You'd have to climb back down and go around to use your key. Also, we have key cards and the doorman can let you in."

It's evident from his broad shoulders and capable hands—not to mention last night—that he's more than capable of reaching the key on his porch.

Another shrug. "I hadn't thought that far ahead."

The Roomba nudges my ankles, wanting to rejoin Ozzy on the balcony. It has no idea how dangerous his company is.

I turn to go back inside. Surely Shonda would agree that chatting up an almost-stranger on my balcony is not safe. Perhaps his niceness is a front. Perhaps he's an axe murderer. Or one of those awful people who prank total strangers and post the video on TikTok.

"I had no idea my neighbor would be awake and on the balcony," he says behind me. He's closer now. "I apologize for scaring you."

I don't turn around. I would like to say that I continue my righteous march into my loft, but his voice is deep and low, all soft rumbles and concerned consonants. He's paying *attention* to me. It's deadly to my self-possession.

I raise my right arm and stab my fingers in the direction of his door. "That's your side of the balcony. This is mine. Have a nice day."

"It's your turn," he says. Then prompts, "To apologize."

"I don't think so." I can see my face in the glass of the slider door. It's tired with a side of grumpy. I wonder what he thinks about it. About me.

"Really?" Our reflections merge in the glass of the slider door. "Not even the smallest *sorry*? You don't even have to mean it. I promise."

His scent surrounds me like flowers in a garden. He smells like laundry detergent and pine. Something outdoorsy and warm and solid. I think it's his deodorant. I think I might have the same one.

"I'm not apologizing to you." I mean it. Shonda wouldn't, Rosie wouldn't, *I* wouldn't. He is totally in the wrong here.

Mostly.

Probably?

I turn around and wrap my arms around my chest. I've just remembered that I'm not wearing a bra underneath my pajamas.

"You could send me an edible fruit bouquet," he suggests. He's shamelessly peering around me into my studio loft. He's taking inventory, memorizing the layout of my place. Which is the same as his.

Real estate is impossibly pricey in San Francisco. My rented condo consists of one smallish room with exposed brickwork on two walls. It's barely large enough to hold my sofa, a standing desk, and my whiteboard. A postage-stamp-sized kitchenette is tucked at the back, and oak-colored stairs lead up to the loft, where I sleep on the same futon I slept on in college. I hope I remembered to shut the door to the bathroom but probably didn't. That's one of the perks of living alone, the ability to pee with the door wide open. Another included perk: to not quite pick up after yourself.

The sweaters I put on and take off with the regularity of a metronome are scattered everywhere. There are socks on the floor. A random flip-flop. And pillows. Lots and lots and lots of pillows. I may not have got around to hanging pictures on my wall, but I have pillows in abundance.

"You really like tassels, don't you?" My eyes follow his to the pink fringe on a lumbar pillow. I *like* my pillows tasteless and over-the-top.

"Not illegal." Unlike scaling the wall of a building. You need a permit to do that. Or at least permission.

"You could give me an apology pillow. It's like a home goods store in there." He laughs, his eyes crinkling with good humor.

"There's nothing wrong with a good pillow." It comes out defensively. I have a pillow addiction and I know it.

Now Ozzy knows it, too. He's counting ostentatiously, taking inventory of my mountains and mountains of pillows.

"Or a pie," he says musingly, as if my apologizing is a foregone conclusion and now we are simply negotiating terms. "I can give you a list of options."

"Excuse me?" The words fly out of my mouth when I should have said *get lost* or *no*. No is nice and simple. I blame Shonda—she's a bad influence.

"I speak all five love languages." He winks at me. "I accept apologies in any currency."

He is SO annoying.

"Climbing the building is illegal, and actions have consequences." I've aged thirty years in the last ten minutes. I am now the age of my mother.

He nods, all seriousness. "You don't want to kiss and make up? Should I send *you* a fruit bouquet?"

"Fruit *what*?"

"Hold that thought." He points a finger in my direction, vaults back over the waist-high wall dividing our spaces, and disappears into his loft. For a moment, I let myself hope that he is gone. I don't think he has a long attention span, and I'm not that interesting.

Somehow, though, my feet refuse to take me inside. It's not warm, and the balcony's chill sinks through my fuzzy socks. I'm not sure how Ozzy manages to run around with so little clothing on.

He comes rushing back like the ocean waves he loves so much, waving a black Sharpie. The cap is AWOL, and notes of ink and alcohol waft toward me.

He poises the marker tip above the bare skin of his muscled forearm. "Tell me what would make you happy. I take direction well."

He scrawls letters on his skin, draws bold loops and tight curves, thick and sure. I'm sure this is some kind of deviant metaphor for his penis. Or for how he would be in bed. *Ask for kisses*, an ill-behaved part of my brain suggests. *Or a date! Take him up on that coffee offer!*

He notices my distraction, and his mouth curls up in a wicked smile. "You've thought of something."

"Go away," I say. "Please."

The adverb feels like a weakness. He hasn't earned my politeness.

A frown puckers his forehead. "Your love language is not quality time spent together. Noted."

He ostentatiously strikes through something he's scrawled on his forearm.

He's all muscles and a light dusting of blond hair beneath the loopy all-caps manifesto he's written himself. He's out of room. Can he write on his abs next?

"We can't be friends," I say.

He hums a whisp of melody. "Pretty sure that's a country music song, but I can't remember how it ends."

"That's not the only thing you don't remember," I say.

He nods, looking chastened. "It was something important. The thing I forgot. I apologize."

It's ancient history. It doesn't matter. "You have a nice day now. Please get off my porch."

I march myself back inside. Then I go hide in the bathroom with my laptop.

★ ★ ★

"Is now a bad time?" Rosie leans over the wall of my cubicle. "Am I intruding? Is something wrong?"

She ogles the enormous fruit basket that is taking up far too much space on my desk. She's on a spy mission, sent to find out who my secret admirer is. My work life and my nonexistent personal life have collided and I'm off balance.

I take my ire out on the fruit basket. It's huge. The size of a hamper. Maybe even bigger than a wheelbarrow. Entire orchards have been denuded to fill it.

"Yes!" I snap.

"Problems in Shondaland?" Rosie snags a grape and chews happily.

"Nothing I can't handle." I walked-ran away from Ozzy yesterday in a righteous huff, fully prepared to hide out in my bathroom for the remainder of the weekend. After a few minutes, however, he'd ceded the field to me and vacated my balcony. From the banging and off-key singing that filtered through the wall, he'd spent the rest of the night working out. This explains why I'm haunted by dreams of his muscles (which are impressive).

When I left for work this morning, there was a note taped to my front door. A big, yellow smiley face grinned at me with tears coming out of its eyes. Maybe it's the crying-with-laughter emoticon? I have no clue; I've achieved the emotional maturity of an octogenarian. A bold *Sorry!* had been scrawled beneath the smiley face. I'd crumpled the whole thing up into a ball and left it in front of Ozzy's door.

That balled-up note now sits in the center of the fruit basket, perched on one of those little plastic sticks for floral enclosure cards.

"Is it my code?" Rosie swallows mock-dramatically. Plucks another grape. If she leans any farther over the wall, she will crash-land into my cubicle. "I knew I should have code reviewed before I committed, and I'm sorry I broke the nightly build. But Noah promised me he rebooted the server, and no one noticed because you're the only one who codes at dark o'clock, and I backed my changes out." She pauses to consume more fruit. I don't think she's truly chastened.

Also, I hate office life. And teamwork. And pretending that I'm absolutely fine with rogue server reboots. I miss my space geodes.

Rosie gives me sorry puppy dog eyes. She is the best intern ever.

"I had a run-in with a neighbor yesterday." I debate asking for more details about her coding fiasco, then decide that I don't want to know. "He and I had words."

"Was he mean? Inappropriate?" She hurls an indignant glance at me. She's my white knight defender in yoga pants. "I can come over and kick his butt!"

"I told him off." Mostly. Rosie looks impressed. And slightly skeptical. She knows that my backbone is made of marshmallow.

"Shonda would be proud. Sometimes the best answer is, 'Yes, yes I *can* kick your ass.'" She trots around the cubicle wall and perches on top of my desk. "Let's debrief."

"And then he sent me this fruit basket."

We both look at the basket. Ozzy's fruit basket is to baskets what a transatlantic shipping container is to an aluminum can. You'd think he was trying to make a point with all this rambutan and dragon fruit. A pineapple perches on top of Fruit Mountain, its rough skin covered in sharp spines. I have so many questions. *How does he know where I work? What if I had a citrus allergy? Did he poison it? How can he motivate fruit delivery people to show up so early on a Monday, and can I apply that lesson to my software team?*

"It's very...generous?" Rosie tries. She must sense my rage because she hyper-focuses on peeling a banana that has been lurking beneath its spinier companions in the basket.

"How does he know where I work?" I grumble. "Is he a stalker? Did he follow me? Track my phone?"

Rosie hypothesizes wildly (Bing! Drone surveillance! A clairvoyant consult!) while I check my email.

I ruthlessly break into her brainstorming. "Mystery solved. He sent me a LinkedIn request."

She deflates. "But at least you made an impression? I'm sure he respected you standing up for yourself."

"Sure." She fishes out the crumpled-up ball of paper. Smooths it out. Snorts. "What?"

She turns the paper so I can read Ozzy's addition: To my dearest, darling ogre.

I hate him so much.

"It's like he knows you!" she crows.

"He absolutely doesn't." If he did, he'd a) know that ghosting a person you kissed is a recipe for revenge and b) know that I am a competitive person. I hate to lose. I click over to the local plant nursery site and send an orange tree to Ozzy. I'll see his fruit basket and raise him a baby orchard.

"Fresh fruit!" Noah skids to a halt. He drops his scooter to the floor.

"Help yourself." I'm making plans to get even.

Five

By ten o'clock on Thursday night, I have wrestled Trip-Friendz's bug queue down to triple-digit numbers. I am Crocodile Dundee grappling with programmatic reptiles in the wilds of Australia. I'm muddy and exhausted, and for the next few hours I plan to hide from the world and mine space gems.

I stop downstairs before I head up to my loft. After Basketgeddon on Monday, I went stress shopping, and a text has alerted me to the presence of my pillowy consolations. They are a menagerie of embroidered flowers and orange tassels. There may be faux zebra fur, as well.

The problem with this step in my self-care plan, however, is that all packages are delivered to the building's mail room. My box of pillows is therefore trapped in a small room that only just meets the guidelines laid out by the United States Postal Service in their *Postal Operations Manual*. Most of the available space in this room is currently consumed by Ozzy, who is chatting up a delivery lady as he shows her pictures of random sea life on his phone. She beams at him, he smiles back, and then they pose for selfies together. Jesus Christ, does this man never go to work or leave the building?

The Code for Love

I zip in, grab my box while he's distracted, and hustle out the door. My usual superpower of invisibility does not work around him for reasons unknown, possibly because he lives to torture me with his incessant cheerfulness.

I make it as far as the mail room door. The wide expanse of the building's communal living space stretches out before me, a sofa-filled game reserve where I am the prey. I've got this. Head up. Walk fast. No eye contact.

"Wait up!" Ozzy bounds after me like a herd of graceful, predatory elephants.

I pretend he's talking to someone else.

The elevator looms in front of me. I peel off to the right and opt for the stairs. Voluntarily enclosing myself in a small, mirrored space with Ozzy is a bad idea, and he won't leave me alone now that he's got me in his sights.

He follows me at a jog. It's the fastest I have ever seen him move. His usual pace is more king of the jungle, a leisurely, masterful, lazy saunter. He sprawls. He takes up space. He occupies not one but two reserved parking spots in our basement garage. I hate him.

Biceps bulge as he juggles an enormous stack of boxes into a one-handed hold. He reaches a hand out to me. "Can I carry that box up for you?"

"Completely unnecessary." Although now I am tempted to order a cast-iron tub and watch him wrestle it up the stairs.

"Did you get the fruit basket?" He peers around his stack of boxes to look at me.

I slide him a look. He sighs.

"You did. You didn't like it. Or are you allergic? Shoot. Does pineapple make you itch? I shot a commercial once with a girl who couldn't stand the stuff."

He does not shut up. Ever.

He talks and talks and talks. By the time we reach the third floor, I am out of breath and he is rounding (finally) into the conclusion of his TED Talk on promoting a pineapple-flavored lip balm. I should tell him that I do not need to know about the weird rash his fabulous costar got when they kissed on set because he was wearing said pineapple lip balm.

As attested to by his social media—which I have not looked at in months—he is a bright, shining, beautiful star. He wears a smile on his face in almost every picture, flashes a self-deprecating laugh in the remainder. Even wiping out, falling off his board, being rolled by a wave, he is joyous. How can he be so perfect even in those imperfect moments? Charisma is his weapon and he wields it like a man-bunned Thor. The urge to retreat, to hide before he can hurt me more, is an undertow sucking me out to sea.

I add to my bucket list moving to a deserted island, a remote island in a frigid lake, an igloo on an iceberg.

He pauses by his door. "Good talk," he says.

It's my turn to say something, but I'm speechless.

A second passes.

An eternity.

"Night, neighbor!" he carols, disappearing inside his condo.

I imagine moving.

Not for the first time, I fall asleep sitting up. I jerk-startle awake from a dream in which I'm piloting a small spacecraft through pineapple-shaped debris. My eyes fly open, my hands instinctively clenching on my laptop as it slides toward the floor. I cannot afford to break my hardware now. We're days away from my demo and four weeks from code complete, and our codebase is anything *but* complete.

Lines of Java spill through my brain, pieces of logic connecting, and I should whiteboard this…it's right there almost… and then the solution I've been chasing for weeks gives me the finger and romps away to get lost in my hippocampus, leaving me 80 percent awake and 100 percent out of luck.

I'm so, so tired, and in less than five hours I need to achieve 100 percent awakeness and go back into the office. This close to our deadline, work from home has been forbidden. This is supposed to make us more productive, but instead just makes us hate each other. One more week of this and my team members will be complaining that they can hear each other breathing.

The problem is the code. Specifically: it doesn't work, despite endless rewrites. I see whiteboards in my dreams. I fix *bugs* in my dreams.9

I must have fallen asleep mid-descent on my ten-minute break, because my space shuttle is crumpled nose-down on an asteroid. *Game Over* blinks on the screen. *Play again?*

I check the bug queue automatically. I've closed more tickets than any other engineer in TripFriendz's history, but it's not enough. Fixing code may be my superpower, but the problem is that the original architecture simply doesn't work. As soon as I fix one issue, another crops up. Like the little Dutch boy with his finger in the dike, I'll be here all night trying to stave off disaster. Not even an octopus with eight hands could contain this mess.

Worse, the director of engineering knows it. The looks I get when I venture out into TripFriendz's communal kitchen in search of caffeine are knowing and sympathetic. My head will be the first to roll as Margie's is safe on her cruise ship. There are tersely worded emails in my inbox. Meeting requests. Noah is sending out his résumé. We are dead men walking.

Thumping noises emanate from the neighboring unit. They are loud, rhythmic, and totally obnoxious. Oh God, Ozzy's exercising at one in the morning. From the sound of things, he is running, singing like he's in a cadence competition and desperate to win first place. He does far too many plyometric exercises. Each jarring thud of his big body hitting the hardwood floors jolts me further out of my sleep.

Time to grow a spine. I set the laptop to one side.

My reflection in the glass slider is more Grim Reaper than confident, kick-ass woman. My tension lines have tension lines. My anxiety is mapped on my face for everyone to see, and I will need a truckload of collagen before this product release.

It's tempting to put on my noise-canceling headphones and disappear back into the Crystal Cluster Cosmos. Pink geodes make everything better.

Something sparkles outside, something far less pleasant than crystal-filled hollows. Thanks to the streetlights, half a moon, and a not insignificant amount of light pollution, it's easy to make out Ozzy's bare feet. They're bare and tanned, like the rest of him.

The bottom of one foot is nonchalantly braced against the half wall separating his space from mine; the other arches up and over, invading my air space.

The enemy has fired its missile. The ball is in my court.

I launch myself off the sofa and out the door. He may call out a "Thanks for the orange tree," but I can't hear him over the sound of my righteous indignation.

I charge over. "Remove *YOUR FEET* from *MY WALL!*"

I whisper-shout in deference to the nine o'clock noise ordinance.

A lazy, volume-agnostic "Hey, neighbor," floats up toward me.

I growl like a werewolf at a full moon. My fingers close around his offending ankle and nudge him back over the invisible line that divides us.

Mistake. His skin beneath my fingers is warm, and there are muscles and tendons, a seductively tensile strength in his ankle. God, what is wrong with me?

The lines of code marching through my brain blip out of existence. I feel Ozzy's body beneath my fingers. I'm imagining running my thumb up his misbehaving arch, kneading his skin. I'm unbending to go so far as licking. Tasting. Biting is definitely on my agenda.

He is entirely oblivious to the need churning in me.

"Good idea! Brace me!"

What on earth... His body *shifts*, surging against my hold, and I make the mistake of looking down.

He's a delicious golden brown all over. The sun has kissed him everywhere, and I am envious. I bet he doesn't even realize how beautiful he is. He moves his body into some impossible geometric shape with no visible effort. His heel is braced against my hand. I am part of this. I should let go, should push him away, but I am stuck. He is an irritating burr that hooks into my leg, the barnacle to my whale, the remora riding the side of my shark.

He's not wearing any pants. This is fine by me. This is—

Danger.

"Where are your pants?"

My question comes out nowhere near as calm and accusing as I would like. My words are, in fact, betrayingly breathy. I blame his boxer briefs. They are a black cotton, pillowy soft and wash worn. The elastic waistband sits snugly below his six-pack. They are also covered with bananas. Bright yellow, cheerful, embroidered bunches of bananas. Bananas are a dick-shaped fruit. I cannot look away.

Even more distracting, now that my brain is on the dick-observation train, is the shape of his...fruit. Ozzy is large absolutely everywhere. His banana is supersized. I have never, ever, not once in my life been served something so large.

"I'm comfortable." Hazel eyes sparkle at me. "Thank you

again for the fruit tree. It is now one of my most prized possessions. I keep it in my bedroom."

"Pants. Now. Please."

I absolutely don't feel a frisson of pleasure at my gift-giving success. It was meant to needle. He doesn't deserve to enjoy it, and I am not warmed by his graceful thanks.

Ozzy is busy considering my newest request/demand. "But I'm in my own home! It's a pants-optional zone. Feel free to remove yours."

We both look down at my pants. The only explanation for this is that he has short-circuited my brain with his pantsless state.

I look down, he looks down, and we both independently come to the conclusion that my righteous indignation has brought me outside with less in the way of pants than is ideal. I'm wearing a fuzzy brown sweatshirt and coordinating lounge shorts that expose my vampirically white legs. I may glow in the dark. Software engineering is not conducive to tanning—or vitamin D, outside time, and sunshine.

His mouth curls up in a wicked smile. "You look like a little brown bear! I'm going to call you Panda."

"Pandas are black and white," I point out. I ache to tell him to back off, that I've had my fill of cruel/unfortunate nicknames, that I'm tired of laughing along with other people's jokes.

"Not the really special ones!" He curls upward in an impressive display of abdominal muscles. His fingers tap mine where they are wrapped around his ankle.

No, wait. He reaches around me to pluck a stray Post-it note off my butt with surgical precision. His fingers don't stray, don't touch me. I mourn that touch I will never have.

I make a note to google pandas.

And also: download a hookup app.

Surely, I can carve out an hour a week for sex. A half hour. I'll eliminate the awkward preliminary meetup for drinks, coffee, or dinner. Skip the boring intro to the book for the good part. Dating sucks and I hate it. Why would you go to a restaurant and pay for an entire meal when you just want the éclair that comes at the end?

His foot flexes. His toes work against my palm.

I will never be able to buy bananas again. I institute a lifetime ban on the produce aisle.

He is still talking.

I tune back in just in time. Maybe.

I fire right back. "Why are you always here? Shouldn't you be out surfing?"

He should live somewhere where there are waves and TV cameras and prizes, right? My knowledge of competitive surfing is minimal despite my extensive post-kiss googling, but this building doesn't even possess a pool.

Also: I have the conversational sophistication of a five-year-old. A shadow passes over his face. It could be a passing cloud, a plane overhead.

"Bum knee. I'm professionally retired." He taps a faint red line that mars the smooth perfection of his thigh. I am the asshole here.

"No more competitive surfing?"

"Nope. Occupational hazard." He shrugs and flows into another position. "Wall Pilates helps." He studies my face. My guilt must be written there in all caps. "And it's not a good time of year for surfing here anyhow."

"Oh." My face burns with embarrassment.

"Hey," he says, far too kindly. "The best waves are January to March. It's June. And you have to watch out for baby seals and sharks."

Wait. *Does* he remember our kiss under the boardwalk? I

hate that I can't be sure, at least not unless I ask him outright, which is a level of awkwardness that I refuse to deal with. I'm drowning in a sea of mortification, and a shark attack might be a blessing.

"I'm sorry?" I force the words out. They don't sound believable but I mean them.

I search his face for clues. Does he or does he not recognize me?

He smiles back at me. I vote: *not*.

"You want to come surfing with me?"

No. No, I do not. I've seen *Jaws* and I like my sharks best in an aquarium. Shark safety is mission critical.

He laughs at the expression on my face. "Just kidding, Panda Bear. I haven't been on a board for months."

"I have a name." And so many questions.

Why no surfing? Was there a wipeout? A rival surfer who kneecapped him? Vicious penguins?

He winks. Now he's trying to embarrass me. You couldn't pay him to end my suffering. "I like it here."

He executes a spectacular backward roll, leaps to his feet (whatever is wrong with his knee does not affect his agility), and then vaults one-handed over the wall. He is in my space.

"Can I come in? To borrow a pillow? A cup of sugar?"

He leans around me, shamelessly peering in my slider door.

"Your place is great!" His big shoulder gently bumps mine. It's a love tap. The barest of nudges. "I love it. Mine is so empty."

I turn away. "Okay?"

He laughs happily and ricochets to the far end of my balcony. He is a ball of endless, irritating energy. "I know, right? Can we online shop together?" He rushes on without waiting for an answer. "We can be shopping buddies! I bet you know all the best places for pillows!"

I must have been a truly terrible person in some former life. Or I'm being paid back for my teenage years when I raged and shouted and trampled all over everyone in my life. It's only fair. I was awful.

"Are you never serious?"

Ozzy replies, "I am very serious about pillows. And tension. You look tense."

He wanders up behind me, and I pretend I don't feel him coming. He doesn't smell like pineapples. Cedarwood, maybe. Lemons and salt. Something expensive and wild. I exhale, evicting the Ozzy scent from my nostrils. Breathing is optional from here on out.

"May I?" His hands hover above my shoulders.

"Yes." I am oxygen starved. That's why I consent.

His big hands cover my shoulders, warm and firm. They knead and squeeze. He finds tight spots, and they magically unfurl like panties dropping. He isn't doing anything a paid masseuse wouldn't do, but my body is on fire and my brain offline.

"Is the surfing retirement why you aren't you still working with Miles to Go?"

I blurt the question out, and Ozzy is on me like a shark on chum. "You read my LinkedIn! Is that where you first noticed me? At a surf competition promoting the app?"

I must be desperate to avoid humiliation, because I prevaricate. "It doesn't speak well of you that you can't remember our introduction."

He crows, "So you admit we've met!"

Twice.

"It's not impossible," I confess.

His hands drop away from my shoulders. I'm disappointed. I won't be tipping him.

Oblivious, he grabs my hands and dances me around in a

circle. I stumble after him awkwardly. "What are you doing? Why are you like this?"

"Tell me our origin story!"

"Answer my question first." I negotiate for time.

Ozzy frowns. It's adorable. "Miles to Go put together all these one-size-fits-all trips, but I didn't want to go to those places alone. How did I know I would like them? Who would I talk to about them?"

I snort. "You wanted a travel buddy? You never travel alone."

His jaw tightens. His frown deepens to something less cute and more pained. "You really shouldn't make assumptions, Panda Bear. It's rude."

"Uhhh..." I stare into his eyes, and he stares back, like this lack of space between us isn't setting off his proximity alarms. Doesn't he have a travel harem? He's so popular. He's sugar and spice, and everything nice. Which I guess makes me snips and snails, but at least I get a shell and a portable home. Snails are the RV dwellers of the gastropod world.

I open my mouth, possibly to apologize, but he says in a rush, "I spent a lot of time on the surfing circuit. Like, a *lot* of time. It's a job that's never done."

I perform the mental gymnastics necessary to pretend that an entire ocean with monster waves is an office. Swap cubicles for surfboards. It's a tough sell, and a little vague, but I think he's saying he worked all the time. We...have something in common besides a shared wall?

Ozzy Wylder. Workaholic.

Possibly lonely.

"Life-work balance." I make a face. "I mean, does that even *exist*?"

He nods vehemently. We *do* agree on something. "When you love what you're doing, it's not even work, right?"

I'm not sure I would go that far.

I shrug.

He shrugs.

"And then," he continues, our strange moment of détente over, "I wiped out, busted up my knee, and left the competition circuit. Which meant I left my friends there, too. Or maybe they were more coworkers. We don't talk much, because all we had to talk about before was work. Waves."

"Don't forget the rip currents." His hands return to digging into the knots beneath my shoulder blades, and it hurts so good. "I'll bet you ran into a deadly sandbar or two. Maybe a shaved ice stand or a tropical lei."

He huffs out a laugh. "Sure. All in a day's work."

The kneading of his hands makes it hard to follow our conversation. "So you're saying you don't have any friends?"

Ozzy nearly slumps against my back. "Not exactly."

"But you've been so busy winning surf competitions that you don't know anyone who doesn't ride a board? And you don't talk to the board-riding people in your life because you, yourself, are not currently riding any boards?"

Another laugh. "I know you! Are you free to travel around the world with me? I'm currently underemployed and looking to take my life in a new direction."

There's an idea tickling at the back of my head. "We would make the worst travel companions in history," I say absently.

And it's true. We would.

But it's...an interesting idea.

I take the five miniscule steps over to my whiteboard and grab a marker. What if... What if the most important variable is *who* you go with and not *where*?

I start sketching out the process to get someone from alone to paired up and on a plane. I fill the whiteboard with shapes and arrows. All the guidelines that the computer will need to perform its one task: matching you with your perfect travel buddy on your perfect trip.

"Don't mind me," Ozzy says. "I can see you're busy."

I dig in. The guidelines would have to be… Yes, that could work… What if I…

I scribble frantically. Draw circles. Arrows. Scrawl notes.

Ozzy colors in my circles. Moves an arrow. Lobs words my way that I ignore because I am in the zone. Asks a million billion questions that I also ignore. Who knew that annoying surfer dudes made for such great inspiration?

I have tried everything—even, at my nadir, podcasts on manifestation—and now I know what to do next.

Ozzy naps on my sofa. He wakes up noisily and rolls to his feet to *go work out and do some stuff, but we should totally do this again!* He looks adorably rumpled as he reminds me to *credit him because he wants a byline.* I bet he'd love the blame command in our version control system.

I work on. And on and on. By the time San Francisco's infamous morning fog has burned off and I can see past my balcony, I have a wireframe and a new direction.

I do owe Ozzy something, I decide. A few clicks of my keyboard and I discover that Amazon will same-day ship cacti.

I can order enough barbed plants to line the entire wall, to turn it into a spiky fortification, a botanical KEEP OUT sign. Take that, Ozzy Wylder. Keep your feet to yourself. I don't need your strong hands, big body, and offensive cheerfulness in my life.

My finger hovers over the Buy Now button. Clicks.

I'll leave it on his doorstep tomorrow.

Six

Fun fact number one: brown pandas really are a thing.

Fun fact number two: the Qinling panda is rare and uncommon. It hides its brown self in some Chinese mountain, the name of which I cannot pronounce, interbreeding and generally refusing to interact with the rest of the world.

I can never, ever let Ozzy know that he is right.

I leave the cactus on his doorstep as little Friday Funday present.

In exchange, he sticks a Post-it of a fuzzy, brown bear on my door. It has curly eyelashes not found in nature and is more blob than bear.

On it, he's scrawled, *GRRRRR*.

The blinders fall from my eyes. They smash against the floor. I am no longer blind. I see. Ozzy's relentless niceness, his jovial good nature, his annoying *helpfulness*—it's all part of his master plan. I've been so caught up in my work that I haven't caught on. My peopling skills are poor, so as always, I'm late to the party and nobody has noticed. I've been focused on TripFriendz, trying to do the best ever job and stand out so that they see me. I thought my efforts had misfired, like a bad spell or a mislabeled Amazon package, and brought me to Ozzy's attention instead of my bosses'.

Ozzy, my neighbor, my dear nemesis, is an evil genius. I'm sure he has a villain origin story. He's doing these things on purpose to irritate me. To get a rise out of me, to torment me. I'm sure it's revenge for his near-arrest. Never mind. I'm on to him now, and the joke's on him.

I am a competitive bitch, and this is war.

In the last three days, I have checked the following off my whiteboard list:

- Sign Ozzy's number up for texts about the upcoming national election. Good citizenship is important. I indicate that he's ambivalent about who to vote for and would love more information.
- Look out for Ozzy's immortal soul by expressing interest in joining several local churches.
- Enter Ozzy in online contests for free airfare, free hotel stays, and a free deluxe tropical vacation if he sits through a short presentation. The timeshare people hound him relentlessly.
- Flood his inbox with emails about Nigerian princes, free AAA car kits, misplaced packages, and Etsy side hustle courses.
- Donate ten dollars to name the world's tiniest snake at the local zoo "Ozzy's Trouser Snake."
- Send him a package labeled XXXL Sex Toys. Spoiler (literally): it's a banana.
- Purchase and detonate a penis glitter bomb (a classic, and I've booked a repeat on the theory that he would never suspect it a second time).
- Send forth my spider army.

I am particularly pleased with this last one. I purchased a thousand plastic spiders from an online Halloween discount site with same-day delivery, and now I'm deploying my arthropodan minions one eight-legged soldier at a time. Ozzy yelped when he discovered the first spider on his balcony two mornings ago, and I've added new spiders every day. Spiders march toward his door, invade his balcony. They cling to his railing and have swarmed his key frog.

Take that. He's been killing me with kindnesses, smiling and beaming, ruthlessly moving into my building. My space. My *life*. He thinks I won't see through him, that I'll be happy with the crumbs of his kindness. I wonder sometimes if our kiss was a prank and I'll understand the punch line later.

A door slams next door.

Ozzy's whistling stops abruptly. He may have started our neighbor wars, but I have taken our battlefield to a whole new level. It is literally raining spiders this happy, hostile Monday morning. I spare a brief thought for the possibility that he has a spider phobia, will stroke out on the spot, and I will spend twenty years in a maximum-security prison paying for my crimes. Worth it? Maybe.

I peer through my peephole, but it's not tuned to the Ozzy channel. My view is limited to a two-foot by two-foot slice of our shared hallway. The carpet is not doing anything interesting. I debate logging into my ring doorbell account but that's so much work.

Gargantuan, Sasquatch-sized feet thump down the hallway. Ozzy has shaken off my spider attack and is going about his day.

I fling my door open. I intend to yell at him to be quiet (yes, I am aware of the irony), but he whirls around like an aquatic ninja and flicks a two-fingered salute (and a spider) at me. It's cool and funny. I steam.

"Good morning!" He beams at me. There's a spider atop his man bun.

"Is it?"

He does not pick up on my subtext. He nods vigorously, and the spider falls to its plastic death.

"You might want to check your car," he advises.

I wait, but he does not volunteer additional information. My brain suggests various possibilities. The car has been towed. He's written rude messages in my dirty windshield. He's planted a glitter bomb in our parking structure, and I will have to demo TripFriendz's app sparkling like an ancient vampire. He smirks. It's as if he can read my mind.

I cave first, sacrificing my pawn for the greater good. My plans are longer term and I need information. "Are you going out?"

Usually, he exits the building in black athletic shorts and an ancient T-shirt advertising a surf shop somewhere I have never been. Workout clothes. He must live on air and influencer fees because he doesn't seem to do any actual work or go into an office. Perhaps he's a trust-fund baby. Or hocked the enormous gold-plated trophy he won at his last surfing competition and is living off the proceeds.

Today, however, he's unexpectedly upgraded to pants with buttons, albeit of the blue-jeans variety. An unbuttoned shirt has been shrugged insouciantly over his T-shirt. This is black tie for Ozzy.

"Hey!" I bellow after him. "Are you going out?"

"Are you interested in my whereabouts, Pandora Fyffe? Should I share my location with you?" He waves his phone at me.

I hold my hand out. "Sure!"

He smells a trap, but it's too late. He's trapped by his own fake good manners. He unlocks his phone and hands it over.

Suspiciously, my information is already in his contacts, which may explain the unexplained uptick in pet adoption emails I've received this week. I share his location with me, regretting that I don't have enough time to switch the keyboard to Uyghur.

Still, there's now an Ozzy dot on my phone. I legally have his phone number. We are digitally connected.

He takes his phone back. Examines it for booby traps. Picks an errant piece of glitter out of the case.

"I'm doing a thing at Aquarium of the Bay," he offers, despite my having shown zero interest in continuing our non-conversation. "For school kids."

"Where's your surfboard?"

He clucks his tongue. "It's not nice to stereotype people, Pandora. I am a well-rounded person with non-paddle-based interests. Where's your laptop?"

"My laptop is none of your business," I say loftily. "I didn't realize you worked."

Unlike us lesser mortals. He rocks back on his heels. He's trying to figure out my angle. Or perhaps he's—wisely—wondering what mysterious but embarrassing packages will show up if I discover his place of work.

"I'm volunteering," he qualifies.

I give him my best sympathetic nod. "You work for free. You shouldn't undervalue yourself. You should at least go for an internship."

His brow furrows as he tries to work out if I'm insulting him. Spoiler: I am. The old Pandora, the one who was terminated, the one who nobody knows her name? That Pandora would have made polite noises and pretended to admire him for his charitable endeavors. Today he gets Pandora 2.0 and the unvarnished truth.

He launches into an explanation about his plans for the

day, which involve escorting groups of impressionable youth through a glass tunnel. Marine life will swim overhead. Biology facts will be imparted. A good time will be had by all. I hear how it's a bummer sharks are never still, because it makes picture taking so gosh darn hard. I nod and smile as if this is the best thing I have ever heard. I've never met anyone more selfless! So giving! Let me toss you in the shark tank and bring your photographic subject to you!

Eventually, he has to give up on making conversation with me and gets in the elevator. Wherever he's really going, he needs to be there and not here. I wave goodbye to him like an airline steward deplaning an unruly passenger. Buh-bye! Thanks *so* much! You have a nice day now!

As soon as the door dings shut, I launch myself back into my condo.

To prepare for our next encounter, I do yet another internet deep dive on Ozzy Wylder. This is strictly for research purposes, and I barely glance at the treasure trove of online shirtless, swim-trunks-wearing Ozzy photos. Maybe I can ferret out his dirty little secrets. When I reveal to him that I'm in the know, he'll fall on his knees. Beg me to spare him. I'll demand he grovel-apologize at the next condo board meeting, and he'll *do it*.

Unfortunately, online Ozzy is disgustingly sunshiny.

I reconfirm that he will turn thirty in three years, making him a younger man to my older woman. He is photographed in public with his parents, voted in the last three elections although he missed the fourth, and has no parking tickets, arrest warrants, or embarrassing TikToks. He started surfing at the age of twelve and has since won more prize money than the GDP of a small country, which could account for his current state of idleness. Oh, and he likes taking pictures of wildlife.

His Instagram has more pictures of seabirds than surf bunnies in the last six months.

Undaunted, I open a new browser tab and sign into ChatGPT. Having exhausted my own mental resources, I set it to brainstorming pranks to pull on your neighbor. It seems I am only capable of assisted fun. ChatGPT chides me for my ill intentions and reluctantly lists twenty harmless pranks. It admonishes me to help clean up afterward and avoid triggering any of my neighbor's phobias. ChatGPT is Team Ozzy.

I give up on computer-assisted mayhem and instead climb over the half wall that separates my space from Ozzy's. It's the work of a moment to steal the key from his stupid key frog. He's practically inviting me in.

I skulk across the hall, open his door, and slink inside. Shit. What if he has a doorbell cam? Or some kind of high-tech security system to protect his surfing trophies? Since it's too late to back out—perhaps I can pretend temporary amnesia and/or confusion about which door is mine?—I look for something to rearrange. ChatGPT advised incremental, daily changes as prank worthy, but my nerves demand this be a one and done.

Ozzy's condo is unexpected. A solitary black-and-white photo of the Hawaiian state bird hangs on the wall. My banana gift lives on in a box on the counter, attracting fruit flies. Instead of a potted plant or a chair, he's decorated with a set of weights. A pile of black nylon gear bags and a tangle of tripods. A television screen NASA would envy. Some surfing stuff.

Since invading his bathroom is a step too far, I settle for rearranging his collection of surfboards. They lean against the wall in a surprisingly orderly line. Who knew one man could own so many? Long, longer, thick, broad—that one might be a boogie board. Orange with white stripes, yellow with Hawaiian flowers, a Day-Glo blue. Pink palm trees, because Ozzy is not constrained by vegetation found in nature. He's compensating for something. Or he's easily bored. When I tug on the closest board, it's like nautical Jenga and the entire row shifts, careening toward me, listing, making an ungodly racket. He's definitely going to know I was here. I shove everything back upright as best I can, reordering as I go.

It seems insufficient. Boring. I could…wrap them in cling wrap? I calculate the amount of plastic product that will be required, add in the same-day delivery fees, and decide to opt for something more cost-effective. The Ozzy dot is still at the San Francisco wharf. Unless he's invented a teleporter or grown wings, I have time.

I watch his dot skitter back and forth, and for a moment I can see the happy, fish-filled scene in my head. He's just so good with people. Kids. Dogs. Probably with random seagulls and trash pandas, too. He's the opposite of me. No one's ever forgotten who he is. I imagine a spotlight shining down on him as he leads his mini fan club through the aquatic exhibits. A ray of golden sunshine. A divine finger pointing at him from on high: this is my chosen one.

It's very motivational. I must win our war.

I scoot back into my condo and retrieve my lipstick. It's a singular, solitary tube that rattles around my empty makeup drawer because I've never bothered to learn what to do with cosmetics. Rosy pink? Optimistically named Tease? Two of the reasons I've never used it. Today is a day for firsts.

I recheck Ozzy's dot—still lecturing his charges on the joys of the ocean—and dart back into his condo. I unsheathe my lipstick and draw a smiley face on each board.

Take that, Ozzy Wylder.

I wake up much, much later, face glued to my laptop keyboard. Ozzy has texted me at some point between sundown and dark o'clock. **I didn't know you liked makeup!**

He accompanies this with a picture of a double-crested cormorant. The bird's feathers are tufts on either side of its head, ruffled, untamed.

Let's do ours together. Pandora? PANDORA! PANDOOOOORA!

He's a cute puppy. The dryer sheet that clings to me. A burr whose barbs have hooked into my leg.

And five minutes later: **Dora?**

Followed by: **Don't make me come over there.**

I text back, Wrong number, before I fall asleep for real.

When I head into the office on Tuesday morning, he's left a message for me. It's written in shaving cream, the letters dripping down my door: THIS MEANS WAR.

Maybe.

His manly shaving cream isn't stiff enough to hold its form. It drips. It flops. He should do something about that because it's possible he's just invited me over for tea.

As if. I consider defacing his door, but I'm short on time. Fortunately, I'm well prepared *and* an engineer. It's the work of seconds to set up my glitter bomb. It's a simple pull tab release, the string tied around his doorknob. As soon as he opens the door, the string will go taut and *BOOM*. Glitterpalooza.

Ozzy will remember me with each tiny, shiny speck.

Seven

Trainwreck.

Disaster.

The Titanic ramming the iceberg over and over is an understatement. Lounge chairs slide off the Titanic's deck and into the water; the lights flicker. The passengers scream.

The director of engineering—"Call me Bob"—sits at one end of the conference table. There are strategically empty chairs on either side of him because no one wants to get too close. That's the kill zone. His arms are crossed over his chest, and he wears a surly glower.

"Who peed in his Cheerios?" Rosie whispers. She sounds worried.

Zoomed to Godzilla-like size, our bug queue is projected on the screen. I'm an engineer who fixes things, but our software is unfixable. As soon as we fix one line of code, another breaks. Not only can our testers not successfully book a trip, but the travel recommendations are wrong. Bob searched for tropical vacations, and our algorithm recommended a cruise to Antarctica. *Abandon all hope, ye who enter here.* We haven't built a brilliant new travel app—we've constructed a new circle in hell.

"I'll pitch my travel buddy alternative. He'll love it," I lie. Bob is clearly incapable of loving anything.

Rosie clears her throat and leans forward. "Remember Shonda. She will guide us."

I admire her optimism. Noah fishes for a flip-flop under the table. He has two hundred bugs in his queue. Casey has three hundred. I have twelve, but I also haven't got more than two hours sleep in the last week. I'm holding my eyes open with my fingers. Lying down under the table and snatching a quick nap would boost my productivity by 500 percent.

Bob cuts into the attempts of Fiona, our project manager, to minimize the colossal number of errors that we've uncovered. "No," he snaps.

He is not a Shonda fan.

Fiona blinks. She opens her mouth.

"This is unacceptable." Bob rolls over her. "How do you plan to fix this? How are you getting this project back on track?"

Rosie nudges me. I inhale. *Go time. Pitch, pitch, PITCH!* "I—"

The room explodes as everyone talks at once.

Noah unhelpfully mimes a bomb exploding; Rosie sits bolt upright on her chair, talking over everyone. I think she might be trying to intercede on my behalf. Six engineers, one director, a random woman in a very nice pantsuit, and the guy who delivers bagels (who has stuck around for no discernable reason) launch into diatribes about what is wrong with Engineering. They have plans, ideas to sell. Loudly. There is hand waving and f-bombs that are entirely inappropriate in an office setting (*but I feel you, Noah, I feel you*). Casey diagrams a piece of code on the whiteboard that looks like it could launch a nuclear missile.

I wait for a break in the noise to share my travel buddy plan. And wait. And wait some more. The director's scowl has carved deep grooves into his forehead and alongside his mouth. He radiates his displeasure as he snaps his laptop shut. He glances at his phone. Tosses his coffee cup in the recycling bin. We're losing him. Oh God, he's leaving. His next stop will be HR and we'll all have an email. *You're fired, effectively immediately.*

"I need a talking stick," I mutter. There's no getting a word in edgewise. No one is listening to me.

"A big club," Rosie agrees instantly. *She's* listening to me. She's an excellent multitasker. "I can shut them up."

She jams her fingers in the mouth—rainbows on her nails, a glittery moon on one thumb—and whistles.

All heads swivel toward us.

Silence falls. Okay, so I really didn't expect that to work.

"Pandora has the floor," Rosie says firmly. "She has an alternative proposal to share with us."

But…my brain freezes, and no words come out of my mouth. Everyone is looking, and looking, and looking, and my slide deck has not magically jumped off my desktop and onto the projector screen. This is the most intensely uncomfortable moment of my life.

Rosie nudges me hard. "Do you want me to run your deck?"

God. Do it. Also, please read the words and give my presentation for me. Director Bob is half out of his chair and Pantsuit Lady has drifted toward the door. I nod frantically at Rosie. *"YES."*

Rosie is up for the challenge. "Travel buddies! A world-class matching algorithm! Dum, dum, *dum,* DUM DUUUMMMMMMM."

She attempts a drumroll on the tabletop. Noah lends her an assist, tapping a percussive rhythm on his side. Bob looks like he may not wait until he's in the HR lady's office to fire us. The Titanic nosedives into the deepest crevasse in the ocean.

Visualize your audience naked. Google promises this works for presentation anxiety. I inappropriately strip my coworkers to their underwear, naked being a bridge too far (plus: Bob). For absolutely no reason, Ozzy pops into my head. I see him sprawled on my sofa, one thick, muscled arm behind his head. The other slides down his chest and into the front of his pineapple-print briefs. He cups his massive banana of a dick and... Am I drooling?

Rosie nudges me again. She may have cracked a rib. I glance down at the bear Post-it that is stuck to the left of my trackpad for no discernable reason.

Shonda, Rosie mouths.

I try to pretend I am a super successful, highly creative media executive as I stand up. Semi-convinced, my knees hold. *Shonda* can walk to the front of the room. *Shonda* is not worried that her shirt is riding up and her pants are stuck in her butt crack. I trip over my own foot, but I make it.

Conversation is starting to resume as I stop in front of the whiteboard and erase Casey's code. It would never execute. There's a logic error in the tenth line.

"Who are you?" Director Bob's backside (which I am never, ever imagining naked) hovers over his chair. He's leaving. Walking out. My opportunity is rapidly vanishing.

"Pandora Fyffe. I'm the chief play officer's replacement." I'm the whole wheat bagel the coffee shop offers when they've just sold the last cake pop to the customer in front of you. I'm second choice. Better than nothing.

"Make this work and the job is yours," he quips and I nod. We have a deal. He sits down—all the way—and looks at me. His face telegraphs, *Don't think we've met.*

Spoiler: we have.

"Yes. Slide, please," I say to Rosie. She dramatically punches a button on my keyboard. "I have an alternate proposal for you, one that will get us to our goal of launching a revolutionary new travel-booking engine."

My voice is thinner than a model at New York Fashion Week. My TripFriendz T-shirt, the open button-up shirt, and blue jeans—these suddenly seem insufficient. I want a pantsuit. A makeover. Armor.

"When's Margie back?" He talks to Pantsuit Lady, as if I'm not presenting. He's so rude. "Soon?"

Pantsuit Lady bends down and whispers something in his ear. They both look slightly constipated.

I forge ahead with my presentation. This Shonda imitator needs to pee when nervous, so the sooner I start, the sooner I can finish and run to the unisex restroom.

"We've been trying to come up with a recommendation algorithm that pairs people with trips." I point to my slide that lays out our current project goals in Times New Roman sixteen-point font: tell people where to go, sell them trips to said locations, rake in the cash. The sunshine-yellow background (which Google promised me is cheerful) ruthlessly swallows up my bullet points.

"I am aware." Bob's voice is drier than the Sahara.

There's a wave of laughter. Someone should have brought popcorn.

I plow ahead. Nod to Rosie, who advances the slides. "But that's the wrong problem."

"Pretty sure it's not," Bob rumbles. He looks personally affronted. Oh God. Was this disaster *his* idea?

There's no way to go but forward.

Briefly, I entertain a plan to run out of the room, down the stairs, and onto the street. I can move into a cardboard box and earn an income begging passersby to fill my empty coffee cup with spare change. Which no one even *has* anymore because who carries cash? It's all Venmo and Cash App and probably some new payment app that just launched yesterday but that my entire engineering team will use to split the bill if we ever have time to go out to lunch.

"Instead of matching travelers to trips, we'll match them to their perfect travel buddy."

Reaction ripples through the room. Bob frowns. My currentAnxietyLevel increments.

I move to my next slide. I've put together compelling stats on the number of solo travelers out there, the atrociously high single supplement charged by so many travel providers, all the reasons why it's cheaper, safer, and just gosh darn easier to travel as a couple. I graph the data points: every year more single people venture out into the world. The straight line goes up and up and up…but the question really is: do they actually *want* to be on their own?

I force myself to look around the room. To make eye contact. "Stop me if you've heard any of these when you travel solo. 'Is it just you?' 'We need a minimum of two people.' 'Aren't you lonely? Don't you have *friends*?'"

There are head nods. Confirming noises. Noah googles on his phone.

I round second base, running for home. "How many times has someone you know blown up your phone with a thousand vacation pics? They're doing it because they want someone else to share the experience with. They want to talk about it. They don't want to be *alone*. It's not that they don't have friends—it's that their friends don't have the same time off or maybe the same interests or even enough cash to tag along. There are *good* reasons why our solo traveler is alone. Case in point…"

Rosie advances to the next slide.

"Noah sent us five hundred pictures of the cookie dough croissant he enjoyed in Paris last month."

"I would have loved a travel buddy," he instantly confirms. I now love Noah, in a completely platonic, workplace-appropriate way. "And yes, I have friends."

He looks anxious, so I move on quickly.

"If a tree falls in the forest, does it make a sound? If you're the only one who sees something really cool, does it count? Will you remember it?"

Rosie is nodding enthusiastically, her head whipping back and forth like a bobblehead doll in a hurricane. She's all in. Color her convinced.

"We're going to find you your perfect travel buddy. We're Trip*Friendz*. And *then* once we've matched you to your new trekking friend or sightseeing partner or whomever, we'll sell you the perfect trip the two of you can take. Together."

Rosie is clapping enthusiastically. "It's matchmaking for the travel set!"

"And this is how we're going to do it," I say.

And then I tell them.

I lay out the algorithm I've come up with. The wireframe. The databases we'll need. The enormous tables of data we'll require to make this all meaningful. The engineers look part sick to their stomachs, part enthused.

Calling this a technical challenge is like opting into a short stroll after Thanksgiving dinner and finding yourself at the base of the Matterhorn with nowhere to go but up. There will be dead bodies (hopefully not mine). Painful scrambles across rock. Way too much snow and ice. Fingers and toes may have to be sacrificed.

"But we *can* do this." I round into my conclusion. I'm sliding toward home plate and a ball is streaking toward my head. I'm so close. "I already have a working prototype for the algorithm."

Bob blinks. Frowns. Blinks some more.

Pantsuit Lady leans in. "How will we get the data points for the travelers? It will have to be opt in, but is it a blind date or do you get to swipe left and right on your potential buddies?"

That feels suspiciously like signing up for a threesome.

"It will *not* be a popularity contest," I say firmly. "We're going to ask meaningful questions and analyze your responses. And then we'll find you your perfect travel buddy and send you off on a trip together."

I sit down. My knees tremble and I have to stress pee urgently. Presenting sucks.

There is a moment of silence and then the usual explosion of noise. But...they're talking about my idea.

Five minutes later I have a green light and a week.

Bob walks up as I'm gathering up my things. Rosie thumbs-ups me behind his back. Then she draws the letter *u* in the air. Or maybe it's a boat? A slice of cantaloupe. *Smile*, she mouths.

Oh. Right. I do my best.

"Nice job, Firth. I see you do want to be the next chief play officer. Make this work and it's yours."

He nods brusquely and steps away. Pantsuit Lady falls in beside him. They're almost inappropriately joined at the hip.

Her question drifts back to me as they walk away. "Do you think she can handle Margie's job? You wanted someone who can lead."

I'm going to brain her with my titanium reusable water bottle.

"I know. But she's motivated." Bob moves toward the door. He may not know my last name, but he does know that I can hear him, right? "And she's here."

I'm stale Cheetos when you need a midnight snack. A paper towel when the toilet roll is empty. The last middle seat on the plane. I turn toward the door. I need to stand up for myself. Sell myself. Do *something*. Pantsuit Lady shoots me an assessing look over her shoulder. And a smile. That seems like positive feedback.

"You can do it!" Rosie sings in my ear. She is my cheerleader. The mom clapping for her awkward five-year-old at gymnastics class.

"I can." It's a vow. I inhale. Believe in myself. I'll nurture the tiny seed of my algorithm plan until it sprouts like Jack's bean stalk.

All of you will see who I am.

Eight

My doorbell rings. And rings. And rings some more.

I give up and open the door. The marauders have crossed the moat and are storming into the castle.

Spoiler alert: my midnight guest is Ozzy.

He shakes his head, looking disappointed. Take a number, I want to tell him. You are not the first person I've disappointed. "You should check before you open your door."

"Right. Because it could be the Big Bad Wolf. Or a political campaigner. Are you here because you're concerned about my soul?"

The corner of his mouth kicks up. Sweet mamaloosa, is he ever hot. He leans against my door frame, which may lean right back. It's the smartest door frame ever. His broad shoulders stretch the limits of a T-shirt with a cartoon fish on the front, and he hasn't shaved in days. Golden scruff roughens his rugged jaw. I am unaffected.

Liar.

He holds out a handful of yellow and green plant life that I take automatically; identification eludes me. Weeds? Flowers? They're all the same to me, although these look suspiciously like something I've seen growing on the curb out front. On the other hand, I've been working non-stop since Bob greenlit my TripFriendz rewrite two days ago. It's possible I'm hallucinating.

"I come in peace. Permission to come aboard?" He's all warm eyes and wicked smile. He's buttering me up. Coming in for the kill. I try to resist but I'm weak.

"Why would I ever let you in?"

He contemplates his weed offering. "To set a good example? As an overture of goodwill?"

Oh, sure. He can't expect me to lay down my arms just because he asks, can he?

I tap a finger against my lower lip ostentatiously. "Your diplomatic skills are lacking, Wylder."

"Let's declare a truce," he proposes, dropping to one knee dramatically. He produces a Ring Pop from somewhere and holds it out. "Will you be mine?"

I toss the weeds in his face. "No, thank you. Can you go home now?"

"Maybe."

"Have a good—" I don't get any further because Ozzy's moved faster than anyone should be able to and is now kneel-lying in my doorway.

"I'm suing for peace, woman."

I don't believe him for a moment, but I'm a busy *woman* and I can make this work to my advantage. If I let him in, I'll lull him into a false sense of security, and he'll never see my next move coming. I examine this new plan for holes but decide it's logical enough for dark o'clock.

"If you come in, will you shut up?"

He mimes zipping his lips. Whatever. I turn and walk away from the door. Settle back into my pillow fortress on the couch.

He's not really here to hook up with me. My past experience with dating confirms that this is a solid data point. He's bored and I'm fun to torment.

He throws himself into the mound of pillows enthusiastically.

I peek at him from the corner of my eye. He looks as if the silence is killing him, and it's only been three seconds. This is more fun than I expected.

He spreads his arms, petting my pillows. He's a pasha reclining on a divan. His bare feet draw my attention down his muscled, blue-jeans-wrapped legs. The dark waistband of his boxer briefs tease me when he briefly jackknifes up to grab a throw and tuck it around us.

I grab my laptop. "Make yourself at home."

Not really, but dear Lord, the silence mocks me.

His gaze dips down, returning my wardrobe inventory. I'm wearing a fifteen-year-old Mathlete T-shirt with a suspicious stain on the hem, no bra, and a pair of fuzzy socks that have more pills than a pharmacy. Both my hair and my pits are unwashed and unloved. He is the beauty queen here.

I am working. Manifesting that it be so. Frowning at my screen. I tap a line of garbage characters, delete it, and start over.

Ozzy jackknifes upward. He reads over my shoulder. I should make him sign an NDA, because my promotion is riding on this project, and I am a deeply suspicious person. Except he's warm. It's kind of nice.

Plus, we've already spent more mostly clothed time together than my last hookup. He raises his hand for me to call on him.

"What?"

He rests his chin on my shoulder. "Permission to speak?"

"Dude. You just did. I could sue you for breach of contract."

He waits. Breathes too loudly. His breath on my ear is fantastic. I still count to ten before I answer him because I'm mean.

"Granted."

"Oh thank God. What are you doing?"

The words pour out of him. He does not remove himself from my person. He is draped against me like my favorite throw blanket.

"Data collection."

"Are you using statistical modeling for your data analysis?"

I twist away from him so I can see his face.

"OMG. Are you smart, too?" He grins. Question answered. "That's so unfair." I mean this with all my heart. "How can you look like that and be athletic *and* smart? Are you personal friends with God? Have you unethically enslaved a wish-granting genie?"

His grin widens. "I'm hearing that you think I'm hot, smart, and talented. Please continue."

I make a scoffing sound. "And an asshole."

Hazel eyes twinkle at me. He's so stinking beautiful. He's also so right here next to me on my couch. There are mere inches between us, no pillows, and our legs are in imminent danger of brushing.

Fortunately for my chastity, my ticket queue fires off lasers. *INCOMING*, Darth Vader intones, signaling the imminent demise of my night.

"You like outer space?"

I am so not telling him that I like to mine for space crystals. I settle for nodding and aggressively typing on my keyboard. There. I've communicated.

"That's cool. I wanted to be an astronaut as a kid." He presses his hand over his heart. "Scout's honor. Not that I was a Scout, but I respect their principles. I had a NASA-themed birthday party twice, mostly so I could eat freeze-dried ice cream."

"So you're food motivated."

He nods enthusiastically. He's adorable. "But I was also a big fan of zero gravity."

"Oh." My typing slows. Coding with an audience is difficult. "So how did you end up surfing?"

"Physics, with a practical application. Spaceships are too theoretical, plus I'm not a fan of sitting still." Big, warm fingers play with my hair, tucking wispy escapees back into my messy bun. "And a surfboard's way cheaper and easier to build than a spaceship."

"Got it." I really need to get on that AI conversation app. I desperately need a robot to hold up my end of the conversation for me. "Not to mention there's more money, more dating opportunities, and fewer chances of imploding in a fiery ball when you reenter the atmosphere."

Ozzy throws himself backward on the sofa. Pillows scatter. His head is now by my hip. "You're a ray of sunshine."

I think that might be his job. His skin is definitely sun-kissed. He glows like a golden god. Alternatively, it's possible he's spent too much time outside and all that sun exposure has fried his brain. He has the tiniest sun lines by his eyes, but that imperfection makes his beautiful face seem lived in, alive. I catalog a freckle on his cheekbone. He's tousled. It's attractive, in an I-just-had-sex way.

I have sex on the brain.

"I call it like I see it." I start my unit tests. These are a thousand tiny blocks of code that each verify that a smaller, isolated block functions. The goal is to be perfect, but my test suite fails five tests in. Damn it.

I need air. Space. A miracle. To curse my coworkers. That last part comes out of my mouth and Ozzy laughs.

"You don't like people much, do you?"

Hatred doesn't compute in Ozzytopia.

"I like people. I'm just highly selective."

His eyes laugh harder. "Do I make your short list?"

"Nope. Not a chance."

He decides to interpret this as sarcasm. "What are you coding?"

My brain requires a reboot. We are different species. He is a lion and I am an aardvark.

"I'm working on a VIP project for work." I don't tell him about the promotion. I don't want to jinx it. "Travel software for booking adventure vacations and the like."

He taps a spot on my screen.

"You'll get a NullPointerException there."

He's right, but I may growl. "Do you want my job?"

"Are you taking applications for friendship? Do you have openings?" He's bright-eyed, charming, made for lounging on sofas and beds. The laughter in his eyes grows; he's having far too much fun. I return my attention to my screen, face burning.

He frowns. "My butt is buzzing."

He reaches beneath him and pulls out my phone. It's imitating a personal pleasure device and vibrating hard.

His brow crinkles as he holds it out to me. "Rosie needs to talk with you, Panda. Also, you have a new match on your dating app."

It could be residual embarrassment—and the Sahara Desert that is my dating life—but I don't yell at him for reading the notifications on my phone. I just take the phone from him, silence it, and shove it under a different pillow. There, problem solved.

Ozzy looks at me expectantly. "Are you on the market?"

"The dating app is for research purposes. The app assesses two people for compatibility, and that's something my travel algorithm also needs to do."

"Uh-huh." The corner of his mouth curls up. His eyes warm. He is 10,000 percent unconvinced.

I glare at him. "So?"

"No judgment." He stretches out an arm. His fingers brush my shoulders. "Everyone does it. But—"

"But, what?"

I really need to work on my conversational skills.

"I'm right here."

He is, indeed. "And?"

"So research me."

What? "Is that a euphemism?"

I look at him, debating. He can't possibly be hitting on me. Can he? For reasons unknown, I don't shove him off the couch. I look, he looks back, and here we are in the land of Awkward.

"Sure," he says. I'm no less confused.

"Are you trying to hook up with me?" I finally blurt out.

I value clarity.

"Yes." He grins at me.

"Is this some kind of joke? Why?"

The dimple in his cheek flashes. "I love helping."

I bet he does. I bet he doesn't realize how tired I am of being the joke, the punch line.

I snap. I do something that's not on my to-do list. It will not write a single line of code, close a bug, or advance my career. I'm not even sure it will make me feel good (I am such a liar).

I lean down into him and fit my body against his.

It's not enough, so I slap a hand down on either side of his head. I am pulling him in like a fisherman landing a prize-winning fish. He wants to help? Have at it, big guy.

"Yes?" I ask.

He bats aside an errant pillow, his naughty grin deepening. "You bet."

Permission granted, I cover his mouth with mine.

His mouth is firm and soft. I can feel his lips curving up in a smile, and I try to kiss it off his beautiful, irritating face. One second I'm plotting his demise, and the next I have my tongue in his mouth, learning his taste, probing for a weak point. I want inside him. I want inside him *now*. He must like this not-plan of mine because he opens up with a groan, his tongue tangling with mine, warm and wet and soft. The rest of him is hard, and I approve.

He cups the back of my head with one large, calloused hand, tugging me closer. We do some rearranging. We lust after each other's mouths. We're two puzzle pieces that unexpectedly almost fit. He's all strength and male power, and I shift...*like that*...and feel the incontrovertible proof that Ozzy Wylder enjoys kissing me. He's sporting a massive hard-on that I would dismiss as absolutely improbable except that of course he's got a jumbo-sized, XXXXXL dick.

And he kisses...he kisses like I remember, except somehow even better because it's happening now, and I've thought about it happening since the first time on the beach. He knows who I am, and his hands are holding me close. We're weightless, floating in this space that holds just the two of us. He maps my mouth with his, and we just work together. Mint and cinnamon are the taste of poor choices.

Oh God. Why am I kissing Ozzy? And why is he so good at it?

Having spent most of my adult life surrounded by engineering nerds, the answer is obvious. Engineers are unshowered, unkempt, and perpetually distracted. We think in process diagrams and whiteboards. Our diet is disproportionately full of Mountain Dew and Sugar Babies. That makes it hard not to jump on a man who smells like sunshine and the outdoors. He's the closest I've been to nature in weeks.

One moment we're kissing, the next lasers fire on my laptop. "The bugs are with you," Darth Vader intones.

I startle, and Ozzy breaks our kiss. We've been kissing for forever and only a second. I want to be one of those people who documents every moment of her life with her phone because this Ozzy, this lazy, sprawled-beneath-me, tousled, sexy-eyed Ozzy needs to be remembered.

He shifts his hips beneath me. "Do you want to go to my place?"

Is that a trick question?

My brain reboots. I frown. "I'm not having sex with you."

We both look at the spot where my vagina is glued to his monster dick. So *literally* we're not having actual, penetrative sex. At this precise moment. But the option is clearly on the table (or my sofa).

"Okay," he says.

Just like that.

"Great." Holy shitballs, this is awkward.

He grins up at me. "But you thought about it."

I remove myself from his dick. My stores of dignity are exhausted and need recharging. I don't miss the feel of his skin beneath me at all.

Ozzy jumps to his feet with far more grace. He doesn't have to use his hands. He's all muscles. Pectorals, triceps, biceps. I didn't even get to put my hands on his lats. Oblivious to my disappointment, he shoves a hand into his jeans and shamelessly rearranges himself.

"Don't touch my doorknob on your way out."

"You know where I live when you change your mind."

He said *when*.

I grab my laptop. I'm so *screwed*, and not in the deliciously, post-orgasmic way. There'd better be a new apartment in my future.

Unbothered by my silent rejection, Ozzy wanders off. He grabs my pink Sharpie and scrawls something on the whiteboard hanging on my fridge. I think it might be a panda bear. Or a cockroach.

"That's *permanent* marker."

"You've got my number! Call me, maybe," he carols.

And then he's gone.

It's the worst prank of all.

Nine

Water balloons were a bad idea, but Ozzy's kiss fried my logic circuits.

I will cling to that belief until I'm dead. One kiss does not a peace agreement make. Blah, blah, blah.

Ergo, I've filled a ridiculous number of balloons with water. It turns out that they're surprisingly heavy and even more awkward to transport, which leads to my current predicament. Instead of conveying them upstairs and positioning them above Ozzy's door, my miscalculations regarding weight and size have run me aground on the door to the mail room. Someone should have sanded it, but did not, and now I've impaled my water balloons.

There is water absolutely everywhere.

I've run my Titanic up against an iceberg and it popped.

I mop the flooded mail room floor with maniacal determination because the sooner I finish here, the sooner I can go lie down and pretend that today never happened. I'm erasing this Friday from my memory banks.

"This is unexpected," Ozzy says from somewhere behind me.

I jump and water droplets fly everywhere. We have to stop these water-based meetings. "I live here."

"So you do." He has a box tucked under his arm. His hazel eyes scan the mail room, come to rest on the puddle I've mostly but not entirely cleaned up, check out the voluminous stack of used paper towel I've deposited in the trash can. ChatGPT was not wrong when it admonished me to stick to pranks that were easy to clean up.

"Water balloons?"

I shrug. *Duh* would be a syllable too far.

"We may have gone too far." He makes it into a statement and not a question.

He's not wrong, but I decide to disagree just on principle. I shake my head, which compounds my water balloon misjudgment because my wet hair slaps my cheeks. I regret my poor life choices.

"Can we declare peace? I'd like a peace treaty."

I summon up enough energy to glare in his direction, but the flame of my wrath has been extinguished by all this water.

Oblivious to my discomfort, Ozzy shakes his head, taking in the disaster I've created. He says something to himself that I don't catch, then sets his package down on the counter. He looks at the floor. "Do you want some help cleaning this up?"

My face burns. I'm spontaneously combusting.

I opt to lie. "I've got it."

To prove my point, I restart my mopping. I liberated my cleaning equipment from the maintenance closet, but it has so far proved inadequate. Pieces of broken water balloon are everywhere. It's rubber carnage.

I imagine what the condo board will say when they pop in for their L.L.Bean catalogs and vitamin deliveries. I won't get evicted, will I? I work a little faster. A good engineer can obfuscate her bugs. I'm hoping the same principle applies here.

"What happened?" Ozzy asks, grabbing the other mop.

I refuse to confess. Once the deluge is gone, it's as if it never happened. "Is anyone coming?"

He disappears, presumably to check the lobby.

When he returns, he offers up a "No."

He mops alongside me silently. He knows, though. I can tell, even though he doesn't say a word. I'm sure he's gloating. He'll kick the bucket of dirty water over when we're finished and rub it in that my prank has backfired. That I'm the loser.

Or not. He mops, I mop, and all he does is empty out the bucket. I don't ask where. I can't afford to care.

When he comes back the last time, there's a squishing sound.

"Uh-oh." He holds up a sodden messenger bag. *My* bag. "Is this yours?"

I wish it wasn't. I wish my bag was upstairs, or at least on the nice, dry counter next to Ozzy's box. Which is, I realize, addressed to me. It has air holes and is labeled Live Poultry. I can feel my shoulders slump.

I'm hoisted by my own petard. Unless there's been a technology miracle, the questionnaire responses that I spent the last two hours collecting furtively outside the corner market are gone. I was offline and the data will not have synced to my cloud account. All that work is gone. Poof.

"Uh."

I sink down onto the mail room floor. I want a do-over on today. I don't want to be sad. I *won't* be sad. I'm manifesting it into existence.

"Hey." He crouches down beside me, and his shoulder nudges mine. He is warm and solid. I am ridiculously mad that he is not soaked.

I ignore his one-syllable overture. I require full sentences.

"Truce?" He extends a paw. Waves it in front of my face.

I consider my options. "Do you admit defeat?"

He snorts. "Are we fighting?"

"Yes," I splutter. I wish I sounded cooler or more put together. I'll take *things I'll never be* for two hundred dollars, Alex. "Do you pay no attention at all to what's going on around you?"

He ignores my question, hopping to his feet. It's a miracle my abs don't hurt just watching him.

"Come on."

"Excuse me?" I would never move again but leftover water has seeped through the seat of my yoga pants.

"Come. With. Me. Why are you so difficult?" He waves his big paw at me again. He believes he is a motivational speaker. That it's a miracle I don't throw myself at him and declare my undying love for his thoughtful words. For insisting on these conversations. Breathing on our shared balcony—*why*, what reason does he have for torturing me like this? It's against the Geneva Conventions. Desperate, I launch my nuclear arsenal. Pew-pew-pew. Our condo disappears beneath mushroom clouds of toxic smoke. Radioactive particles. Fission byproducts.

Ozzy is unfazed. I get to my feet, mostly because my butt is wet.

He sighs dramatically. "Why are you fighting with me?"

Because he started it.

"We're not. I barely know you exist."

He levels a look at me. It's part smirk, part warm amusement, part annoying. I can't decide which part I hate most, but they're all in close contention. "Sure you don't. You're mad at me about the Miles To Go kiss."

Boom. Whoosh? Does a nuclear bomb make a sound when it lands? I'd google, but I am floored. Ozzy grabs the remnants of my water balloon monster and tosses them into the communal trash can. I let him.

Because...

He remembers…

The kiss.

I am not a stranger. He did not forget me. The ground shifts. The mail room's second-rate laminate flooring is pulled out from under me.

He scans my face. "Did you think I forgot?"

Again: *Duh?*

I don't know what to say here. Fortunately for me, Ozzy is already talking. It's a miracle he paused for breath long enough to kiss me.

He shakes his head. "Wait. Did *you* forget? You did."

His lips turn down. He looks away, frowning at the hapless wall of mailboxes on the other side of this too-small room. He blinks slowly, speech drying up, and I feel him pulling away. He looks…hurt? It's not an expression I associate with Ozzy. He's not supposed to know what it feels like to be on the outside, looking in. From my point of view, I'm the injured party here. We kissed each other, but he's the one who walked away. If he's known all along who I am, what we did together, why hasn't he mentioned it before?

He frowns. "I thought—"

Whoops. Did I say it out loud?

His face flushes. He tries again. "I thought you didn't want to talk about it."

"Wow. There *is* something off-limits in your conversational arsenal."

He gives me a look. "Did. You. Forget?"

I shake my head.

He asks the obvious question. "So why didn't *you* mention it?"

Our kiss looms between us. It's growing bigger, deeper, hotter with each passing second. By the time I reach the safety of my condo, it will be Godzilla-sized.

I grab my poor bag and trudge out of the mail room. Ozzy follows. Is this a draw?

Am I conceding defeat? Is *he*? Nothing about this feels the way I expected it to. I spend the yearlong walk to the stairwell rehearsing my answers to his question. *Oh—that kiss? It was so long ago, such a solitary, unimportant kiss, so short! Kisses are like shoes: I have so many!* Believable? Not so much. I imagine my next kiss and how the person I kiss will be all the things Ozzy is not. I'll kiss someone softer, curvier, who fits into my arms? My imagination wraps us around each other and she's so into me and me into her. She'll be nothing like Ozzy. We'll kiss in the car or the park, in front of my door when she drops me off after our bookstore date or on my sofa like regular people do. There will be no sand, no ocean, no barbarian rushing out of the darkness and overwhelming me with his *Ozziness*. People won't wonder why she's dating me. We'll match.

When we reach our floor, Ozzy pushes the door open and holds it.

He doesn't move. He's glued to the door like the sexiest of doormen.

"You hate asking for help." Amusement fills his voice. "No. You hate *needing* help."

He's right.

Just to prove him wrong, however, I march past him. My messenger bag bangs soddenly against my hip.

Ozzy looks concerned. "Do you want some rice for your electronics?"

What I really want is an Apple Genius Bar, but it's far too late. "How do you know I have electronics inside my bag? It could be anything! Tampons, library books, a teacup poodle."

He smirks. "You're more connected than a cyborg, Dora. I'm surprised you didn't short-circuit when *you* got wet."

He makes an unattractive popping sound. Flares his fingers

out. Is that me meeting a wet demise like the Wicked Witch of the West? He'd make a terrible charades partner.

"I have funeral arrangements to make," I tell him.

My tablet requires a ceremonial burial and a panicked replacement.

"Our kiss wasn't that bad." His shoulders hunch. "But I won't mention it again."

It wasn't bad at all, even if it wasn't much longer than the walk to my front door.

I think about that first time we met, how I didn't overthink things. Life threw a man at me, and I kissed him. Easy-peasy. Two mouths met and dreams flared to life. Fantasies. I built an entire pipe dream based on five minutes in the sand. *This could be the start of something amazing*, I'd hoped.

Ozzy keeps pace with me. Stops when I stop. Smirks as I scoop up a handful of wee baby spiders. "They're procreating!"

"You never know where you'll find one," he says darkly, then swipes at an errant streak of now-fossilized shaving cream that I missed when I erased his THIS MEANS WAR message.

When I shoot him a look, he mutters, "You started it," and steals one of my spider children.

"Are you—"

"What?"

He swings around to look at me. It's been a day, and I'm tired, but I think he's concerned about me. It makes me uncomfortable.

"Do you need anything?" he asks.

Oh, the things I need. His brow is furrowed, his hands on his lean hips now. I can tell it's absolutely killing him that I won't admit that I could, in fact, use help. A miracle. Divine intervention and a forty-eight-hour day. Since I still half blame him for the mail room debacle, however, I play dumb. "Like?"

"Rice," he suggests. *Lame.*

I'm sure the last time he ate refined carbohydrates was a decade ago.

"I'm good." I jam my key in the lock. I've got this.

Ozzy leans in. He might brace himself against my wall with a hand. "Do you want help?"

He means *my help*.

Because that's what he's asking.

Do I want *his* help?

Will I accept it, or will I mark it *return to sender*? It'll be like a rejected Christmas present on December 26 tossed in the exchange bin at Walmart.

I shrug. No big deal. He'll get over it. He'll be fine.

"You can come in," says the stranger who's taken over my mouth.

Ozzy follows me inside.

I guess we're doing this: him helping, me letting him. It's so weird.

I dig out a ten-pound bag of rice and shove my tablet in there, but the patient is on life support and we both know it. It shows no sign of life, no pulse of light. While I wait for rice to fail me, I check my backups and discover that, yup, I've got nothing. The tablet didn't sync before it swam, and I've lost a hundred questionnaires.

"Bad news?" Ozzy asks.

Can I help dances in the air between us.

I'm too tired to fight, so I admit the truth. "I lost my data for my demo."

He huffs a laugh. "That sucks. Can we recreate it?"

It's weird, this being part of a *we*.

I fall back on my default mode: sarcasm. "Do you know two hundred people who are available now to fill out a semi-invasive online questionnaire about their travel and hygiene habits?"

He looks like he has questions. I forestall them.

"I'm coding a new travel app, but it requires data. There's an online questionnaire that quizzes people about their travel likes and dislikes, does some personality analysis, asks a bunch of stuff that gives my algorithm the data points it needs to find a traveler their perfect travel match—and their ideal itinerary."

I can't quite hide the flush of pride I feel. This is my brainchild, my project, and it's really—*really*—good. Still, I wait for him to make the obvious jokes about dating apps.

"I'll bet it's great." For once in his life, he sounds serious.

"It is." Oh, my God, it is. I am good at this, and I can do this.

Ozzy looks at me. "I'll fill it out. Your questionnaire."

"One down, 199 to go." I am a fount of optimism.

Still, I text him a link to the online survey. He brings it up on his phone, hums to himself for a bit before asking, "Can I share it?"

I shrug. "Sure. It's not a government secret."

He nods and flings himself on my sofa. Pillows scatter.

"Do I prefer solo activities or traveling with a group?"

I am immediately defensive. It's not the most original question, but it works. "Trust the process, Ozzy."

He tucks his tongue into his cheek, a gesture I did not know existed in real life. Squints. Moves the tablet closer to his face. His nose is leaving Ozzy-shaped smudges on the screen.

"Are you farsighted?"

He ignores me.

"Do I need to stay connected to work while traveling?" He clucks his tongue. "Did you write these, Dora?"

"I think we need to revisit your definition of *helping*." I latch on to his phone. I'll clear his browser cache, and it will be like this whole nightmare never happened.

He won't be defeated and tugs back. Somehow, I crash-land on the sofa next to him.

"New foods or familiar friends?" he muses. "That sounds almost cannibalistic."

He taps away, writing a book rather than answering my multiple-choice-single-answer question. I try to sneak a peek. He'll be the adventurous type. Bold. Ready to eat fried tarantulas or fertilized duck eggs. Hapless puffer fish. Ant larvae.

"What's the last new thing you ate?"

I don't want to answer his questions. It's not as if we'll ever travel together. It's pointless. "I already took the survey."

I roll my eyes so hard that I see stars. Stars. God, I want to be in my spaceship so badly.

"Answer, please." Ozzy is a relentless taskmaster. "If I'm answering your questions, you should answer mine."

I try to remember how many items are on the survey.

"Mochi doughnuts," I mutter ungracefully. "I went to Japantown last month."

He crows. "I knew you were a sweet girl!"

If looks could kill, he would be dead.

Fortunately for him, he moves on. "Preferred options for nightlife?"

"None." I'm an inside girl. A hermit.

He makes a buzzing sound. "Unless you turn into a comatose vampire, you have a nightlife. What do you do with it?"

"I...work?"

"Have you considered getting an actual life?"

"What do you do?"

He grins. "I help you with work?"

"Okay, but when you're not holed up in my condo, what do you do? Where do you *go*?"

He shrugs. "I take pictures. I run. I swim. I disappoint my loving parents by taking insufficient interest in my future."

There's so much to unpack there. "You don't go out?"

"Those things count," he protests. "Where else should I go?"

"Where do people go out to?" Now it's my turn to shrug. "Bars. Movie theaters. Pop-up taco trucks. They date. They talk to other human beings. Just finish the survey."

I have used up my quota of words for tonight. For this lifetime. I groan. I might slap my hands over my eyes. I am more dramatic than a seven-year-old in a school play. Who knew what he'd ask next?

Strong hands tuck me up against a muscled side, anchoring me when my bones threaten to melt. I'm seconds away from oozing off the couch. Moving to live on the floor. Time is warping.

I think I doze off. My couch vibrates and rumbles beneath my cheek. It's warm and deliciously solid.

Ozzy groans. "I don't know how you do this for twelve hours a day."

"What?" I blink back awake.

"Blue light is bad for you, Panda Bear."

"Are you done? Because I need to go solicit 199 people to overshare about their travel habits with me."

Oh God. I have to talk to strangers. Ask them for help.

"Yeah?" He sits up, sliding me gently onto the sofa.

"Thank you for filling out the survey."

"Sure. I like helping you."

That shuts me up. What am I supposed to say? Thank you? Give him my to-do list? We barely know each other, and yet he seems to have my back. Ozzy Wylder might be a surf star, but he's surprisingly down-to-earth. He's a decent man.

A decent man who I kissed.

"I'm done. So are they."

"Who?"

"Friends of mine," he says. "People I've surfed with. I sent them your link and they filled it out."

He's actually done it. He's helped me out. Replaced my missing data by—I check my laptop—soliciting what appears to be the entire surfing community and their surf bunny friends. His social media reach is impressive, too.

"It's okay to ask for help." He stands up with a groan, stretching.

He says this easily, as if it's just a matter of words. As if it's no big deal. As if we're possibly, truly friends. Or at least not enemies. But I'm remembering our kiss, remembering how good it was and then how bad, when he waltzed away from me. I got lost in the crowd then. I couldn't keep up, didn't (if I'm forced to be fair) know how to. He makes it look so easy, this reaching out. This *connecting*. It's not fair to be mad at him for how easily relationships come to him or how quickly he's fixed my blunder, especially since I *am* grateful. He has helped. It's just that I really wanted—or maybe needed—to do it myself. I need everyone to see *me*.

Ten

Three hundred seconds.

As in, that's how long I set the timer for before I dive into my spaceship. People have sex in less time. Since it's crunch time at work and mere days before my demo, I need to limit my diversions. I hurtle through the near empty vacuum, making for my favorite asteroid. Stars stream past my viewport in a burst of light. No time for photos. When I land, faster than is safe, my ship wobbles. The world tilts forty-five degrees. No sandworms, no fatal space debris, no meteoroid. Victory is mine!

As soon as I'm suited up, I sprint out the hatch, land hard on the rocky surface, and take off for the gulch. Forty-two seconds into my countdown, I'm tunneling into a vein of glittering pink, scraping delicately at the asteroid's surface. Bits of nickel-iron float past me. My gloved fingers close around a rough pink stone. It's translucent, like a gummy treat, and the size of my fist, its surface rippled and cratered. Holy shiny balls. It's the biggest space diamond ever.

I grab it. I might fist pump because this is so awesome.

Clang.

Clang.

CLANG.

I jump reflexively. The world is ending. Space monsters have invaded (I unfortunately coded them into this universe on a grumpy day, proving you truly do reap what you sow). The space diamond slips out of my fingers and bounces down, down, down into a crevasse. It winks a fuck-you up at me.

CLAAAAAANG.

Since I'm running on no sleep, I rub my eyes and consider my retrieval options. Also, murder. Satisfying, vengeful felonies. Klaxons sound. Sirens. Lasers. *You are a screwup*, Darth Vader intones from my work laptop. The one thing programming for a living has taught me is that there is never, ever enough time and that coding sprints are not for the weak.

When the timer goes off, I'm still mourning the space diamond I almost had. My apartment is a mess of abandoned snack wrappers, empty coffee cups, a bra (my least favorite implement of torture), socks, blankets, a blizzard of sticky notes and half-erased whiteboards. I turn back to the piece of code that has been frustrating me for the last two hours. I've got this. I've fixed worse, so I'm not too worried.

CLANG.

I'm merely deafened. Unable to focus. Absolutely 100 percent peeved. Who works out at two in the morning?

Ozzy's phone number winks at me from the whiteboard on my fridge. I can't even rage-erase it because he used a goddamned *Sharpie*. The pink kissy heart he scrawled next to his digits days ago mocks me. *You will have to TALK to me.*

I am surprised by the (unsuccessful) lengths to which I'll go to avoid that.

Wall banging? Fail.

Passive-aggressive notes? Also fail.

Beaten down, I concede defeat and shoot him a text: **How's your hearing? Are you deaf from all that noise?**

Punching the Send button is satisfying, but then I instantly want to unsend it. Questions invite Ozzy to engage. I want to exile him to an ice floe in Antarctica.

Ozzy's response is to add music to the clanging. He is diabolical. After ninety wasted seconds glaring at my phone, willing him to reply and/or turn down his volume, I give up temporarily and go back to work.

My laptop spawns bugs like a cicada brood emerging from a seventeen-year hibernation.

An hour later the clanging ceases, but the music continues on. And on. And on. Perhaps his weight-lifting apparatus has fallen over and he's trapped. Maybe he desperately wants to turn off his music but can't. It's...possible?

I code sprint for thirty minutes and then I'm done. Ish. I stumble upstairs to my bed. My beautiful, beautiful bed.

Must. Lie. Down.

The clanging restarts.

"You hate me." Before I can think it through, I'm down the stairs, feet slapping against the floor.

I slam my door. *Take that, Ozzy Wylder.* Take a right. Sprint the ten feet to his door (aka the portal of hell).

Feet planted on his doormat, which features two procreating pineapples, I hammer on his door. There's a mutant seashell the size of my head by my right foot. Somewhere out there in the ocean there's a crab the size of a dog. I hope it pinches Ozzy's balls.

I hammer some more. The soundproofing issue must be limited to the wall between our lofts because it's remarkably silent in the hallway. There's just a whisper of music. I'd lie down here and go to sleep, but Ozzy would just step over—or on—my body on his way out in the morning.

The door flies open mid-hammer. I fall forward because the laws of gravity are in full effect.

"Hey, neighbor." Strong hands catch me and reposition me on my feet.

I should thank him. Or do it again. Except my brain goes offline.

Middle-of-the-night Ozzy wears just a pair of low-slung athletic shorts made of black nylon. The shorts stop just above his knees. Dip over his hip bones. Frame his perfect, perfect V-cut. He hasn't bothered with underwear and the synthetic fabric leaves nothing to my imagination.

Ozzy is oblivious to my staring. He removes his hands from my person and does that sexy wall slouching thing. "What's up? How are you?"

"Uh," I manage.

He waits.

I stare.

"I'm good," he prompts. He glistens in the light. The sweat sheen should be unattractive. He should need soap, a shower. Instead, I want to lick him. Drink him in. I am drunk on Ozzy pheromones.

"Are you cold?"

"Excuse me?"

He smiles kindly. "You're not dressed for the weather."

He's the one who is half-naked. Maybe he's confused by all the music. The constant noise has scrambled his logic circuits. Except. *Crapitty crap crap.*

I refuse to look down. "Are you interested in what I'm wearing?"

The smile morphs into a devilish grin. "If I say yes, will you be offended?"

His eyes dip. Mine follow. Oh God. In theory, I know what I put on my body seven billion hours ago. I'd rather forgotten, however, just how ratty this particular pair of sweatpants is. There are holes (and not the artful, distressed kind). A bleach stain from where I wrestled with some AWOL chili sauce. The waistband is folded over to keep them up, which means three inches of my cotton granny panties are visible. Ordinarily, I'm pro comfort panties. Mine are breathable *and* they're covered in tiny spaceships. Right now, though, they feel like a tactical mistake. His eyes bounce between my spaceships and my braless boobs in a tank top I bought in high school. I have no bra. No shoes. No armor. I soldier on. I will die on this hill.

"Please keep the volume down."

I've come prepared. I hand him a printed sheet. It's the noise regulations for the condo in eighteen-point font. I've highlighted the key sections.

He looks down, brow furrowing. Sighs. "Is this your love language, Panda?"

"These are the relevant rules. You're too loud." It feels like my face is red. My eyes sting now like a school of jellyfish has taken up residence on my corneas. I'm so tired. So…something. I should turn around and go to bed.

Yes, bed would be brilliant.

Okay.

I'm not moving.

"Uh-oh." Ozzy shakes his head.

What?

"Quick! Come in!" He shoves the door wide. It hits the wall and flies back toward us. He stops it with one big hand.

I am tired—and ever nosy—because I do as he says. Three steps inside his evil lair, and I can confidently say that the only thing he has added to his loft since my felonious prior visit is a pile of camera equipment on his kitchen counter.

He shuts the door behind us with exaggerated care. "Whew!

We were in violation of the no-talking-in-the-halls-after-ten-p.m. rule."

As if he cares. "Did you lure me in to kill me? Toss my body over the balcony?"

He resumes leaning against the wall, propped up on one bare, broad shoulder, grinning at me. I refuse to fidget with the hem of my tank or cross my arms over my chest. Let him look.

"Your evil lair is looking a little spartan, Sir Surfs-a-lot."

Now he looks delighted. "Why are you here, Panda?"

"Because you don't answer your phone," I grit out.

He walks over to the weight bench and picks up his phone. Types something. "Answered."

I scoff. "My phone is in my place."

Along with everything else except myself, three insufficient articles of clothing, and my key card. Wait. Where is my key card? I look around. On the ground. Pat my nonexistent pockets. *Crap.* I've locked myself out. The maintenance guy won't come on-site for another four hours. The security dude hates me. I allow myself the luxury of closing my eyes for five seconds. I sway ever so slightly.

Ozzy keeps talking (because of course he does). "Is there a problem? Did you miss me?"

"As if. Why are you like this?"

I'm on autopilot now. I spit out some random words, try to inject a little barb into my tone. Mostly, though, I'm thinking about how today sucks. To-do lists and random Java classes from the TripFriendz algorithm float through my brain like soap bubbles. The bugs, the code reviews, the big-ass presentation I have to deliver tomorrow (today?) to sell that algorithm and land my dream job.

I imagine I must look one part manic, one part frantic. All parts of me are tired. I kind of want to lie down on Ozzy's floor, pass out, and wake up tomorrow.

Instead, I list against his wall. I look nowhere near as sexy as he does. I'm both tired and wired at the same time thanks to my caffeine consumption. "Fuck," I tell his floor.

Ozzy pads toward me. Bare feet appear in the corner of my vision and fingers tip my chin up. I should smack his hand, but I don't.

"Are you okay, Panda?"

No. I'm not. "This is your fault."

He hums, neither agreeing nor disagreeing. "Why?"

Am I acting like a toddler having a meltdown? Yes, but I'm so tired and he's so right here and I snap.

"Panda?" Ozzy's voice is steady.

"I'm locked out and I don't have a key frog."

"We'll fix it."

He *is* good at breaking and entering. We've established that. I should definitely not look him in the eye. I shift so I'm staring at the metal torture device he keeps where other people park a nice, comfortable sofa.

The silence is comforting, but I can't help but notice him anyway.

I have a thing for Ozzy.

And it pisses me off.

It may be a free world in which he's a rent-paying, semi-law-abiding citizen, but I need him to leave.

I need him out of my space and my building.

I need...to delete all traces of kissing from my memory banks. Nothing good can come from this.

"I hate you," I tell him.

I'm in a fury trying to make sense of tonight. This week. My whole goddamned life. I can fix this. I'm in charge. And yet I give up on contemplating the tasteful ecru paint job on his walls. Instead, I do the worst possible thing. I'm locked out, running on no sleep, juggling my nightmare job, and I place the cherry on my own shit sundae.

I angry cry.

My eyes well up, and I stand there and cry in front of Ozzy Wylder.

My main engine comes online and I'm accelerating, rocketing at him, moving so fast that I'm not docking, I'm crashing. He mutters, "Whoa," but his arms come around me.

Ozzy is a master hugger.

My hands hit his chest and slide up. I switch gears so fast that I am dizzy. I wrap my palms around his neck and yank his beautiful face down to mine so I can kiss him. My mouth covers his. *Nope, nopity, nope. We can't have sex.* Once he gets his penis inside me, it'll be an open-door policy. There will be *no* boundaries. I have to live *next* to him for the rest of my life. Or move.

I slip my tongue into his mouth anyhow.

He presses his mouth against mine. He licks away my tears.

He cups my face and kisses me back, swallowing up the angry words I itch to toss his way. He's so, so good at this. His lips are warm and firm, so much fun in contrast to the annoying rest of him. I like Ozzy Wylder's lips, to infinity and beyond.

He likes me back. He makes a rough sound as my tongue explores his mouth. I'm inside him, under his skin. His hands cradle my face, his body bends over me. I expect him to break off the kiss, to step back and tease me. To declare himself the winner in this competition. To yell *Psych!* He should. I would. Instead, he keeps on kissing me, pulling me closer against his big body and the enormous hard-on he's sporting.

I kissed him for no good reason. Maybe to prove that I don't want him for real. That we have no chemistry. That he's just a pretty face that I can take or leave. But my body likes its new proximity, and it feels so good to let go and lose myself in the sensations.

My fingers tangle in his too-long hair. I pull it free from its stupid, stubby man bun. Use the glossy strands to tug him closer. His shampoo smells like sage and coconut. He's sunshine and sex on a beach.

When he finally pulls back, we both breathe like sprinters at the finish line. Oxygen is in short supply. I gulp it in. I want to devour his mouth some more and then move south. I want to get under his skin and under those stupid, sexy shorts of his. But maybe he doesn't really want to be kissing his hateful neighbor. Maybe he'll laugh now and point me toward the door and realize all the reasons why the two of us boning is the world's worst idea. Because it's a terrible idea. Top ten worst ever. He's my neighbor and a jackass. I'm just a surf bunny. An Ozzy stan.

"I hate you." I grab his hands, pushing up on my toes so I can reach his throat. Lick a path up his skin and latch on to his ear. "You drive me crazy."

"And you talk too much," he rumbles. Pot, kettle.

He solves the talking problem to our mutual satisfaction by covering my mouth with his. He sucks my bottom lip into his mouth, teeth nipping, tongue stroking inward. I am on fire. I can feel every inch of him.

His hands roam everywhere because he's a master of coordination, stroking down my arms, over my ribs, tracing the curve of my waist and hip. He squeezes, lifting, and then I'm pressed against the wall, legs wrapped around his waist. Ozzy has the best ideas. I hook my feet around his back.

Teeth nip at me.

I bite his bare shoulder. Lightly. Delicately.

I'm marking him. He tastes delicious

I stare at the pale pink crescent I've made in his skin. I've never felt this needy or this reckless before. He's not a casual hookup, someone I picked out on an app. I miss that set of unspoken rules, the script for how sex goes, but this is Ozzy—he barrels ahead. And there's no time to feel awkward or unsure because he fists the hem of my tank top with one hand. His other squeezes my butt. I hear him say my name. "Pandora."

I look up.

"Can I take this off?" His cheeks are flushed—apparently, he *does* have some blood that hasn't rushed south. Pupils dilated, lips parted, he holds my gaze. He's leaning into me, angling his body toward me. The hand holding me up squeezes, his thumb finding a tear in my pants and drawing circles on my skin. He's just as into this as I am. It's astounding.

"Do it," I say. And then, because I'm not conceding anything, "Let's see if you can make me like you."

He barks out a laugh. "Are we…?"

He's taking too long. I jerk my tank top up, pulling it over my head. It flies off into outer space, and his hand cups my breast. I make a rough sound. *Yes. Please.*

"We need ground rules," I say. It comes out more moan than words, which is his fault because, God, his *thumb*. His fingers are calloused, the skin deliciously rough. Is it all the surfing? I have no idea. I don't care.

"Okay," he agrees. He's staring at his hand on my boob, his fingers teasing the swell, heading for my nipple. "Okay."

"Once. One and done. We get this out of our systems." It's a solid plan—my *usual* plan—but the words get swallowed up by a needy whine because his thumb finds my nipple and it's amazing. And not enough. He adds a finger. Pinches gently. I tighten my grip on his shoulders so he can't let go without using his words. Which I need to hear. "Do you agree?"

Not that I think he's going to be struck with eternal lust for me, but it's important to be clear.

"Yes," he groans. "And you're really okay with this?"

"My body likes you, asshole." I thread my fingers through

his hair, tugging. Kiss him hard. When we come up for air, I add, "But if you say that you told me so, there will be consequences."

He laughs. He'd thought about it.

I bite the tender skin beneath his ear, and he bucks against me. His dick bucks in his shorts. He likes that.

"Noted." He exhales roughly. "So just to be clear, you want to have sex right now. With me. But only once."

"Yep." He still talks too much.

He also returns my bite with interest. His teeth press against my ear, move down my throat, pause at my shoulder. Holy crap, he's strong. He lifts me up so he can feast on me.

"Is it negotiable?" His mouth finds my breast. Kisses a hot, sharp path. Sucks the skin just above the swell of my breast. "I feel like we should talk this out."

New rule. "No talking."

He looks up at me. Hazel eyes dance with laughter and something else. His mouth is. On. Me.

"Compliments? Dirty talk? A safe word!"

Heh.

"Do *you* need a safe word?" It's important for partners to communicate, but I don't think he's inviting me to reenact *Fifty Shades of Grey* with him. My safe word is to use no words at all.

"No." He gently bites down on my nipple. My back arches. In my experience, boobs are the quick pit stop on a road trip, something to fly past and not someplace you'd choose to linger. Ozzy makes me rethink that. He's not interested in rushing, in getting on with the fully naked part of our hookup. His mouth pays attention to me, kissing, nipping, soothing the erotic sting. He kisses like there's nothing else he'd rather do, and I don't know what to make of that.

When he finally lifts his head, we're both panting.

"Can we...?" he asks. Stops.

I've never seen him at a loss for words. He's always the winner in our battles. He's bigger, stronger, far more likeable.

"You make so much noise," I scold him. He's not chastened. Something hard pushes up against me, eager to say hello. "You keep me up every night. One of us has a job." It's humiliating how he's always in the back of my mind. He's made a space for himself in my head. I can't evict him. "I bet you want me to notice you. Want me to come over here and take you in hand."

"Great plan." He exhales roughly. "Let's do that tomorrow."

"I have work commitments tomorrow. Tonight or never." I sound more than a little dazed. Ozzy has that effect on me.

He shifts me effortlessly in his arms. Walks us both toward the stairs like it's no big deal and he could carry me for hours. Across deserts. Through raging sandstorms. Is he like this with other girls? I'm not like this with other guys.

He kiss-walks us upstairs to his loft, muscles bunching beneath me as he climbs the steps like they're nothing. He pauses halfway to the top, but not to catch his breath.

"Bedroom. Yes or no?"

"The asking for verbal consent is sexy, but why are you still talking?"

He curses and tosses me over his shoulder. We fly up the stairs. I pinch his ass, smack it once, too. I've never been into spanking games—they're so much work. Ozzy has me rethinking my choices.

He drops me onto the bed and stands over me, looking down at me as if I'm a sex goddess. Beautiful. I ten out of ten recommend my own view: his erection tents his stupid workout shorts. His dick is thick and long and totally on board with our hate-fuck plan. I yank my sweatpants off. My panties, too, because I'm not dressed for seduction. Ozzy watches me like I'm his favorite YouTube channel, and not a mediocre hookup he picked out on an app and is now second-guessing.

"You should tell me to go home." I'm naked now, but the words burst out of me, angry and honest. My bad ideas are apparently contagious. We can do this just once, right? Hate-fuck each other out of our systems. It sounds like a plan to me.

"For sure I should. But then you'd be all alone, Panda. You'd miss me."

Why am I the only one naked? "Don't call me that."

The corner of his mouth crooks up. "But you're my little bear, cuddly and full of claws."

"No more talking," I order. I'm naked. This is... Unease rears its awkward head. What if he doesn't like nerdy, pale, curvy engineers? What if...?

I don't need to risk his rejection. But I also don't want to go home. I've crossed the boning bridge and I'm not leaving unless he tells me to. I reach for him, irritated, and tug his shorts down.

Oh my God. He is *so* up for this.

"Still in?" He fists his monster dick, showing it some love. It kicks in his hand.

"I may need a picture. Your dick is one of the Seven Wonders of the World."

He laughs. "All my cameras are downstairs."

Then he's reaching for me, and I'm sliding across his sheets—blue-and-white ticking, something that belongs in a beach cottage and far nicer than my synthetic ones—and he's positioning me on the edge of the bed. His hands push my thighs wide, easing them apart to make room for his oversize self. "Yes?"

"How about right now, hurry up, and of course?" I narrow my eyes.

"Yes." He kisses along my thigh. "As you wish." More

kisses. Higher. "Yes." This kiss is the highest of them all. "I like the begging."

I'm too close to the brink of an amazing orgasm to complain. Much. "Think of it as an order."

"Yes, ma'am." He kisses closer but not close enough. I fist his hair, twist my fingers in the lush strands. I want him to put his dirty mouth on me. And his hands. Definitely his dick.

We still hate each other.

But I love this.

"Such a good girl. You deserve a reward."

"I do." He eases my legs farther apart, and then he gives me my reward.

His mouth closes over me, kissing and nipping, licking up and down my wet pussy. "Are we good? This is okay?"

He's still asking, not telling. He won't actually go where he's not wanted. We both know that if I told him to go away, to stop, he would.

I hook my feet behind his back again. "Please."

"The magic word." He drops a kiss on my forehead. What the ever-living fuck... But then he's rolling on a condom. Things are moving in the best direction.

"Just this once." I'm reminding myself. "We can't do this again. I just need to get you out of my system."

He gives me a look. "It's dick, not an engagement ring."

One hundred percent agree. Thumbs-up. They don't sell this at Tiffany's, although that's a missed opportunity in my opinion.

"Feel free to not propose," I growl.

He rocks me against his dick, taking his sweet time.

Tomorrow will be awkward because I'll have firsthand knowledge of my neighbor's O-face. The scent of his skin. That the length of his dick has been underestimated by his legions of online fans. He's a superstar and popular. People voluntarily hang out with him. I am none of those things, but right now he's mine. I'll just walk away like I have from every other hookup. I don't have relationship skills, anyway. This could never be more than a one-time thing.

"Bored?" He groans against my mouth, pushing in, taking more of me.

When I mumble something, the bastard laughs. He's so beautiful.

And evil. He rearranges me, big hands gripping my hips. He slowly pushes inside, his thumb circling my clit. The reason for his fan club is clear. Someone somewhere must be able to resist him, but I am not that woman.

Still, I make a token effort to regain control. "Can we hurry up? I have a schedule to keep."

The bastard laughs. "Is there a sex checkbox? Am I on your list? I think I need some reassurance. Compliments. Tell me something nice."

"Are you for real?"

He's laughing as he sinks deeper. "Does this feel real to you?"

It's just sex, but it feels...

It feels...

He fills me up, his hands guiding me into a rhythm we both like. I stretch to take him. "Slow or fast?"

I push up, taking him deep. He makes a guttural sound. I whisper against his ear. "I pick fast."

His fingers grip my hips, pulling me down, pushing me up. He's working me over and over on his dick. I like sex and it's been a while, but he lights me up without even trying. There's nothing casual about this, so we'll bone each other quickly and pass out from the orgasm.

"One time." I am manifesting this. "To get it out of our systems."

His hand slides between us, finding my clit. "Ask me."

I counter. "*You* ask. Start with 'Thank you, Pandora. You're amazing.'"

He pulls back, grinning at me. He's so pleased with himself. I'm sure he hears nothing but positive feedback. Five-star reviews. A Best of 2025 banner. I'll hate myself for this tomorrow. Which is perfect. We'll fuck, get it out of our systems, and move on. In opposite directions. My hookups have never come back.

"You're rude." He sounds amazed.

"Stick around. I'm just getting started." I squeeze his ass. Then I clench around the tip of him. *Hello, please come on in.* "Are we doing this or not?"

"So impatient," he marvels.

I roll my eyes. "Kiss me or shut up."

"Panda." His voice breaks. He groans something as he pushes deep inside me. A curse, praise. His social security number. I don't care because he's *right there* and I'm chasing the electric sensation.

I hold on tight, legs wrapped around his lean hips, heels digging into his back. Another thrust. He's driving me up the bed, the headboard slamming into the wall. It's delicious. It'll leave marks. He picks up the pace, pounding into me, deliciously rough, his arms braced on either side of my head. Our foreheads touch. His eyes are closed. I'm watching him come and then I'm tightening around him, gripping him tightly, riding his dick as I come.

You're amazing, Panda. So good. Oh God, I'm—

Me, too.

Me, too.

Eleven

I don't slip out of Ozzy Wylder's bed in the dead of night. Our hate-sex fuckathon is no Olympic vault. I don't run down the mat, spring onto the table, perform fabulous gymnastics midair, and then stick my landing. It's not over and done within ninety seconds.

He makes me come. I make him come. Sometime after 3:00 a.m. I stop counting. By 4:00 a.m. I need a sports drink. Electrolytes. Carbs.

Naked Ozzy is irresistible. He senses my weakness for his body and tosses the sheets onto the floor. He becomes even more outrageous and outspoken. He dirty talks. He whispers compliments. I'm going to walk bowlegged into my presentation.

Ozzy falls asleep at five. He has an arm wrapped around my waist. One hand cups my boob, which he declared his undying love to forty minutes ago when we ran out of condoms and I suggested he fuck my tits instead. My legs ache, my vagina demands a vacation, and I can see why Ozzy's so popular. He's sprawled on his back. He looks cuddly and adorable.

I still hate him. Mostly.

I sit up cautiously. I need to leave. Abandon the sex ship.

I've banged my neighbor and arch-nemesis. I can't avoid him without breaking my lease. I will forever have to avoid the mail room, unless he forgets who I am again. It's possible. Embarrassment is an unpleasant caboose on the orgasm train.

After unwinding Ozzy's arm from my midsection, I tiptoe across the floor. It's good that he's a minimalist, because his loft is as empty as the rest of his unit. He has a mattress on the floor, but no headboard. I judge him for his lack of furniture, and never mind the stupid, beachy sheets and his deliciously puffy duvet that pretends to be a cloud.

He shifts. He mumbles. It's a miracle he didn't talk the whole time we were banging. I stare back at his naked, hot body and briefly consider taking a picture. I sort of want the souvenir, but my phone is in my loft, plus it feels creepy. Ethics suck. I settle for a mental snapshot and file it under "so much fun, so bad for me."

I find my sweatpants at the top of the stairs, but my panties have vanished into a black hole. Oh well. Since my tank top is downstairs and I have to visit the lobby for a replacement key card, I steal one of Ozzy's T-shirts and his hoodie. The hoodie is from a surf spot somewhere exotic. A palm tree frolics over my left boob; a smiling sun exhorts me to *seas the day*. I'll get right on that.

Before I can launch myself down the stairs and carry off my act of theft, Ozzy rolls over and opens his eyes. He doesn't bother grabbing for the sheet. I hold my breath. Is he awake for real? My last hookup slept like a hundred-year-old vampire at dawn.

"Don't go." His voice is sleep roughened. Sexy. I want to crawl back in bed with him and forget about my career.

I should apologize for waking him up. Or make more noise. Run?

"Places to go," I blurt out. "Code to write. Presentations to make."

There's a moment of awkwardness after I share my calendar update. Well, I feel awkward. Ozzy is just himself. He hums some more. Rolls to his feet. Flashes his tight, bitable butt at me, which is probably unpremeditated because he bends over (I snap another mental picture) and swipes his shorts from the floor. I edge down the stairs while he pulls them on.

He follows me, bounding like a gazelle. "Do you want to get breakfast?"

"No."

I estimate there is twenty feet between me and the door. I pick up speed.

"Coffee?"

"No."

"I feel like we should talk about what happened."

I don't. Ten feet. Five. A large, inked-up hand presses against the door in front of my face, then rapidly retreats as if its owner has just realized that holding me hostage could be misconstrued.

"I want breakfast," he says. "Coffee. But I'd settle for a thank you. Maybe a thank-you card." He runs the offending hand through his hair. It stands on end. "Should I take it personally that you're sneaking out?"

Ozzy likes to do the leaving. Noted.

I open the door. I have to tug on it because he's still mostly in my way. "Why are you following me?"

"I'm seeing you home," he grumbles.

"I love—live—ten feet away from you!" My Freudian slip has me blushing, but fortunately he's too busy rolling his eyes dramatically at the ceiling to notice. His look says he plans on being inflexible on this point.

"Shoes?" He holds a pair of blue athletic slides out to me. I'm barefoot, so I take them. They are ridiculously too huge. They slap against the soles of my feet as I stomp toward the elevator. I can't risk the stairs in these. I'll stumble-slide to my death.

"I could get the new key for you," he volunteers.

"I've got it."

I step into the elevator when the door opens and then jam my finger on the Close Door button.

"Out." I shoo him away when he tries to join me. "Let's never talk to each other again."

"You don't hate all of me," he announces as the door closes.

He's right.

That unhappy thought sits in the back of my head as I get a new key card from downstairs. It's disturbingly present as the elevator crawls back up to the third floor. It has not been vanquished by the time I'm back in my place.

I have sex hair, a cotton-candy beehive of a mess on top of my head. It takes me a good hour to de-sex-marathon my person and get ready for work.

When I come out, there's a coffee cup on my doorstep.

Despite my lack of sleep and sore inner thigh muscles, I make it to work on time. Rosie and I consume cup after cup of coffee in preparation for our midmorning demo and follow it with doughnuts.

Exhausted from my all-night sex marathon, I stumble into the unisex bathroom to finger comb my hair. The beard burn on my throat announces: Ozzy was here. I debate painting over his mark with some concealer, but it seems like too much work. Instead, I section my hair and pull it forward on either side of my face. I'm in incognito mode.

Rosie is not fooled. She points to my lips accusingly. They are fuller, redder. They announce to the entire office: Pandora got laid last night.

"I have so many questions," she says, whipping out her

makeup bag. She eyes my hair and adds a mini Drybar brush to the pile on the counter. "And no time. I need a full explanation of where you were last night, young lady."

"I'm older than you." I inspect myself in the mirror.

"Details," she prompts. "Please. What happened, with who, and when?"

"My neighbor," I mumble. "Ozzy. Last night. His place. OMG. Am I surfer groupie now?"

Rosie makes a WHAAAT face. She's confused. "Who?"

"My neighbor is—*was*—a celebrity surfer."

"Ooooh." Rosie abandons her hair and makeup attempt to peck frantically at her phone. "Was the sex good? Did he live up to his reputation? Is your surfer Ozzy WYLDER?"

I squint at her. "Do you follow surfing?"

This is not a work-appropriate conversation. She is an intern. I am her team lead, even if lately we've veered into friendship territory.

"No, but I'm projecting my own celebrity crush onto yours. It's—"

"Don't tell me." I'm mortified. I should stop this conversation.

Rosie redirects herself. "I thought you were rehearsing your presentation last night."

She means: *There's no sex in our slide deck!*

"I was, but my neighbor was making so much noise that I had to ask him to turn his music down. And then he wouldn't, so I yelled at him."

Rosie stares at me as if I'm a stranger.

I shrug. "And then we hate-fucked. The end."

"I'm not sure you hate each other as much as you think you do," she observes. She drags the brush through my hair. "Also, when I said be like Shonda, I didn't mean that you should apply her year of yes rule to your sex life." She pauses. "Not that that's a bad idea. We should ask Shonda if she tried that."

As we are never, ever going to meet Shonda Rhimes and interrogate her inappropriately about her sex life, I just nod.

"At least you're relaxed," Rosie observes. This of course has the effect of making me poker up.

Still, I hold it together. Rosie runs the slideshow for me, mouthing helpful prompts when I lose my train of thought. The presentation is just ten minutes and I'm overprepared. Plus, my code is solid, my prototype fully functional. I'm trying to make this a no-brainer for my audience, so that they'll green-light the full development. It requires me to sell, and then sell some more. Point out all the ways my redesign of our app makes it better. More likely to sell a thousand vacations. *Awesome.* I'm unexpectedly grateful for Rosie's help. I'm not rowing this boat entirely by myself. I have a wingwoman.

By the time we reach the last slide, the executive team (who have an average age of twenty-three) want a go-to-market strategy and to know who my target audience is. Bob repeatedly asks if my algorithm is a "sure thing," oblivious to the inappropriate overtones of his question. The venture capitalist, who is representing the company board and who is brilliant at turning ideas into money, sprinkles phrases like *total addressable market* and *customer acquisition costs* into the discussion. I'm terrified of looking stupid in front of him.

I've only ever wanted to be seen, and seen by everyone I work with, in any capacity. It's simultaneously my main motivation and the albatross around my neck, which leads to me working day and night in order to code more, better, perfect. The heart of Pandora Fyffe is a computer chip that tries to substitute codes for feelings, and then when people treat her like an automaton, she curls angrily up in her shell. Win or lose (and I'm all in on winning), the people in this room *see* me. It scares me.

What if I'm not enough?

As much as I want this job, as much as I believe that I *can* do it, my instinct is to demur and make myself small and unnoticeable. There's a permanent seat on the sidelines with my name on it. But I'm choosing not to sit down. I'm standing up. Speaking out. Rosie believes I'm enough. Of course, she also mentioned once that she's a terrible underachiever because she hadn't dropped out of Stanford to launch a billion-dollar business in her parents' garage.

She's bold. Beautiful. Boldly beautiful? Her bleached-blond hair has orange streaks today, and she's painted pink daisies on her thumbnails. She changes them once a week to match the flowers she brings for her desk. She spends more time painting her nails than I do sleeping.

I want to be her when I grow up. I make a note to share my admiration at a suitable point in the future while I launch into my conclusion. "The new algorithm will find your perfect travel friend. You'll never have to adventure alone."

"And the data for the matches comes from questionnaires?" Pantsuit Lady is flipping through the printout of my slides. Rosie put them into binders.

"Yes. The algorithm predicts your travel personality based on your answers."

We review the number of entries we have already, which is less than I would like but more than I need to be statistically significant. I've had the entire team standing in front of grocery stores, bars, the local REI with their tablets. We've used a service that pays starving students to fill out online surveys. We've begged our friends and families. Ozzy begged his.

"We're just getting started," I promise. "And we already have ten thousand profiles."

"A good start," Bob says absently. He's flipping through the questionnaire on one of the tablets Rosie handed out. It makes a sad click when he sets it down. "Show us."

"Excuse me?"

"Run it. Find your match." Bob doesn't volunteer. I bet the last time he took a vacation was when he was twelve.

Since no one else is volunteering, I run the algorithm and wait for it to spit out my results.

We only have the wireframe mockup that Rosie made this morning. It's not sophisticated. Or beta tested. There's a cheesy counter that increments through the ten thousand or so entries that we have. I'm fully expecting it to make a farting sound and declare me unmatchable when a cute kitten releases a bunch of colored balloons. *TAA-DAAAAAAA* is spelled out in eighty-point neon pink font. I glare at Rosie. She giggles.

Match found!

Everyone leans forward. My photo flashes up on the left side of the screen. On the right side is…Ozzy.

What. The. Fuck.

Our dream itinerary is equally suspect. A map of—I squint—Tijuana pops up on the screen. A long, red, snake-like ribbon spools south from Mexico's most infamous border town to the tip of the Baja California peninsula. Not only have I been condemned to spending time with Ozzy, but I'm being asked to do it in a desert. On a *road trip*. I'm sure my ideal trip starts with one of those first-class airline suites with gold-plated showers and luxury chef service.

"There's a bug in my code," I hiss to Rosie as the room explodes in conversation. Life-changing sex aside, I can't stand him. We can't travel together.

"Roll with it," Rosie hisses back. "The show must go on."

I keep my panicked thoughts to myself as the executive team loudly embraces the idea of Ozzy as their first-ever match.

The Code for Love 133

He's a celebrity! He's fun! Sending a plain-Jane engineer on a trip with him would be awesome publicity!

My (admittedly quiet) protests are ignored. The marketing team rhapsodizes about the value of a highly publicized, glamorous road trip with a charismatic celebrity. It's perfect. Who *wouldn't* want to match with a celebrity?

Me.

I slam my laptop closed and canvas the room for support. "I don't have time to go on a road trip!"

Unfortunately, Bob is fully on board with the idea. "Make time."

I gather my thoughts and counter-propose: "Let's match everyone in the room. We'll do someone else."

There's a token vote.

I lose.

No one thinks I should stay happily ever after in San Francisco. Everyone thinks I should go on a Mexican road trip with the world's favorite surfer. I don't remember telling them that I know him. I suppose they assume that if we have his data, we have a connection. It hasn't occurred to them that I am not BFFs with each of our ten thousand respondents.

Rosie squeals happily beside me. She would take my place in a heartbeat.

Bob marches up to me while everyone else files out of the conference room, enthusing about how viral a social media campaign starring Ozzy will go. "Andromeda, I feel that you're not entirely on board with the idea of field-testing the algorithm."

You think?

Also, my name is Pandora.

He's already barreling ahead, though, so I wait.

"But this is important. Mission critical." He tosses in some other phrases he's likely memorized during his overpriced evening MBA program. "Jeanne tells me you'd like to be considered for the chief play officer opening, and a successful candidate would make this road trip happen. She'd get Ozzy Wylder on board, and then she'd knock the ball out of the park."

He smiles patronizingly at me. He's forgotten our last conversation, where he assured me that if I made this software launch happen, I'd absolutely, for sure, most definitely be his new chief play officer. Apparently, I need a contract written in blood.

I grit my teeth.

And nod. Very, very reluctantly.

I refrain from stabbing him to supply myself with said blood for our contract.

Oblivious to my rage, Bob flashes me a thumbs-up. "Make this happen, and I'll make things happen for you. Give me a successful social media campaign. Pictures. A story."

I nod again. Decide to believe him. *Again*.

"Good talk." He gives me another smile and wanders out, presumably to book me and Ozzy a camper van. I'm not sure why they think I'll be able to convince him to go.

Oh God.

I have to convince him to go.

"Ozzy Wylder. You. A confined space. We should sell the movie rights. Can I come as tech team?" Rosie's eyes are starry. She thinks I've just been given an all-expenses-paid vacation. This is going to be the road trip from hell. "We're gonna bust out of our boring nine-to-five! Van life will be amazing! This is the best internship ever!"

Mmm-hmm. I have always (not) wanted to sleep in my vehicle. To drive for hours and hours when a plane could get me there so much faster. To poop in the wilderness.

Of course, Rosie wants to bring the rest of the engineering

team in on my amazing "opportunity," and I have to field their questions, including the how-do-you-know-Ozzy-Wylder explanation. They are impressed. Moderately interested on a unipolar scale.

I only hope Ozzy feels the same way.

Twelve

Rosie follows me out of the conference room and back to my cubicle. Noah high-fives me. Enzo waves as he tears by on his scooter. He might mean *late, I'm late for a very important date* or *surf's up*. I slap my palm against Noah's and say nothing to Enzo's disappearing back. I have bigger problems than my nonexistent communication skills.

I slump down into my desk chair. It has been a thousand hours since I last sat here. "How do I pitch this to Ozzy?"

I grab a whiteboard and wait for inspiration to strike. Any. Minute. Now. Rosie drops onto the yoga ball across me.

"Are you dating him?" she squeals. "I need updates! A relationship status!"

Relationships move at light speed in Rosie-land.

"Who's Pandora dating?" Noah follows her in.

I fake intense interest in the whiteboard cradled in my lap. "No one."

"Ozzy Wylder," Rosie says.

My face burns. "Am not. Can we focus on the real problem here?"

"I heard there's a TikTok of you two devouring each other on a beach," Noah offers.

What?

Not only did I not consent to any recording of beach time activities, but the news of my algorithmically perfect match with Ozzy has traveled faster than data packets on the internet.

Rosie's still spouting questions. "Was there actual mouth-on-mouth action in this alleged video? Or was this 'devouring'—" her air quotes are so exuberant that Noah has to lean back "—taking place on a southern continent, so to speak?"

"Jesus! No!" I'm appalled my coworkers think I would make a sex tape and share it with the internet.

"I would totally be up for some geographical adventuring with Ozzy. He's built. He's hot. Even if he totally sucked in the bedroom, I could just look at—"

"Just stop." I do not want to discuss Ozzy's dick with Rosie, even if I can provide valuable eyewitness testimony about its magnificence. "My having slept with him has nothing to do with this road trip!"

"You had sex with Ozzy?" Noah's shock is palpable.

Rosie has follow-up questions. "Did you take photos? Does Neoprene downplay or in any way exaggerate his goods?"

"Do the insides live up to the packaging? How did the two of you meet?" Noah wants to know.

My stomach clenches. Rosie makes a "give it up" gesture. Or maybe it means "come on"? That there's a fly in the room? Whatever. I don't speak hand. "He lives next door to me."

There's a moment of silence while Rosie and Noah consider the intersection of my sex life with Ozzy's. Noah's dumbfounded, leaning toward incredulous, which is not flattering.

Rosie gets out her phone and taps with the determination of a woodpecker drilling into a pine tree.

"This is the Ozzy Wylder in question, correct?" She holds her phone up.

On her screen, #SexGodOzzy—yes, he has his own ridiculous hashtag—flies across the surface of the ocean. Dark board shorts hang low on his lean hips, his chest is a naked masterpiece of muscles and ink, and a terrifying mountain of water rises behind him. Personally, I'd be curled up in a ball preparing to die, but he's laughing. Foamy bits of the wave wet his hair. No big deal. Also, I suspect he's inhuman. Possibly an alien warlord checking out Earth as a possible conquest.

"The world couldn't handle two of him. Yes."

Noah looks impressed. "*You* know *him*."

"I do. I believe I mentioned he's my next-door neighbor."

"You had sex with him."

"Inappropriate."

"Wow." Rosie makes a sucking sound. "You told me you did, so technically you started this conversation."

"Can you just help me figure out how to convince him to go on a road trip with me?" Noah opens his mouth. "Bribing him with sex is not an option."

His face falls.

Rosie scratches something off her whiteboard.

"Professional options only, please."

Rosie sighs. "Well, I guess you could always just talk to him."

Stalking Ozzy is harder than you would think. Plus, once I find him, I tend to want to kill him (except when I'm riding him like my own sex stallion but…details). I could knock on his door. Text. Move into the mail room, order him something perishable, and wait for him to collect the lure. The next step, however, would have to involve either casual conversation or groveling.

The Code for Love

Mulling over my (non)options, I head out onto the balcony. Everything is in its place, my outdoor egg-shaped chair buried beneath a stack of pillows. My spider plant has sent its babies through the railing and into Ozzy's territory. It may be taken hostage. Sent running back for the border…

As if I've conjured him up, Ozzy saunters out his slider door. Maybe stalking isn't as hard as I think?

Our eyes meet. Mine dive south, checking him out. Tonight, he's wearing faded blue jeans and a battered green T-shirt advertising a taco stand somewhere I've never been. He heads toward me confidently, as self-assured here as he is on the water. And in bed. And up against his wall. I tell my brain to stop it. He's my nemesis.

He stops just before the half wall that separates our spaces and holds up a whiteboard that's shaped like an apple. There are two annoying perky green leaves and a stem on top. On it, he's written: *GROUND RULES, PLEASE.*

Yes, in all caps.

The neon green marker clashes with the red of the apple outline.

I open my mouth. Come on out, words. Please be sharp and witty.

Instead, I'm silent. Befuddled.

I blame Ozzy.

When I fail to respond to his written overture, he erases the words with the hem of his T-shirt. I barely resist the temptation to admire the V-cut that his industrious scrubbing exposes.

Ozzy writes, the muscles in his forearm flexing. Then he writes some more. He's recreating that famous, never-ending Russian novel about a French invasion gone awry. Congressional budgets are shorter. Finally, he finishes and holds the board up for me to read:

You declined further personal contact with me. You said to never, ever speak to you again. As a modern male with excellent boundaries and listening skills, I am honoring your demand for silence and a cessation of spoken conversation.

Oh.

He adds a smiley face. He has excellent writing skills. The letters are strong and uniform. I'm sure he was the handwriting star of his fourth-grade class.

He's never going to let me live this down. "I take it back."

I identify the grin that lights up his face as *evil genius*. What will he do? More to the point, what will he say?

He nods. Agreement is good. "Great."

"Okay." I am a pirate, and he is the ship I'm boarding. I've dropped the plank between our two vessels and now all I need to do is walk across it. Easy-peasy.

He spins on his heel and saunters back toward his door. What?

"That's it?" I need more words. Nouns. Verbs. I'd even take an adverb.

"Yeah." He waves the hand holding the whiteboard. I need Rosie here to interpret. Is he giving me the bird? A mutant peace sign? Jazz hands? The slider door closes behind him. The music starts up again.

Executive summary: that did not go well.

I retreat inside and tap ChatGPT about possible next steps (grovel, the chatbot suggests), reject said steps (write a note of apology, it suggests), and then check in with Rosie for an alternate opinion (why is he not speaking to u? she texts back, followed by: what did u do?). Neither computer program nor human has a flattering opinion of my people skills. I guess it's true that I alienate people with my imitation of a hedgehog. Still. It's not them, it's me.

Think, Pandora, think.

An idea pops into my head. A wonderful, awful, terrible idea. It costs me thirty bucks and it's worth every penny. Imperfect soundproofing and my overfamiliarity with Ozzy's music? Correlation. Loud music resulting in my desire to seek him out and yell? Causation.

I barely resist the urge to fist pump as my newly purchased Wagnerian opera soundtrack floods my loft. The windows vibrate. The floor shakes. For good measure, I sing along with Isolde. *Take that, Ozzy Wylder. I'm loud and annoying, too.*

This is exactly what Shonda would do. She'd 10,000 percent sing like nobody is watching. Listening. Whatever. My knowledge of opera is limited to the look-inside option for *Opera for Dummies* but...this tune isn't bad. Almost catchy. I can't dance, but I do some lunges and perform a stretching video I downloaded years ago but never started. I bounce up and down. Throw my arms up in the air. My heart thanks me. My lungs wheeze. It's possible Ozzy texts. Knocks on my door. It's impossible to hear anything.

Seven long arias later, Ozzy starfishes on my slider door. *Gotcha.* He catches my eye and sinks to his knees. He's pleading. Or praying dramatically. According to the internet summary, Isolde is either scream-singing about her love for Tristan or (my personal opinion) she has the world's worst head cold. The aria is all hacking, nasal syllables. I make Ozzy suffer an additional thirty seconds before I pause the music (also, we *do* have a noise ordinance in the building).

I open the door. "Yes? Am I allowed to speak to you, your highness?"

He's shaking his head. "You have shit taste in music, Panda."

Imagine that. "Did you enjoy it?"

Now the look he sends my way is positively aghast. "Were you killing a legion of very sad Germans in here?"

Isolde was opining on Tristan's sexiness in a foreign language. I'm not a heathen—I'm a monoglot.

I break out my best haughty tone. "I love opera. I plan on listening to it whenever I'm working."

Subtext: you heathen.

Now Ozzy looks pained. "You work like twenty hours a day."

I smile. "Yep."

He deflates visibly. He's got the picture.

Imagine the horror, Ozzy. Emotionally tormented sopranos assaulting your eardrums every waking moment.

Being Ozzy, he rebounds quickly. He perks up and nods his head enthusiastically. "You like German opera. Do you speak German?"

I cannot let him win this game. "A few phrases."

Two words: *biergarten* and *schadenfreude*.

He launches into an animated conversation. He and Isolde must be BFFs.

I blink. My choices are limited. "*Schadenfreude?*"

"You don't speak German." He pouts briefly.

Whatever. "I have a proposal for you."

"Is it indecent? I'm not sure how I would feel about that."

I give him a look. "Strictly work related."

"Pandora." He sighs dramatically. We are no longer on a nickname basis. "I am not a sex worker."

Super.

"Do you remember that questionnaire you filled out for my work?"

Now it's his turn to give me a very Ozzy look. "There were *one hundred* questions. On a scale of one to invasive, I give it a seven."

Life may come too easily to him. "Data points are important."

"I was asked what I like to do with my hotel room towels. My breakfast preferences. My evening activity of choice."

Why is he so difficult? I am *so* frustrated. "Data. Points."

His forehead crinkles. "Did you look at my answers? I feel like my privacy may have been violated."

I ignore him, although my face is definitely, almost certainly ladybug red. I just need to ask him my question and convince him to agree, and yet our conversation is derailing. "The database knows."

He wanders past me and throws himself on my sofa. Clutches a pink throw pillow to his chest.

"Come in." Unable to help myself, I ask, "What's *wrong* with you?" Remember the plan, Pandora. "Let me rephrase. May I proposition you now?"

He shoves the pillow over his face with a groan. Mutters something I decide to take as an affirmative.

"You're invited on an all-expenses-paid Mexican road trip." I carefully slide the invitation I've created into the palm of his hand. "Here is the itinerary."

He is silent for a moment. Then he shifts the pillow off his face and holds up the invitation. It's a scroll tied with a red ribbon. Rosie suggested this would read as classy but fun, although I'm now rethinking that choice. He pulls the ribbon free. Sets it gently on the sofa. Unfurls the paper. Reads.

The itinerary the algorithm proposed based on our questionnaires starts outside of Tijuana and follows the highway down the Mexican coastline. It meanders past tiny fishing villages, makes pit stops at not-so-hidden surf spots where Ozzy has won various surfing championships. There is something called the Sea of Cortez. It ends in Cabo San Lucas, that dramatic spit of land with the famous rock arches where Mexico gives up and falls into the ocean. We are supposed to exhaust ourselves at the wilder party bars and then throw ourselves into the bone-crushing summer surf in dramatic fashion at Cabo San Lucas.

As I hate traveling, I suspect the algorithm was forced to work overtime, has become sentient, and decided to punish me for its long hours.

Because it has proposed we do the road trip from hell in a romantically cozy camper van.

"No, thank you," he says.

For once, we are in agreement.

This is bad. I regroup. Think fast. Come up with nothing. My job promotion slips through my fingers.

"Why not?"

Somehow, I've gravitated to the couch. Since standing over Ozzy seems rude, I sink down beside him.

"It's like a victory lap. You get to go back to all the spots you conquered on your surfboard. Revisit your glory days. Take a bow." I stab my finger at the last line on the scroll. "And then you get to star in a spectacular charity surfing demonstration in Los Cabos. There will be applause, Ozzy, and people giving money to worthy charities."

I make a note to ask the TripFriendz executive team to find a nice NGO to sponsor.

"I'm not surfing," he says.

"Well, it's not like I can step in for you there."

He turns. He's a shark smelling delicious, vulnerable tuna in the water. "Are you coming with me on this hypothetical road trip?"

"Sort of?"

"Are you inviting me on a really complex date, Panda?"

"Not…exactly?"

The fingers of the hand not holding the scroll tap on his chest. "Explain it to me, please."

"I've told you about my work." He nods. Pinches his thumb

and forefinger together and then eases them apart a miniscule amount. I interpret this as an invitation to expand on the information I've shared. "Well, I coded an algorithm that matches two people as travel buddies and then algorithmically picks their best itinerary. It uses the data points from those questionnaires to pair people up. When I demoed the algorithm for TripFriendz's executive team, it paired you and me together, and now my bosses want to send us on a Mexican road trip. Together."

Mentioning the camper van seems unwise. Baby steps.

He reexamines the scroll. Perhaps I should have gone with the slide deck that Rosie talked me out of. She claimed presentation software didn't scream authentic or approachable. I don't see what that has to do with anything. Especially with convincing Ozzy to go with me on what amounts to an extended date from hell.

He jams the scroll into his back pocket. Paper crinkles. "Do you want to go on a romantic road trip with me?"

"It's not romantic."

"Will the camper van have an adorable miniature Jacuzzi? Twinkle lights?"

Okay. So, the camper van secret is out of the bag. He can clearly read.

"No."

He looks disappointed.

"Ten days in a tiny van and not an ounce of romance?"

My mad internet skills assure me that the toilet is a pull-out pot that lives under the kitchen counter (unsanitary and exposed) and showering relies on solar heating (thus bound to be short and unsatisfying). Spectacular Mexican scenery and really fabulous Instagram pictures cannot possibly compensate for these dire living conditions.

"Romance free," I assure him. "Also comfort free, likely hot, and going absolutely nowhere I would choose to go."

He looks at me. Oops. There's probably no walking that back.

"I hate traveling," I confess.

To my surprise, Ozzy nods. "I'm not currently a fan, either."

Isn't he a jet-setting international athlete? I mean, he probably gets to stay in five-star luxury hotels, the kind with butlers and minibars that charge you a hundred bucks for a tiny can of Pringles, but still. I'm bewildered by his lack of enthusiasm.

He, on the other hand, may be bewildered by my traveling plans, but he also smells an opportunity to torture me. "But you want to do this anyhow?"

Want is a strong word. "Need."

My word choice is a tactical mistake. Ozzy's dimples come out to play. He knows he has the upper hand.

"Tell me why, Panda. Convince me. Sell me."

"You get a free vacation," I lie. I'm 99.99 percent certain TripFriendz's marketing team plans to work Ozzy to the bone. What he saves in cash, he'll make up for in sweat equity. "You'll get to go to the beach. Surf. Eat tacos. In exchange, you put up with me as your roommate and we take a few happy pictures for TripFriendz's social media. When we're not promoting the app, we can go our separate ways. You'll barely notice me."

Let's hope he has no idea just how small a camper van is.

Ten days locked in a closet on wheels. For my dream job.

Assuming that we don't kill each other, our lack of murderous intent will show that the algorithm must be true. If I prove the algorithm is accurate, I get to be the new chief play officer. It's a mathematical proof. Oh, the new leaf I could turn over. I could be the fun boss. I could work with a team that actually knows my name. Stay in one place for a year.

Two years. Until I'm sixty-two and take early Social Security. Tell work stories at family Thanksgiving and Sunday dinners that make people laugh with me and not *at* me. High school reunion bragging rights. Reserved scooter parking. My name on a cute little business card. *Health insurance.*

I want this more than anything, and that is therefore the one thing I cannot tell Ozzy. It's his job as my arch-nemesis to thwart me, and he's very, very good at...thwarting.

"But we'll be travel buddies," he says. "Paired up by your algorithmic matchmaker."

"*Fake* travel dating," I emphasize. Oh God. I'm losing him. I shouldn't force him to road trip with me. I'll be cranky. Miserable. Hot. I will not smell pretty or share my space well. I *hate* leaving my house. "In a cute camper van."

"Uh-huh." His voice is low and rough. "It's okay to admit that you just want to have me to yourself, Panda."

"You're delusional. And my name is Pandora."

"And yet you want to spend ten days sleeping with me."

"Think about it."

He lobs a throw pillow gently at my head. "You would hate it."

I shake my head. I'm not sure if it's a *yes* shake or a *no*. Or just convulsions at the thought of so. Much. Travel.

When I say nothing, he says enough for both of us. "What's in it for me? Still not sold. Let's whiteboard it!"

He bounces up, ab muscles flexing (thank you, God) and bounds into my kitchen. Grabs the whiteboard from my fridge and inspects my dick artwork. "You've underestimated me, Panda bear."

I have and we both know it.

He uncaps a marker. "Reason number one?"

"Excellent publicity for your brand."

He writes it down. Adds a doodle of a palm tree. "But I'm

out of the surfing business. Washed up. Revisiting surf spots will hurt my delicate sensibilities. I'll be tormented by what I can't have."

My eyes narrow to semi-slits because the last time I checked his social media—approximately twenty minutes ago—there were zero statements about the end of his athletic career. I don't believe him.

"Free travel," I try. "All the ocean you could want. Way better surf sites than what's outside our window."

He scrawls a new bullet point. "See above—no more surfing. Plus, there's more to my life than surfing."

He can't mean it.

But for one moment, I'm finishing his sentence. *There's you.* I'm in his head, we're sharing the same thought. It's just the two of us and it's perfect.

"Days and days of unlimited opportunities to torment me." I don't like this, but it's true. "Pranks. Jokes. Complicated revenge plots. You'd have time for all those things."

He points the marker at me. "Do you know what I think?"

"Nope!" I tell him, hoping I sound unconcerned.

He smells my concern. "You're desperate. You have to get me on board."

"Well…only because my boss is a moron, and my algorithm has a bug in it. I'll fix my code, and you'll be booted off the trip. You should agree now!" Enzo claims that it's important to instill a sense of urgency when you're pitching. Make your audience think that their opportunity will dry up faster than an uncapped bottle of nail polish remover.

"Very compelling," he says dryly. He tosses the whiteboard marker to one side and collapses dramatically on my sofa. "I am overwhelmed by your arguments."

"Really?"

"No." He crosses his arms over his chest.

"It's not just about you helping me out in exchange for a free vacation, though. I know you're between careers."

"I am a very busy man, and it's not as if helping you with your career will get my new business off the ground any faster. I need start-up funds, Panda bear, and I can't pick those up on the beach like a seashell."

"I'm hearing that you want to be paid." I write this down in my phone app. It comes out as *wants ppayign* but note-taking makes me look serious rather than desperate.

"Sure." He shrugs. Grins. "But I could just pander my good looks and popularity on Instagram. Pick up some brand endorsements. Take my dad up on his offer of gainful employment."

His grin is now more grimace.

Okay. He also has daddy issues.

I frown. "But you're retired? And possibly want to stick it to your old man? I'm picking up on some conflicting messaging here."

"Let's just say that I'm out of the sports business, which is *very* disappointing for him. And as I enjoy thwarting his expectations for me, I plan to stay out." Ozzy closes his eyes. Apparently, it's nap time.

"So…no surfing."

Ozzy nods.

I draw on my extensive experience with post-unemployment job interviews.

"And you want to go in a new direction."

Another nod.

"And your father disapproves, but that's…a feature and not a bug?"

And…another nod. Winner, winner, chicken dinner.

"What is it that you do want to do?"

"Wildlife photography."

Huh. That explains the nene picture on his wall and all the birds on his Instagram.

"But breaking into wildlife photography takes time," Ozzy says without opening his eyes. "Cash, too, although that's not the most significant issue."

I refrain from pointing out that he just said money was a factor. I'm supposed to be *wooing* him.

"What I really need are the right opportunities," he continues. "A solid chance to break into the field. And I would prefer to do it now, rather than in ten years. Wildlife photography is highly competitive and there are limited jobs. I'm building my portfolio, but I need a high-profile job. Gallery shows. Magazine covers."

His confidence is mesmerizing. He's not content to just shoot photos—he plans to conquer the entire industry. I want to say I don't understand his thirst to do something new and to do it well, but I get it. Possibly because that's why I'm begging him to come with me to Mexico; his agreement is a gating factor for whether or not I land my dream job. So, yes, I understand dreaming—and working to make those dreams a reality.

I add *pya oof National Geographic* to my list.

"Can you get me a photography gig with national exposure that will let me shoot unique photos of wildlife that showcase my style?" he asks.

"If I do, will you go with me on a Mexican road trip?"

"Sure." The corner of his mouth quirks up. He hums a bar from the *Mission Impossible* soundtrack.

Watch me, Ozzy Wylder.

I whip off a quick email to Bob:

Ozzy's in but he has conditions. We need to hire him as our photographer for industry-standard rates. He can do destination landscapes for the site, chronicle the road trip, maybe activity photos. It'll be the prototype for other TripFriendz users uploading images of their trips, and we can use his pictures for the big product launch.

Bob responds almost immediately, proving that no one in software engineering has a life outside of work. **Okay.**

I hold up my phone for Ozzy to read. "You're hired."

He sits up and stares at me, and I stare back despite my plan to be professional. Persuasive. His face is so beautiful. None of the teasing remains. He just looks me over carefully, nodding his head.

"Is this what you want?"

"It is."

"I feel like I should make it clear that this will not be a giant sexathon. I am not a booty call."

"I'll resist." It turns out that you cannot, in fact, die of embarrassment. Or spontaneously combust.

He's beautiful. Popular. People—guys, girls, everyone—want to be around him. In him. On him. He has a waiting list longer than a Birkin bag. We had our night of fun, but it's over. Exactly as I told him it would be. I have no business feeling disappointed.

"Okay," he says. He winks at me. "See you in Mexico, Panda."

Thirteen

My spine is a waterfall of sweat. It trickles down my back and soaks the waistband of my panties. They are my brand-new, just-in-case panties: pink, frilly, made of a synthetic nylon that is darling but ludicrously unbreathable in the Mexican sunshine. No one (aka Ozzy) will see them, but just in case… I'm covered.

Rosie is concerned. "Have you been stood up?"

"He'll show." Ozzy is already on vacation time. He didn't spend Day One of the Great Mexican Road Trip with us in our Tijuana Beach hotel, and now he's thirty minutes late for Day Two. I'm terrified to turn cellular data on on my phone to track him as I'll have to sell a kidney to pay the bill. The rest of the social media team (Roz, Thom, and Lore, whose jobs are unclear to me, but require constant attention to various electronic devices) seem unconcerned by his absence. They lounge around the parking lot, debating names for the camper van. Berta is winning, although Van Gogh is unfortunately also a contender.

After eleven hours of hotel air-conditioning, the heat of

the parking lot is stunning. I want to retreat inside and never come out.

"Should you call him? Text? Was he flying in directly?" She is applying blueberry-colored lip gloss in the side mirror of the second van, the far less cute but much more practical one that the social media team will be traveling in. She's here because she begged. And also, because I feel like I owe her. If she wants to spend her internship in Mexico that's on her, and I could use a friendly face.

We were warned that crossing the border from San Diego into Tijuana can be slow, so everyone except for Ozzy flew in yesterday. As we'll be trapped together in a camper van soon enough, I didn't insist that he travel with me. Was that a mistake? What if he went to the airport intending to fly to Tijuana but instead ended up in Hong Kong or Bali?

I opt to text. **Where r u?**

His response is almost immediate: **MEXICO!** He attaches a photo in which he's wearing a sombrero.

Not helpful. U R LATE.

He leaves me on read.

The shorthand grates, but Rosie assures me it makes me seem like less of a fossilized dinosaur come to life and roaming the colorful if gritty streets of Tijuana. I pace restlessly to the street, phone in hand, debating whether I should attempt hacking into a satellite to determine Ozzy's precise location. Palm trees line the road, alongside buildings that seem to be mostly cantinas, taco stands, bars, and dance clubs. The smell of grilled fish and corn fills the air.

I fan my face with my white straw hat (beach chic!) and flap the hem of my TripFriendz T-shirt. The itinerary that the algorithm provided is doable if I don't melt first:

1. Day 1. Arrive in Tijuana.
2. Days 2 and 3. Drive down the coast past Rosarito (photo op!) and picturesque places with names like El Descanso and then hang a right to Valle de Guadalupe for wine-tasting and vineyards.
3. Day 4. Motor past Ensenada.
4. Days 5 and 6. Cross the peninsula and push on to San Felipe and the Sea of Cortez, where we will engage in various highly photogenic marine activities.
5. Day 7. Visit a string of tiny, idyllic beach towns with names like Cielito Lindo and Puertecitos.
6. Days 8 and 9. Playa El Pescador
7. Day 10. San Juanico. Swimming in the Pacific Ocean.
8. Day 11. La Paz. Whale sharks. The ocean.
9. Day 12. Finish line! Los Cabos.

In addition to the summary sheet, I have an hourly breakdown of our schedule. Lists of scenic spots for photos. Restroom breaks. I am *not* peeing behind a cactus or in a bucket camper van toilet. If we drove nonstop, it would take only twenty-two hours, but we'll be breaking the drive up with nightly stops. Because *fun*.

Despite our proximity, there have been limited opportunities over the past week to talk. He's sent me a Pinterest board of possible road trip pit stops, but my work hours have made it difficult to chat in person. Once or twice, I've spotted him at the TripFriendz offices. He and Bob are BFFs now. There have been introductions. Everyone is very excited about the possibilities of our match.

I'm relieved when he finally puts in an appearance. Given his love of dramatic entrances, I half expect him to parachute in from a helicopter or rush the beach on a Jet Ski. The taxi makes an impression, though. It's a vintage white Cadillac with an enormous orange sombrero stuck to the roof. Two equally outsize rooster cutouts decorate the front wheel wells, and someone has tied a skull to the grill. The social media team lunges into action.

Ozzy hops out with a small duffel bag and a much larger camera bag. Despite his presumably brief acquaintance with the driver, he exchanges phone numbers as well as cash. They've really hit it off and make plans to meet up the next time Ozzy is in Tijuana.

I'm not sure what to do, so I wait for him to notice me. To give him credit, he does look past the other team members to find me.

"Hey." He saunters my way. He's in cargo shorts today, the kind with a million pockets, and a white linen shirt that's open over yet another T-shirt. This one is the pale green of a ripe avocado. There's a cactus printed in the center of his chest, above the words Can't Touch This.

Roz—whose name is far too similar to Rosie's—stops snapping pictures of Ozzy and says to us, "Meet our van, Berta. I'll let you two go inside to check it out."

Ozzy and I both stop, registering the fact that we can't fit three people inside this tiny, miniscule, far-too-small, mustard-colored van.

Perhaps natural law doesn't apply. Maybe it's like that Quidditch World Cup tent that actually is a four-bedroom en suite with a full kitchen and bath. I can manifest it, right?

Nope. When I take a step forward and stick my head inside the wide-open sliding door (there will be *zero* privacy), I'm practically touching the far wall. But as I check out my new home away from home, I realize I have a bigger problem. Or rather, a smaller one.

There's only one bed. It's a mattress on a platform built into the back of the van directly behind the driver's seat. There are two pillows and far too little real estate.

I have to share that bed with Ozzy, and the last time we did that, we had sex.

Fuck.

Fuck, fuck, fuckity fuck.

Or rather, *no* fucks.

I will give no fucks, receive no fucks, and this will all turn out to be a really vivid stress dream. Clearly, pursuing a promotion at work is not good for me. I should raise llamas. Start an Etsy business. *Anything* else, really.

I back out of the camper van so fast that I collide with Ozzy. And by *collide*, I mean my butt grinds against his front. His hands settle on my hips, steadying me.

I cannot road trip with this man. I simply cannot.

Someone from the social media team yells, *"Queso!"* Everyone around me—including Ozzy—strikes a pose. I am surrounded by grade A influencers and am the odd woman out.

To be fair, this is part of the job. I am going on an all-expenses-paid Mexican vacation for work, and part of that work is making nice for TripFriendz's social media. To be even fairer, however, I am not and never have been a photogenic person. I freeze. Grimace-smile. Wonder if my hair is *really* stuck to my nose or if it just feels that way.

There's a momentary pause while the social media team adjusts its expectations downward. I can hear them wondering if they can just shoot me from behind (yes, please) or photoshop Ozzy over me in all of their shots.

Ozzy, of course, is in his element. He jumps up into the van—no hands, he's such a show-off—and takes "y'all" (apparently, he's now an honorary Southerner) on a "tour of our sweet ride!"

Ugh. These are going to be the longest ten days of my life.

The cameras on sticks, the GoPro-looking thing, and the ten tons of electronic devices peel off and follow him. He's magnetic north to their compass needle, black shirt to their cat fur.

Rosie elbows me. "Get in there."

She's far too optimistic. The van will explode if we add one more person. Lore has squeezed inside with Ozzy, who is enthusiastically testing out the bed (firm) and then opening and shutting the hatch in the roof (we can stargaze!). They don't need me.

Rather than add to the traffic jam, I make myself useful and run through our predeparture checklist. I review the itinerary. Make sure we have the printouts of the Google maps because I am *not* reenacting Exodus and wandering in the Mexican desert for forty years.

Ozzy pops up through the hatch. He balances on the van's roof. The social media team spills backward, snapping furiously. "I can surf up here while we drive!"

His hair billows as if he's in a shampoo commercial. His skin is golden, tanned, beautiful. I, on the other hand, am sweaty, dusty, and my pits smell. Against my will, I take a picture of him with my phone. He's worth remembering.

Eventually, he climbs down and people yell for a group shot. We obediently cluster together and drape ourselves over Berta. Someone lounges on her hood while Ozzy and I crouch-stand inside and pretend to wave. The executive team joins by Zoom because they cannot stand to be left out of the fun.

"Best chief play officer evah!" Lore slaps Ozzy on the back. Ozzy grins and thumbs-ups him.

I tell myself I misheard.

It was a slip of the tongue

A mistake.

But the executives are beaming and winking from the screen of Lore's tablet. Everyone is smiling at Ozzy.

Rosie's head swivels. She's enraged on my behalf. "Say what? That's *Pandora's* gig."

"Who's Pandora?" Lore asks.

"*Pandora*. This cranky, prickly person standing next to me." Ozzy frowns. "The one with the lists and the sticky notes. Pretty sure you've met."

Bob talks over Ozzy, as if afraid he'll let the cat out of the bag. "There is an opening for chief play officer, as Margie is not returning. We want to use this road trip as a test run. See how things shake out. May the best man win."

I don't think that's a slip of the tongue.

Rosie clearly agrees with me because she steps forward. She's ready to rumble, to defend my honor, to grab Lore's tablet and *end* this unfortunate Zoom call. I grab her arm as a precautionary measure. Measures will be taken, but not yet.

There is no silencing her, however. "What about *Pandora*?"

"Pandora is also a candidate," Bob adds hastily. He's looking at Rosie the way you would a large snake that you just discovered by your trash can. "Ozzy and Pandora are our top two."

Rosie is not letting him off the hook. "So how do you determine who wins?"

"Whoever does the best job at representing the chief play officer on the road trip. Likes, posts, on-brand content, amazing pictures. Sell TripFriendz to the world!" I'm pretty sure Bob is making this up as he goes along. Also, it seems borderline unethical. Possibly a violation of OSHA. How has Ozzy gone from a freelance wildlife photographer to job-stealing future boss?

Nevertheless, Bob ends the Zoom to a round of applause. Someone produces snacks and tequila cocktails that are a terrible idea, because some of us are driving. More pictures are taken, some of them even by Ozzy, who ignores my sotto voce suggestion that he takes pictures of *snakes*.

"Let's roll!" Roz tosses the keys for the camper van at Ozzy and me. Ozzy's arm is longer and he catches them.

He hops out of the van and strides around to the driver's side. My stomach sinks. I'm losing already.

I charge after him. I hate driving, freeways, and vehicles with poor visibility, but Ozzy doesn't get to win this, too. I slide my body between him and the door.

"When I said there might be opportunities for you at Trip-Friendz, I didn't mean my job." I glare. Refuse to blink.

Or cry. Because this is now a competition. A ten-day job interview. Ozzy will sabotage me. He has an unfair advantage. People *like* him! He takes the best bird photos ever!

His hands curl around my waist. He lifts me off my feet and sets me to one side. I breathe in ocean and salt, sun and warmth. Forget selling vacation packages—we should bottle him. We'd make a fortune. I'm eye-to-eye with his cactus.

"I'm sorry, Panda," Ozzy's voice says from somewhere west of me.

He's not sorry at all.

"This is *my* job," I tell him. "Go get your own somewhere else."

His forehead crinkles. Poor baby.

"May the best person win," he says magnanimously.

I ignore him.

Olive branch spurned, I take pictures while he climbs into the driver's seat and rearranges everything to suit himself. I snap close-ups of the van and then flat lays. My cute pink suitcase with my wide-brimmed straw hat and guidebook spilling out. Flip-flops on the desert sand with a pair of sunglasses shaped like mariachi-waving cacti. I'm terribly motivated. I'm not at all discouraged. Well, mostly.

By the time I'm finished posting to social media, the vans are loaded and ready to go. Rosie has magically acquired a piñata from Piñata Alley. Ozzy inhales food from a roadside vendor that will absolutely *kill* his intestines. Pupusas. Those aren't even Mexican—they're an El Salvadoran import. I judge him ruthlessly.

I climb into the passenger seat as there's no evicting Ozzy from the driver's seat. It's fine. I'll insist on taking turns. Steal the keys. Wait for his ill-advised snack to send him running to the nonexistent bathroom and *then* steal his seat.

I play the silent game as we head out onto Highway 1.

"I didn't know they were going to give me your job," he tries. "Come on, Panda. You believe that, right?"

He has a bridge for sale. Timeshares. An extended car warranty.

He makes another attempt. "It's important."

As are my wishes and wants.

"I need this chance," he says.

Nope. "Seriously, how does ruining my career prospects fit into your vision of wildlife photography? We hook up, I bring you on board at my work, support your career ambitions—" because they meshed well with mine, but details "—and then you stab me in the back and go for my *job*?"

"It's complicated." He has the good grace to look guilty. Slightly. I mean, on a scale of one to ten, he's registering about two and a half, so I'm not swayed. He can talk all the way to Cabo for all I care, but there's no explaining this away.

"Do you know what's *complicated*?" I hiss. "Coding an *algorithm*. Why do you want my job?"

He gives me one word. "Networks."

And then he rests his case with a sheepish look. *Goody. That explained everything.*

"Can you please give me more words? Perhaps an entire sentence?"

"Travel companies collaborate with local guides and naturalists. There will be opportunities to visit places and scout for animals to photographs. I'll gain marketing experience."

I scrunch my eyes shut in pain. *Marketing experience* sounds like *miracle from God* when he says it. I could try to explain that working for a travel startup isn't...

"Do you think it's going to be one, big wildlife party?"

I cannot understand his enthusiasm. Overexposure to software startups, probably.

He lifts a shoulder. "It's a chance."

"It's *my* chance."

"They haven't given the job to me," he tells the steering wheel.

Yet, we both add. I'm thinking it. He's thinking it. Plus, Bob loves him.

"I won't give up without a fight." I hope I'm threatening him, but I might be trying to give myself a pep talk.

"I would expect nothing less," he says solemnly.

"This isn't a game."

"Because you would never play those."

Yeah, my words seem less than believable when you consider my pranks. The spider army. The glitterpalooza episode. "You started it when *you* climbed up the wall. Who does that? And then you were so annoying. I had to do something." Although perhaps I could have tried just talking to him. Or suing him in small-claims court, like any self-respecting American.

My stomach clenches as I scan his face. Maybe I read too much into our road tripping together. Maybe I was hoping for something more than just business. He meets my eyes.

"Do you want me to take you to the airport?"

"What?"

"I don't want you to feel trapped. This is a small van, and everyone's going to throw us together. Do you want to go home?"

"Are you trying to talk me into *quitting*?"

"I'm trying to be thoughtful!" He throws his hands up in the air.

"Hands at nine and three o'clock!" I shriek.

He chuckles devilishly, taking an eternity to lower his hands back to the steering wheel. Because truth is, our neighbor wars were just the warm-up act. He knows it. I know it.

I whip out my phone and work on my to-do list. Give up on my cell phone bill and search for service so I can google *van pranks* and *how to sabotage a job interview*.

Ozzy is unfussed, of course. He taps out a salsa beat on the steering wheel. Stops for a red light and then waits patiently while a man runs up and washes the windshield. I'm not sure where to look when he squirts cleaner on my window. Ozzy hands him some cash when he finishes. Asks him something in Spanish. Naturally, they're best friends by the time the light changes.

"Do you want to pet the zonkey?"

I'm trying to process his non sequitur when he gestures excitedly toward the side of the road. *Oh, right.* A brown donkey-looking animal with black zebra stripes on its legs glares into the windows of our van.

I sort of do, but that's not going to win me my job back. "We have a schedule."

"So that's a no?" He looks disappointed. Briefly.

Then two hundred yards later, he's disregarding my wishes—exactly like he did with his job-stealing shenanigans—and pulling over onto the side of the freeway with the gusto of a NASCAR driver realizing he has a limited-time pit stop window. Berta's tires squeal. The contents of the van shift alarmingly. We're not even all the way out of Tijuana yet. Our first break is not scheduled for another hour.

"Do you need a water bottle to pee in?"

"Tree." He jerks a thumb toward the rock-studded, sandy, and absolutely barren roadside. There is a single, solitary bush. It has zero leaves and a few twiggy branches. "But no."

He hops out (taking the keys with him) and descends on a roadside vendor sitting on a blanket, surrounded by hundreds of brightly colored *alebrijes*. The whimsical folk art creatures bob and move, stirred up by our dramatic arrival. There are turtles and peacocks, a butterfly with pink and green wings. A lizard bird samples the air with a lime-colored tongue.

I consider taking Ozzy's place behind the wheel, but he has the keys. Also, I hate freeway driving. I'll take over tomorrow.

He's back almost before I know it. The vendor is grinning and waving. *Alebrijes* spill from Ozzy's cupped hands as he climbs in and deposits his treasures on the console between us.

"I need a dinosaur," he confides as if we're best friends.

"Get used to disappointment."

He pulls a face. "I have three nieces and a nephew. I have orders. A shark, a giraffe, and a dinosaur."

I've never thought of him as an uncle or a family guy. It's only logical that he has parents. Siblings. An evil villain origin story.

"For you," he says. He plucks a panda bear from his herd. "A peace offering."

He holds it out to me. It dances on his palm.

"Great, thanks." Perhaps he'll autograph it later for me and I can sell it on eBay. I take a picture of it lolling on his palm. This is war and he's just handed me a weapon.

He darts an amused glance at me. "Do you want my face in that, partner?" He pronounces it *pardner* as if it's me and him against the world, in this together, buddies.

"Eyes on the road, please." Our caravan are the only vehicles on this stretch of road, but traffic safety is important.

He laughs. It's a delicious, deeply amused laugh. His happiness indicates I'm no risk to his future employment. I'll show him.

"We could totally off-road here."

I look out the window, but I can't rebut his stupid claim. We drive past scrub brush, rocks, a *cardón* cactus stretching impressively prickly arms up into the sky. I settle for taking more pictures.

Another amused, inquisitive glance. "Do you want to play a game?"

"Nope." I am immediately, deeply suspicious.

"Road trip bingo," he suggests. "Scavenger hunt. I Spy!"

His social media posts will be awesome.

"How about the Quiet Game?"

He takes his eyes off the road. He bops me on the nose. "Nice try, Panda."

I check the odometer. We have sixty miles until our next stop. I cannot kill the driver. Work-from-home is difficult when you're locked up the state penitentiary.

Fourteen

"Red."

"White."

"White."

I attempt to play peacekeeper. "Both."

Everyone glares at me. I've spoiled their game.

I hate wine. It gives me a headache, and we've tasted a dozen varieties since arriving in Valle de Guadalupe vineyard three hours after leaving Tijuana. The valley is so dry, hot, and choked with vineyards that we could be in Greece. It's also super chic, full of in-the-know Angelenos and pop-up dinners held beneath two-hundred-year-old oak trees, at alfresco sushi bars, or in wine caves. I think up a dozen ways to abandon Berta and flee back to my San Francisco loft. I fantasize about life on an ice floe, just me, the penguins, and a nonhostile polar bear. I dream of alone time in an air-conditioned room.

After shutting down Ozzy's attempts to play with me (and/or kill me with good cheer), we'd driven down Route 3, La Ruta del Vino, the Pacific Ocean sparking on our right and the desert shifting sharply upwards into mountains on our left. Unfortunately for me, Ozzy does not know how to stew silently. Instead, he hums, sings, loudly proclaims the beauty of the rocky terrain, the cacti, the buzzards hovering overhead. He's deeply in love with the rolling hills with their stupid, shrubby, prickly bushes. He's never seen anything more charming than the white adobe buildings that sprout of nowhere with their tiled roofs.

And now we're here, at our third and final vineyard. It's rustic yet modern, chic but charming, insert your adjectives here. The marketing team and Ozzy have cooed over every grape vine, terracotta tile, and barrel room.

Me? Tannins disagree with me. The sun disagrees with me. Camper vans, motion sickness, and forced proximity? Also disagree with me.

"Let's buy them all!" Ozzy crows. He's ready to stack Berta with cases of wine. He wants a monthly subscription.

His shirt tonight is one of those black athletic numbers made of clingy artificial fibers. It gift wraps muscles that would make a god jealous. He attracts attention wherever we go. I can feel myself weakening. He's pulled his hair back in his usual man bun and is frowning adorably into his wine glass. He's not his usual, ebullient self. He's a little tousled, not quite smooth, probably from being pent-up in a moving vehicle with me. Hopefully, he's contemplating a new career path as an enologist.

It's been eight days since we had sex. Since I got underneath his shirt, got my hands on his divine body. It is nowhere near long enough to dull the edges of my memory. I drag out my mental snapshots and pour over them. Ozzy lounging in bed, bare-skinned, sheet wrapped around his hips. Ozzy moving over me. In me. My face flushes. I know what he looks like *naked*. There is no going back from this.

"Panda? You okay?" His voice is concerned. I force myself to nod.

"I'm great! How are you?"

"The drive wasn't too much?"

My throat squeezes. He says *drive*. He means *fuck*. He's wondering if I mentioned to the TripFriendz executive team that we jumped each other just over a week ago. He's barreled down the Mexican highway imagining that he might lose his chance at my job if they find out. The joke's on me. No way anyone will believe my algorithm is impartial and accurate if they learn what happened in his loft.

"All good." I give him double thumbs-up.

"You sure?"

I nod vigorously. There's no time for panicking. Or memories. *We can do this just once… But then you'd be all alone, Panda… You'd miss me…* My vag squeezes remembering our sex marathon. My skin smelled of him for days. The sex was amazing. Not that it matters. We're not doing it again.

Valle de Guadalupe? Officially checked off the list. We've visited the vineyards and taken all the pictures. Likes trickle in slowly on TripFriendz's Instagram. Ozzy's fan club comments in gushing terms on the photos he's somehow managed to share despite hogging the driver's seat all day. Most people don't bother to type anything; they sprinkle colorful hearts, smiley faces, a flame emoticon.

Someone sets their empty wineglass down and yells: "Photo on the roof!"

Ozzy slides me a look. He can see how much I'm into this suggestion. I'd rather file my taxes. March barefoot through the Mexican desert. Re-architect the TripFriendz app.

"Ding! Ozzy elevator!" He holds up his hands. We both stare at the ink on his forearms. He's out of space for anything else.

"Sure. It'll be a great shot." I try to be a team player. It may kill me.

"Going up," he says. He wraps his hands around my waist and lifts me onto the roof. I scramble briefly for traction, my foot slipping, but he's got me. He doesn't take the easy out and let his competition tumble to the ground.

"You're strong." My mouth starts a conversation without consulting with my brain. Idiotic things come out. I rearrange myself, trying to deflect his attention. Sit crisscross applesauce.

"Thanks. I work out." Ozzy handles the weird compliment like a professional before remembering that his working out irritates me. He makes an *oops* face. He assumes a surf stance for our audience. Rubs his knee and readjusts.

"So what's it like to surf?"

"It's like walking on water. On a good day, you're just flying over the ocean. No wings, no fancy gear, just you and the waves. I couldn't believe people would pay me to do it. It was good to me."

Past tense.

"Even if you're not competing, you can still go out, right?" Making conversation on a rooftop is awkward, but I feel like we're really talking. For the first time, we're not fighting. We might be listening to each other.

"Panda." He beams at the camera. He knows what he's doing. "It was a *bad* wipeout."

He pokes at the scar on his knee. Shrugs. Pretends everything is great despite being land-bound.

"And so that's really it? Forever?"

I try to imagine never coding another line. I fail.

He mimes shaking a Magic 8 Ball. "Cannot predict now."

Wineglasses are handed up. We obediently pretend to toast each other. To TripFriendz! To bread, without which there would be no toast! To travel buddies! We smile too much. Laugh overloudly. Thom wanders away—we've bored him.

When my glass clicks against Ozzy's, wine sloshes onto his hand. He sits down next to me and licks it off. Our eyes meet.

"Is this okay?" His voice is hoarse, his smile painted on his pretty face.

It's too soon after our sexathon for me to have forgotten how good he is at this.

"So much fun." I try for perky. I might read murderous. Ozzy flinches.

"Is that what you want? Fun?"

"It's what everyone wants. A good time. Keep it light. Keep moving." I smile like this is the best idea ever. I'd never ask for something more.

"And that's what you want from this trip?"

"Fun is good." I pretend to mull it over. I imitate Rodin's *The Thinker*, hunched over, deep in thought. I am downright pensive.

Are we done yet? My head aches. From the travel, from being on. From so. Many. People. I rub my face. There's a carpet of stars overhead, though, bright spots floating in the inky black. I flop backward. My head ends up on Ozzy's thigh. His fingers rub my hairline. It's hypnotic. Soothing. I never want him to stop.

A new bottle of wine is passed up to us. I pencil in fatty liver disease on tomorrow's agenda.

When the sound of lasers goes off on my phone an eternity later, I'm almost too exhausted to care. Driving and Ozzy are a lethal combination. Plus, wine. I reluctantly remove myself from his leg and sit up. I edge over to the open hatch in the camper van's roof while Ozzy watches me, amused.

I scramble awkwardly through the hatch and onto the bed.

At least the landing's soft. Ozzy thumps around overhead as I pull up our bug tracking app on my phone.

My team has missed me. Our work queue is bursting with critical issues, bad code, new feature requests. I call Noah back on Slack and have him walk me through the ticket he just opened.

"Can you fix it?" He is already moving the ticket into my queue. He flags it as a blocker.

I send it back to him. "I'm out of the office."

"But you're the only one who can fix it," he whines. "No one knows the code like you do. It will take me days, but you could be done in ten minutes. I can't believe you won't help."

He's wildly optimistic about my coding skills. The social media stuff doesn't seem as important, not compared with this. Without code, we don't have a product. Without a product, there's nothing to market, at least not ethically. "I'll look," I sigh. "No promises."

"And maybe you can redo the front-end UI? Zhuzh it up a little?" He's a five-year-old asking Santa for a pony. Tickets pepper my queue like mosquitoes.

I whip my laptop out and sign in. Until now, I've always been sort of in the background—a temporary employee who may or may not stick around. Now they need me. It will only take a few (hundred) minutes. The wallpaper on my desktop is a picture taken in the Crystal Cluster Cosmos. Imaginary gases swirl around an asteroid.

"What on earth did you guys *do*?" The code is a mess. This is mission impossible.

"Give the bug to Amir. He can fix it." Amir has been working for TripFriendz for twelve days; he has yet to successfully set up his laptop. "He wants to learn the front end."

There's a round of laughter from the table outside where Ozzy is racking up popularity points.

"No, I need you to do it."

"Why me?" I click. Update to head. Watch as my workspace fills with errors.

"The other engineer is rude. You're so much nicer."

This is my first blue ribbon. He hands me the gold trophy. I am drinking champagne out of the cup, and my team is hoisting me on their shoulders.

"All right. Let me see if I can fit it in tomorrow." Maybe I can code while we drive.

Ozzy's feet pad into view. He's come in search of me.

"Can you do it now? I was supposed to be done an hour ago." He sends a meme of a begging puppy dog.

"Wait," I say, but he's hung up on me. Slack plays whimsical hold music and informs me: you are alone in the huddle.

Ozzy sighs. "You let them take advantage of you. Tell him no. I can call him back for you."

I'm embarrassed. Hot. And also: exhausted. I want to lie down somewhere quiet and sleep for a week. "He needs my help."

"He *needs* you to cover his ass."

I dig in. "I'm a team player."

Lore pops his head in, which puts an end to Ozzy's unwelcome comments on my workplace habits. He wants to show us a reel he's put together of today's travel highlights. It's mostly shots of Berta rumbling down Highway 1 with the ocean on one side and the desert on the other. Ozzy and I are two bickering dots in the front seat. At the end, Ozzy flashes a peace sign out the window.

"It's good. I love the music." It's fairly generic, but I'm trying for positive feedback.

Lore's smile lights up his eyes. He has the goatee of a pirate. "Awesome!" He hangs out in the open door of the van, like he maybe wants to have a conversation. "There's a hot tub, and some of us are hanging out later. Seems like a good way to unwind."

"Super. It sounds like fun."

Once again, I am questioning the accuracy of my algorithm's results. The social media team will be spending tonight in posh canvas tents with twinkle lights. In the spirit of authenticity, Ozzy and I do not get to glamp alongside them and have instead been relegated to Berta's less luxurious embrace. Remembering the swoopy canvas ceilings and tasseled throw pillows on their beds results in twinges of envy. I want a tent. A bed. Quirky word sculptures decorating my bedside table. *Indoor plumbing.* There's no way my algorithm should have condemned me to camping.

"You could join us?" Lore looks at me eagerly.

Before I can process his request, Ozzy interrupts. "Sorry, she's busy. Do you have the engagement numbers for today's posts?"

Lore hands over a tablet. He's still smiling at me as he slinks away. He's been schooled.

It's after midnight when our teammates turn into pumpkins. They stagger to their posh tents, excited about the possibilities of glamping. They carry darling little lanterns. They fall into actual beds.

Berta is parked in a spot carved out of the vineyard. She swelters in the heat that lingers, looking worn-out and dusty from today's drive. We're too late for cooler weather but too early to pick grapes for breakfast. The vines have flowered, and the petals are falling away from the tiny buds to reveal the baby grapes.

Ozzy slides the door open. Heat rushes out. This will be our first night sleeping in the van; I half expect one of our teammates to pop out from behind a grapevine and pap us, because the expression on my face is stunned. The TripFriendz executive team is clearly not worried about personal space, boundaries, or potential sexual harassment lawsuits, because the single, solitary bed has shrunk to even smaller proportions since we left Tijuana.

I continue to worry about the one-bed situation, despite the decidedly unromantic nature of bedtime in a camper van. First, we have to rearrange all of our day stuff to get *at* the bed, and then there's the lack of bathroom facilities to contend with.

Ozzy brushes his teeth with my bottled water, spitting into the dirt. I brush away at his side. We are an old married couple. Despite our recent sexathon, I wriggle into an oversize T-shirt and sweatpants inside the van with the curtains closed and Ozzy locked outside. I'm mildly embarrassed when I re-open the door, but I'm not putting on a show for him.

I have bigger problems anyhow, starting with the world's smallest mattress. Ozzy is huge. Even if we wanted to, I'm not sure sex is possible in such a cramped space. I eye the bench behind the built-in table, but it's maybe three feet long and I'm not a sadist.

Ozzy has a solution. "I'll take the sleeping bag outside."

I scour the inside of the van, but spot no camping supplies. "Is it an imaginary sleeping bag or an invisibility cloak?"

He whips a colorful blanket out of his duffel bag and waves it like a cape. "I have this fabulous Mexican blanket!"

"Okay." If he wants to sleep on a five-dollar flea market blanket in the Mexican wilderness, I don't feel it's my place to stop him.

"That's not your line," he mock-whispers. "This is the part where you tell me, 'Have a nice night.'"

He disappears outside with his blanket.

We're not friends, but we're no longer mortal enemies.

Fifteen

"The engagement numbers aren't exactly where we need them to be." Roz delivers this news on Day Five with the grim calm of a surgeon after breakfast. Bad news: the cancer has spread, and we'll have to cut off your head.

While most of the team makes excited noises and thumb furiously on their phones, I scribble ideas on an oversize sticky note. I would give my kingdom for a whiteboard and a marker, but I am engaged. On point. The best team player ever.

Ozzy has his arms stacked behind his head. He lounges, occupying 98 percent of the banquette in the tiny roadside diner where we fuel ourselves with bitter coffee and pancakes.

As his fake travel buddy, I am forcibly perched on the southernmost tip of the bench seat. His toes prod my hip, seeking new conquests. I inch my troops north, exerting a slow, steady pressure on his marauding digits. I gain two inches of seat.

Most of the content on the TripFriendz channels so far goes something like this:

Sunshine-filled pics of Berta's interior. She looks chic and boho.

Stunning action shots of Mexican wildlife, looking primal and gorgeous. A black-tailed jackrabbit snapped by Ozzy in midflight as we thunder past. Turkey vultures frozen in time, ospreys wheeling, a desert iguana sunbathing on a rock. Once, a rattlesnake lurking near the highway's edge.

Gorgeous shots of Ozzy in activewear. Surfing on top of the van. Flashing his trademark grin at the camera. He high-fives our audience. Gives them a thumbs-up. He lounges in the bed. Pulls back the curtains. Mans the wheel while snapping endless beautiful photographs. Who knew he could multitask?

There is one picture of me. It's too close. My hair is messy, my eyes half-closed. My bra strap is exposed—and it's not one of those cute, lacy numbers. Someone tagged it #BadPictureMonday.

It's a tough audience. Someone accuses us of appropriating van life for nefarious corporate purposes (probably true). More people comment on our current location. TripFriendz has shared a live map with a cute little VW Vanagon booking it down the peninsula. A weather psychic predicts a hurricane is headed our way. Tarantulas are mentioned. The possibility of bandits (survey says: Ozzy will either kick their asses or trade me for a free pass). Whether the van's stationary periods are due to Ozzy and I having van-rocking sex or traveler's diarrhea. The odds are three to one in favor of parasites.

I flip through the posts again. Reread the comments.

We are boring people.

Someone suggests we make a sex tape. Feedback noted.

"So what can we do differently today?" As much as I hate to admit it, I'm not a social media expert. I'm an engineer. I can troubleshoot an Instagram bug, but I don't know why people spend hours watching a puppy reel.

Ozzy may be asleep now. I debate poking him in the ribs and decide against it.

"The quality of our posts isn't where we need to be."

"We should be more organic," someone chimes in. Tim? Thom? He greeted me today with a "'Sup" and introduced himself, even though we'd been introduced in Tijuana. There is justice in the fact that neither of us can remember each other's name.

"Humor," Lore offers. "We could do funny behind-the-scenes content."

Rosie waves her hand wildly. *Pick me!* "Inspirational quotes about travel!"

Roz grimaces. "*Good Housekeeping* magazine ran an article on those last year." Translation: even my grandmother can do better than that.

Beside me, Ozzy has expired from boredom.

"Let's hit the road," Thom suggests. "Think on it." He's clearly hoping that the inspiration fairy will visit.

Ozzy comes alive, and we race each other outside to Berta. As he has the obvious advantage with his strong legs and superior lung power, I award myself a handicap and pretend to fall, throwing my arms out with a loud "Shizzballs!" Ozzy pivots gracefully and puts his hands out to catch me. Sucker. I duck under his arm and lunge for the driver's seat. He won't pry me out of there when the cameras are rolling as he has his family-friendly image to maintain.

"You cheated."

He sounds so shocked.

"I think on my feet."

"You pretended to *fall over*!"

"And you should have let me face-plant." I shrug. "It's not my fault you're a decent person."

He tries to decide if that's a compliment or an insult and then gives up. "Surfer, Shark, Wave?"

Now it's my turn to look confused. It's a very brief moment of confusion, though, because Ozzy is happy to explain at length about the surfer version of Rock, Paper, Scissors. The media team films away as he demonstrates the positions (hands steepled on his gorgeous head for shark, wavy horizontal hands for wave, and the classic surfer pose).

We draw the first two times, our waves battering each other, but on our third go, my shark devours his surfer.

"Loser," I crow.

I regret my victory as soon as I inch us out of the parking lot and onto the road. I've forgotten just how anxious driving makes me. When I'm behind the wheel, there are infinite possibilities for catastrophes. Fender benders. Complete immolation on Highway 1. Destruction of company property.

After an hour on the road, however, I revise my concern level downward. The van cannot go faster than forty miles per hour. It's disappointing that speeding isn't an option, particularly when the social media team passes us in their air-conditioned, fuel-efficient vehicle. Roz has found a motorcycle somewhere, and Rosie rides pillion behind her, arms wrapped around her waist. She may be in love.

"Our van is a slug," Ozzy complains.

I give him the evil eye. "Don't be mean to Berta."

I ease us around a tight bend and mentally high-five myself for my caution. A cow stares back at me from the center of the road. I toot the horn. The cow refuses to budge. Ozzy snaps a photo.

"Berta?"

Don't be offended he forgot your name, Berta.

"I'd like to reintroduce Berta to you," I pat the dashboard. "She's a classic girl who enjoys vintage clothes, life in the slow lane, and starring as a Pinterest pinup gal."

Ozzy pretends to shake an imaginary hand. "Enchanted."

He cocks his head, listening intently. "You're a Scorpio! Me, too! We have so much in common."

A pause.

Apparently, our van is talking back.

Ozzy nods. "You totally should have a topaz-studded license plate."

"Are you done?"

"What's that? We should plan your birthday party?" He looks at me. "Berta wants a really big party with a bouncy house."

"It's June."

"October will be here before we know it! And reservations for the cool stuff book up fast."

I have to stop myself from nodding in agreement. I am not planning an imaginary birthday party for a car. By October I will be the chief play officer and will have forgotten all about this road trip from hell. Berta will be someone else's van by then, and Ozzy will have moved on.

"I need to get her flowers." Ozzy throws himself backward dramatically. The seat squeaks.

We trundle down the highway that connects Tijuana to San Felipe. My map is overkill, as there is only the one road, an asphalt serpent that winds steadily south, stretching from last night's winery all the way down to Cabo. Desert stretches away on one side of us and the Sea of Cortez on the other. Mountains hem us in. Heat rises off the sand, the salt flats. We are driving into the center of the earth, and I am on fire.

Today's plan is:

1. Drive to San Felipe.
2. Fish for our dinner (because TripFriendz is both cheap and opportunistic).
3. Ride ATVs around the famous sand dunes at sunset.

4. Eat our catch of the day at a restaurant on the Malecón that has been bribed/paid to cook said fish.

My algorithm may have spit out a list of destinations, but the details are 100 percent generated by TripFriendz's marketing team.

It's super-hot in the van. We roll the windows down to try to cool off. This morning my white shorts with their cute little lobster print seemed like a fun idea, as had the gingham-checked blouse tied at my stomach. Now I'd embrace public nudity. When I adjust the visor to try to cut the sun's glare, Ozzy's gaze is glued to the bare strip where my blouse stops and my shorts begin. I drive barefoot, hair up. I dressed for Cannes, for a yacht and for poolside service. Instead, I am being spit roasted like a rotisserie chicken.

Ozzy has also half dressed for a day on the water. His green board shorts hang low on his hips, revealing a band of black boxer briefs. His T-shirt is tossed on the console between us. He is barefoot. He slouches in his seat, all golden-skinned and godly.

"My latest post has two hundred likes," he announces.

"Surf bunnies."

"Wow. You're mean. They like me for my personality."

I'm sure they do.

Ozzy scrolls, taps, flicks an image up. Down. He writes an entire novel and peppers it with wave emoticons

"You're not winning this job."

He puffs out his cheeks. Exhales roughly. "You are so impossible," he growls. For once, he's not smiling.

I shrug. We lapse into sullen silence. I sweat through my blouse.

Eventually, he starts yelling out directions from the map app on his phone. He spurns my printouts ("Antediluvian, Fyffe," he scoffs, so when our cell phone service drops twenty minutes later, I make him eat his words). I'm still surprised, however, when Berta rolls to a gentle, exhausted, spluttering stop in the middle of nowhere. We are not in Kansas anymore.

Clumps of heavily branched cacti rise ten, thirty, maybe fifty feet into the sky. They form a forest of upside-down, lumpy octopuses.

"Your navigational skills are subpar," I accuse.

He mock-gasps. "You thought I wanted to go San Felipe?"

"The next stop on our itinerary?" I one-up his theatrics. "Why, yes! I *did* think that was where we were headed. Instead, we're…"

"Somewhere better." He's already opening the door. His feet hit the sand. The puff of dust that floats my way is intentional. "Come on. We don't need that map."

"Where?" I need a plan. Coordinates. A rescue beacon.

"Valle de los gigantes."

"We're in the middle of nowhere!"

He slams Berta's door shut, then leans in the window he didn't bother to close. "Two words, Panda. Giant. Cactus."

He's as excited as Christmas morning. All he's ever wanted are spiny, flowering succulents. I roll my eyes, cross my arms over my chest, and say, "Nope."

"It'll be fun."

The label I would use is certain death. A sign warns in the direst of terms that we must abandon Berta in order to enjoy the "miracle" (the sign's words, not mine) that is this cactus-opia because only 4x4 vehicles can handle the terrain. To call the dusty track a road is optimistic. It is a trough of beige-colored sand crisscrossed with tire tracks. There are no humans in sight. No bathrooms. No water. We will die out here, stuck in a wash.

"Your loss." Ozzy shrugs and turns. Strides away. He's not

looking back. Or waiting. He belongs here. His body is made to conquer mountains.

"I'm leaving you here!" I bellow after him.

He laughs and raises his hand. Which is holding my *phone*.

I award him a point in this game we're playing. He's taken my pawn. Sunk my battleship. If I abandon him here, I'll lose our social media war. I doubt there's an Apple Store within two hundred miles of here—and I can't google it because he. Has. My. Phone.

"Sure. I'll just follow you." I roll up the windows, grab a bottle of water, double-check that Berta is locked. There's at least one thief in the area.

I trudge after him. It's too hot to run and I can't be bothered. Plus, I've used up my worry quota for the day, what with worrying about our hookup, the kissing, the sex. Knowing what he looks like naked. He's seen my O-face. We know things about each other.

Ozzy, on the other hand, is supremely *unworried*. He's dismissed it. Or compartmentalized it. Gotten over it. Over me. I can't move on so gracefully. I think about it constantly, about his big body moving over me. How he held me close, made me feel safe, and then made me... I wanted... We did so...

Some things can't be forgotten.

Like the man waiting for me in the shade of what has to be the world's biggest cactus. It towers over him.

He frowns. "Where's your hat?"

I point, hopefully in Berta's direction. Giant cacti are interchangeable. "Someone hijacked me."

"This will be better," he offers.

Right.

"Panda."

I make finger frames. I pretend I know what I'm doing. Snap an imaginary picture that will never go viral.

"Panda Bear."

"You know my name."

He holds out a phone-shaped olive branch. "Fine. You win."

We contemplate a cactus.

"Are you having fun?" His face is so close to mine. Dappled with sunshine, striped with cactus shadows.

I wipe sweat away from my hairline. Why didn't my algorithm pick Iceland or Antarctica? I would kill for thirty minutes in the ice cream aisle at the grocery store. "This is a job. We're not really on vacation."

"Fake travel dating," he says mock-solemnly. "Fake relationshipping."

"For a ridiculous reason," I add.

"Because TripFriendz needs some fake PR."

"Completely harmless." I shake my head, fake sadly. "It's temporary, of course."

"Just until we reach Cabo." He nods gravely. "But."

"There is no but." I give in and snatch my phone from his outstretched hand. I take his picture. I'm too close, his face is all nostrils and dusty cheekbones. It's a Salvador Dali Ozzy. I'll post it as soon we're in San Felipe. He deserves it.

"But you know how the story goes."

"Tell me all about it." I wander past cacti. The sky is impossibly, blazingly blue. There's nothing but sun and sand.

"I shouldn't spoil it."

I snort. "You started it."

The light in his eye is warm. There's a spark of something there that I can't quite put a name to. I want to lick him, I think. Taste that patch of skin beneath his ear where he's tender, salty-sweet, vulnerable. I didn't kiss him there during our night, and I have kiss regrets. Missed opportunities.

"In the story, we catch feelings. Real ones."

I run a cautious hand over the base of a cactus. It's hard and smooth, the skin pebbly against my fingertips. "Totally against the rules."

"What are we going to doooooo?" He flails dramatically, but that spark in his eyes is bigger.

"We've lied." I take another picture of him. His arms take up the entire frame. "Misled people. We're master manipulators."

"There must be consequences," he agrees.

"Of course. Even if we did it for the right reason. The best of reasons." While I don't endorse lying, my algorithm is the lifeline TripFriendz needs. I don't fail to recognize the importance of my technological contributions, even if I'm floundering on this job interview from hell. Our lies—that we are happy trip buddies, that my algorithm did a bang-up job when it paired us together—will keep us all employed. My coworkers like getting paid and not sending out a thousand résumés to get just one stupid phone-screen interview where you're trying to guess what a disembodied voice wants you to say, and your cell signal keeps dropping and it's horrible. I don't want to do that again.

"And then it's real," he says. "The end."

"It's my favorite book."

He nods. "Mine, too."

We wander around the forest of giant cacti for what feels like hours. Ozzy christens them, because "you named the van so it's my turn to name our children." We pose like supermodels. Ozzy catwalks as I record him. He's highly photogenic. Me? Not so much. There are a few of me that aren't awful, though.

Mostly, this is because he sneaks up on me, capturing me before I can freeze and make that weird face I wear in all the Fytte family photos.

He hands his phone to me. "Keep or delete? Do you like these?"

I thumb through them, seeing myself through his eyes. It's weird. "I'm not photogenic. Can we find one where I'm not imitating a dusty mouse spotting a hawk?"

I've been told more times than I can count that I pull strange faces in photos. I'm always the one with her eyes shut, and I've definitely got a lazy eye. It's fortunate I never lusted after a career as a model, since I'm wearing the Mexican desert like it's an exotic dusting powder in most of these.

The look he gives me is something, although I'm not sure what. "You want to know what I see?"

"Not particularly," I say. "Although I'm sure you'll tell me."

Ah, brutal honesty. How I love thee.

"You look strong. Capable. Not afraid to get dirty or meet me head-on." He shrugs. "It's a good look. Pick one, please."

Ozzy waits patiently while I flip through the pictures again. And then again. "This one," I decide finally.

It's the one he likes.

I hand him back his phone, and just like that the moment is over. He flashes a thumbs-up in the shade of a *cardón* that must be sixty, a hundred, a thousand feet tall. There's a hazy shimmer to the air now. When I inhale, every breath is superheated.

I follow along behind Ozzy, kicking up dust and small rocks with my feet. Thirsty-looking brush makes walking in a straight line impossible. They make me stagger just a little, and I'm glad when we're safely back in Berta. When Ozzy announces it's his turn to drive, I just rest my forehead against the passenger-side window. I think I might be allergic to cactus. My stomach roils.

It's just overexposure to Ozzy. Sleeping with my irritating neighbor isn't something to feel good about. It's not part of my plan to get my life back on track. I don't have time for detours. If Ozzy wins this competition—assuming he hasn't already—he'll be my boss, and we'll never, ever be able to have consensual sex again. Plus, I'd have to quit and never speak to him again. I'd end up living in a box on a sidewalk. I'm in this to win this, I remind myself.

Sixteen

Roz throws up her hands. "You ditched us."

"We detoured."

Ozzy straddles the bench, his hands tapping out an upbeat rhythm on his thighs. He's switched to a pair of loose khaki chinos. A white T-shirt hugs his chest the way I secretly want to.

Roz groans. "We had a *schedule*."

"Uh-huh."

"And so, you wandered off and took pictures of…giant cactuses?"

"Cacti," I mutter. *"Cardón."*

The drive to San Felipe lasted two eternities and a half, as our detour to visit oversize succulents took us thirty kilometers in the opposite direction.

In my journal, I'll describe it as hot, bumpy, and nauseating and never mind that when the road turned curvy, Ozzy's arm appeared around my shoulders, anchoring me.

Now, predictably, I'm slumped in exhaustion at a cantina table at the very tip of the Sea of Cortez. Mountains pepper the horizon, and there's a strip of creamy sand and mud because the tide is out. Salt scents the air. And fish. Crustaceans. Crabs. Decapods. There's no mistaking the distinct aroma of seafood. My stomach twitches.

Roz discovers the reel of Ozzy strutting like the desert's his runway. I may be yelling WORK IT, BABY because I'm the supportive kind of travel buddy. Roz closes her eyes briefly.

I blame Ozzy. He started it.

"We were supposed to ride ATVs," she accuses. "And fish. I had everything booked."

"Van life is about going off grid," Ozzy counters. "Living in the moment. Exploring. Having fun."

"And yet everyone on the internet thinks you're off making the van rock," she counters right back. "Banging. Hooking up. Sometimes they even think you're doing it together."

"Why is everyone so interested in my sex life?" Ozzy grumbles.

Objectively speaking, he is Beauty in this non-relationship, and I am Beast. He's good-looking, takes regular showers, and pays attention in bed. Hooking up would be fun, but, as I don't want to join his fan club, there will continue to be his and her sides in the van.

Thom considers it. "If they bang, it could be great for numbers."

Roz answers too quickly to not have already thought about it. "It could go either way. Maybe people love a travel romance, an everyday girl falling for a hot athlete—or maybe they're jealous or judgy or decide that TripFriendz is *really* in the dating app business, and then all our launch plans will go out the window and we'll have to find new partners and rebrand the website."

My inner engineer barely suppresses a full-body shudder. "We're just driving around together."

"In a van with a bed. You could pull over on the side of

the road at any time and do it." Thom decorates the map in front of him with a NSFW doodle.

Rosie returns from the bar with a bucket of ice-cold Coronas and limes. "Who's having road sex?"

Everyone looks at me and Ozzy.

"That's an HR violation."

"Does TripFriendz prohibit workplace fraternization?"

"You could step in now," I hiss at Ozzy.

He shrugs. "We didn't have sex today."

Strictly speaking: true.

"How about yesterday?" Roz looks suspicious.

"No."

Rosie looks like keeping my secret is killing her. "Let's move this along," I suggest. Then with heroic maturity, I say, "Ozzy's content turned out great."

Phones are exchanged. Captions are suggested. Hashtags. Magic incantations. Lore edits a reel that will likely win an Oscar. There's the barest niggle of an ache in my head, a gentle pounding.

I caption the picture where my thumb ended up over Ozzy's face: Insert travel buddy here. I doodle a smiley face on my thumb.

Roz still looks skeptical. She's also my sunburn twin. We both have bright red noses. I frame our faces between my fingers and snap an imaginary photo. Caption: Rudolph the red-nosed reindeer?

The evening drags on. We're on hour two thousand when a waiter delivers a butter-drenched dinner of octopus and spicy *aguachile* and Rosie returns from yet another trip to the bar.

She has made an important discovery. "If you can eat all the peppers, you get a free T-shirt!"

This prompts the immediate delivery of an entire flight of

spicy peppers to our table. The pièce de résistance is a mescal-soaked habanero. It's a stupid challenge and Roz loves it.

"We'll have Pandora and Ozzy go against each other!"

She's decided to capitalize on our hatred for each other. We are two bucks, horns locked, vying for supremacy.

Ozzy groans. "Do we get a vomit bucket?"

"Does this look like a Roman banquet to you?" Roz shoves a plate of peppers in front of him. He looks unconvinced.

I stare at my own plate, trying to fast-forward the night. This is the second worst idea, ever. Only hooking up with Ozzy was worse.

He pokes at the peppers, investigating. Bile rises in my throat. I'm going to lose. The seagulls wheel hopefully overhead. The sun is a fiery ball of angry orange that refuses to go down.

A waiter by the name of Miguel Ángel demonstrates how to eat the pepper. He urges us to dig in.

"Can't do it, man." Ozzy is politely regretful.

It turns out that Ozzy, Mr. Perfect, cannot handle spice. His eyes will run, his face turn red. He demonstrates this for us with remarkable goodwill by licking a pepper. Somehow, he makes this look sexy rather than stupid. Neighboring diners look over. Catcall.

Roz face-palms. "We cannot use this," she mutters. Ozzy unleashed is rated R.

She comes up with a new plan. "Engineers against socials. Ozzy can be on your team, Pandora."

Naturally, I'm doomed to lose. Or to achieve Pyrrhic victory. I've got Rosie, Ozzy, and the tech guy. Ozzy mumbles, "Dear God, send help, pleasethankyouamen," and hums a bar of "Amazing Grace" before voting himself in as our pit crew.

The first man into the breach lasts one bite. Rosie makes it three. Thom is chewing with pained deliberation, Roz urging him on.

I am a desiccated corpse. Something once human but left out in the desert. Sweat beads my brow. Not a few dewy drops but the steady drip of a faucet. My sunglasses have left a white mask around my eyes. I am a rabid racoon.

Rosie shoves the plate toward me. "Win it for us, Pandora!"

She is counting on me.

Ozzy drops down behind me. His thighs bracket mine as I sag against him, gathering my thoughts. It's harder than it should be because parts of Ozzy—specifically, his dick—are rooting for me.

"You've got this, Panda." He breathes the words into my ear.

Across the table, Roz grabs her pepper. I fist mine. We're two Wild West gunwomen going mano a mano. We nod to each other. Thom smacks the table with his palm. "Go!"

Roz is quick, but I'm faster still. The first bite is bitter and grassy. I try to swallow without tasting but there's a wildfire rampaging across my taste buds. The smoky flavor of the mescal is not enough to put out the flames.

Ozzy's arms are around me, supporting me. "You've got this," Rosie screams. She believes in me, too.

I'm a porn star, moaning. I work the pepper in my mouth. I swallow.

Roz taps out. She's done. Out for the count.

Rosie raises my hand in victory. Our plate is empty.

"Are you okay, Panda?" Ozzy shields me from the others. His hand cups the back of my neck, petting the skin there.

"I'm great." The words sound like the croaking of a frog.

"This is a stupid game," Ozzy snaps to our audience. "What are we, twelve? She's really sick."

Roz mutters fiercely. Thom is googling on his phone.

Someone—Ozzy—argues with whatever the group has decided. I have stopped processing language—I speak only Misery now.

I force myself upright. Dig an elbow into his rib cage because I shouldn't be the sole sufferer. Smile around the table. Look at me! I'm so much fun!

The world whirls, mocking me. It's a Tilt-A-Whirl of fiery red sky, ocean, sand, shrimp. I'm never eating again. I stagger away and huddle beneath a palm tree. I'm a cat hiding beneath the bed in pain. A hedgehog bristling its spines.

Ozzy won't leave me alone. "You look awful," he tells me, handing me my winning T-shirt.

"We can't all be pretty boys."

"Are you sick?"

"Doesn't matter." I focus on the most important thing. "We won."

His voice sounds like sunshine when he says, "You won, Panda."

"Woo-hoo." I fist pump feebly. Attempt to sing "We Are the Champions," but the words get stuck in my throat. They're all mixed up with pepper and mescal. Maybe I'm allergic to them, too. Ozzy's forehead is crinkled into an adorable little pucker.

"You're so cute." I have no filter. "So beautiful. Should we bang?"

"Are you sure you're okay?"

"What would you do to get our job?" I really want to know, but the world tilts again. He tucks me against his side. I pinch him. "You need to tell me. I need intel."

"The job's not what matters here."

We both pretend he doesn't help me stagger to the van. He slides the door open for me like a gentleman. He pulls the covers back on the bed, and I throw myself onto the mattress. In the window's reflection, I'm undone, my hair wild, my face flushed a sickly red.

Ozzy hands me a bottle of cold water, and I pass out.

"Hey. Panda. Panda? Panda?"

"Whassup?" I slur. It must be midnight. Eternity o'clock. I should be... I should... Shudders rack my body.

"We went viral!" He sounds excited. Must be nice. I am nice and horizontal. "We broke the internet with our Surfer, Shark, Wave video!"

Footsteps come closer. He's let a herd of elephants into the van. "Panda?"

He places a cool, rough hand on my hot forehead. It feels so good. I porn-moan.

"Hey, Panda." His voice is softer, concerned. He removes his hand, and I want to cry. "I've gotcha."

It's so black that I must be in space. It's also hot. So very, very hot. Maybe my rocket ship has broken up on entry? I'm burning up. Send help.

Mission control is hailing me: Panda. Panda. PANDORA.

"Whassup?" My mouth is more dried out than the space food NASA serves its astronauts. All the water has evaporated from my body, sucked into the atmosphere.

Someone strokes my forehead. "Open your eyes for me."

I mumble, turning into those delicious fingers.

Time skips. Bounces. Laughs in my face. No, wait. That's Ozzy laughing. I am so funny that he's amused. I award myself a bonus point in our competition.

I must crash on an ice planet after I smash through the fiery atmosphere. Maybe it's Antarctica. A tentacled sea monster drags me down into the water, and I flail to get away. It has a hundred billion trillion arms, and there is no escape.

I do my part for humanity and yell, "There's something in the water!"

Ozzy shushes me. "It's just you and me. Five more minutes."

His hands press on my shoulders, brace my back. He's my replacement spine.

"You're in cahoots with the sea monster." This is only partly true. The cold makes my legs cramp. A brown skua wheels overhead, a hungry avian predator.

"I'm helping you. Stop fighting me."

When I do as he says (it's a red-letter day), he eases me all the way into the water. It's so, so cold.

"Whhhhh..." Even monosyllabic words are beyond me. I try harder. "Whhyyyyy?"

"Shhhh," he says. "This is good for you. You're sick."

"No." I have the vocabulary of a two-year-old. "No."

"You have a fever," he tells me. I hear the frown in his voice. "We need to bring it down."

"From the crash?" I'm up to five words. I'll be kicking his butt next.

"From heat exhaustion. Too much sun for my Panda Bear."

"Is this a cryotube?" An ice cube bobs in the water, and I realize what this is. I'm in an *ice bath* in a *tub*. "Are you harvesting my *organs*?"

All my brain cells are on vacation. They've gone on a road trip without me.

I grasp the front of his T-shirt. "I need my kidneys. You can't have them both. Just one. If you ask nicely."

"There are easier ways to get a spare kidney, Panda. But thanks for offering to share."

His beautiful face is just a cover for his plotting. "I'm in a tub full of ice. I've heard this story before."

"Urban legend." He dismisses my legitimate concern with a patient sigh. I turn my face to enjoy the cool breeze.

"No harvesting?"

He answers me, but I'm drifting, the channel flipping. We're out of range. Ozzy moves closer, holding my head above water. His T-shirt must be soaked.

"Come here," I whisper. I try to fist the cotton—it *is* wet—and tug him down, but he's an immovable rock. He does what I want anyhow. He leans in, and I ask my question. "If I drown, do you get the job by default?"

"Jesus, Pandora."

I turn my face into his palm. My lips brush his skin. His hand is wet. I squint up at him. His T-shirt is definitely soaked. His hair is damp and tousled. The pieces of him that I can see look like they've been battered by a wave. "You and the ocean are BFFs. You like it so much."

"Sure I do." His voice has an unfamiliar edge. "This is so much fun."

"Sorry," I whisper. "You like the ocean. I like outer space."

"Oh yeah?" He is stroking my arm. "What's so great about a whole lot of nothing?"

"You're so mean." I pout. "Space is wonderful."

"Tell me more."

"It's the best game ever." I think I sigh. I don't think I care. "I wrote it."

"Scary smart," he hums. "With your super brain."

"You can play it with me."

He's saying something, but I'm slip, slip, slipping away again. "When you're better," I think he says, "I'd love to play with you."

The next time I wake up, I'm swathed in heavy, wet cotton. Ozzy's wrapped me up like a mummy or…

I surface, flailing. "Piñata."

"Hey," he soothes.

He's made a piñata out of me, and he'll break me open looking for prizes.

"I'm going to lose." My voice is mournful. It quivers thanks to the ice he's surrounded me with. "I can't win our popularity contest if I can't play."

I should be embarrassed at how whiny my voice sounds. I will be, later. Why are we in a bathroom together?

I didn't realize we had a tub in the van. Berta has been holding out on me. She has hidden wonders.

"We're in a hotel," Ozzy tells me when I ask.

"Bet Roz is mad."

Ozzy snorts. "Don't care."

"You'll post embarrassing pictures of this. Hashtag Nurse Ozzy."

"Of course I will. Drink this for me," he says, shifting me. He holds me with one arm and presses a bottle against my lips.

I drink. It's sweet and cold. I want to have this bottle's babies.

"We need to get you hydrated."

Something tugs on my arm when I move. I roll my head to determine the source. It's almost too much effort. "There's a needle in my arm."

Veins don't just sprout medical equipment. Do they? "Am I special?"

"You bet." His hand gently moves mine away from the needle site. Serious Ozzy is unfamiliar. His mouth is drawn in a cranky, unhappy line. "Let's leave that alone, okay?"

"Okay. Don't be upset with me. I can be good. But you don't have to stay."

I was the worst rage monster in middle school. And also, in high school. It took ages for me to learn how to regulate my emotions. Now I almost never melt down. People don't like me when I get mad.

"I want to," he says quietly.

"Are you mad at me?"

Six Ozzys bend over me, enough for a dancing troupe. A herd. A platoon. There can never be too many of him in this world.

He laughs quietly. "Thanks."

I think I said that last bit out loud. I've given away my strategy. I dream that he makes me a promise. Everything will be okay.

I like this dream best of all.

I'm sweating. Shaking. My bones are fault lines, my skin one big tectonic plate that shudders and pushes, trying to come apart. Ozzy holds a plastic water bottle to my mouth. He's waterboarding me. Yelling at me to *drink it all, dammit, Panda Bear.* This is bad. I open my mouth to tell him that he's so not in charge of me but it's too much effort to talk. I drink obediently. I have no idea where my body is storing all this water. Perhaps I've turned into a camel. It's hot. The Sahara has relocated to Mexico.

Ozzy. Ozzy can google it for me. He won't want to road trip with me through a desert. I can ask him. In a minute. Just a minute... My clothes stick to my body. I am drenched with sweat.

"I'm moldy. This is so gross. No, no, *no*. This isn't part of my plan." I should spring out of bed. There's no time to lose.

Big hands gently press me back. "Easy, Panda."

Nope. I'm losing time. Points. Popularity votes. *All* the likes. There's probably a new Instagram algorithm by now, and I need to reverse engineer it so I can finish beating Ozzy.

"You have to tell me if I'm being a pain."

"You're not." His voice is soothing.

"And if I'm losing ground. In the contest." This is very important. "Don't let me fall behind. Don't leave me."

I'm the slowest swimmer, and there's a bull shark approaching the pod.

"I'll take care of it. I promise. And you're not a pain."

"I hope not." I chew on my lip. It's like hardtack. "You won't like me if I'm a pain."

I'm so pathetic.

Something ice-cold is pressed against my lips. I drink. Whine some more. Ozzy does what he promises and stays.

"I've got you," he says. I think I make him say it over and over. I'm sad and needy.

The next time I wake up, rosy sunlight filters through the glass doors that lead outside. I've slept the night away. Possibly a century.

I've also teleported in my sleep because I find myself in a king-size bed, surrounded by a heap of sage-green pillows. I've either been magically transported or Ozzy has seriously redecorated. I spare a glance for the white walls, rustic wooden beams, a hammock strung in front of a sliding door that's closed. Beyond the glass is a balcony, the tops of palm trees, and through them, the familiar blue of the ocean. The air conditioning hums, set to arctic.

Out of the corner of my eye, I spot a monstrous bathtub. It's big enough to double as an ark. There's a crumpled towel on the floor. My shoes.

I jerk upright, a damp sheet falling away from my chest. I'm not dead. Not embalmed or tucked away in an Egyptian pyramid. I'm

"You seem better," Ozzy says. He's leaning against the headboard next to me, my laptop resting on his legs. Because he hasn't left me. I take in his bare feet and missing shirt and am ready to declare myself cured. He looks ready to take on the world.

The smile I give him is shaky. "I'm good to go. Let's hit the road. Check off some stops on our itinerary."

He snorts softly. His expression declares, *You're full of shit, Pandora Fyffe.* He looks me over, inspecting, and I bristle.

"How about we stay put for a while?"

"Itinerary," I counter.

He mimes tearing something up. I assume it's our schedule. A piece of paper that has made him very, very angry. An ancient love letter to his long, lost love.

"You're not ready," he says.

"Am, too."

"Are very much not."

The amused smile gives him away. I look down, down some more, and barely manage not to have a heart attack. I've lost my clothes. The borrowed tank top I'm wearing sticks unpleasantly to my breasts. My nipples are hard, but not in a sexy way. I'm a load of clothes that's sat in the washing machine for a week, mildewed and damp.

"I plan on living a long life to torment you."

"Please." He nods solemnly.

We have a deal.

Seventeen

"Doctor Wylder," I say.

"Yes, Ms. Fyffe?"

"I really think it's time you let me out of bed."

"My bill will be astronomical." He sounds thoughtful. "You may have to sacrifice that kidney after all."

I glower at the ocean. It's been the longest two days ever. Which makes no sense because I only remember about thirty-six hours, which leaves twelve unaccounted for. I'm sure pictures will surface, or blackmail will ensue. And it's not like I don't enjoy alone time—it's just that the van is small, the world is big, and Ozzy hovers like a mother hen. I have no idea why I decided that we should come back here and torture ourselves with poor ventilation and no leg room. But I did. Here we are.

Somehow, he's convinced the others to mostly stay away. They came once, muttering about schedules and lost opportunities, and he shooed them away. The only living creature I've seen since was a weird racoon-like critter that appears to be nocturnal. Last night he brought his missus, and I fed them bananas. Then there are the birds, waves, and the plethora of fishing boats carrying loads of blue shrimp that I will never, ever eat again. It's downright pastoral, the kind of thing someone takes a picture of and then you see it blown up to nightmarish proportions at a travel convention with the words Visit Authentic México! and then a horde of North American tourists will descend like locusts, and nothing will ever be the same.

A small eternity passes while I consider the dangers of mass tourism.

"Hey, Oz," I say.

"What?" He huffs. I'm under his skin now. He can't get me out. Still, he pretends intense interest in the unfamiliar surfboard he's fixing.

"I've never spent two days in bed before. I don't think it's necessary."

He sets the board down and looks up. He's got all his stuff spread out on the floor beside the bed. Partly because the van is small, but mostly it's so he can annoy me and prevent me from sneaking out of bed. Apparently heatstroke is debilitating and I am supposed to rest up. The built-in table has camouflaged itself like a cuttlefish to match the small mountain of masking tape, fiberglass cloths, wax, knives, acetone, paint brushes and who knows what else. He's moonlighting as a surf shop.

"I should have taken you to the hospital."

Because I'm sure my nonexistent health insurance works in Mexico.

I put that thought in time-out with other unpleasant thoughts. Thoughts like: the Valley of the Giants tried to kill me, and I may be terrified of giant cacti for the rest of my mortal life. Or: Ozzy saved me. I probably owe him for that.

Instead, I say, "I'm bored. This is unproductive. I'm so behind."

"Live in the moment, please."

I make a face. "Also, I stink. I need a shower. My laptop. The Wi-Fi password."

"You're beautiful." He says this like it's a fact: Australia is wider than the moon, bananas are radioactive, Pandora Fyffe is beautiful.

"You have a thing for dirty women?"

That came out wrong.

He benevolently refrains from making a sex pun and instead leans against the bed, tipping his head back. Upside-down Ozzy is my favorite. "I thought we'd established that I like you."

I have follow-up questions. What kind of *like*? To what degree? Is this the pleasant like you have for the friendly barista who makes your coffee when you're barely civilized and squinty-eyed with fatigue? A thumbs-up on a social media post? Or something else.

I say none of this. Instead, I go with, "You're holding me hostage."

"I'm insisting you recuperate."

"You're hovering." When upside-down Ozzy frowns, it looks like a smile. "Go for a walk. Out. Go surf."

He arches a brow. It's a teeny-tiny smile. "San Felipe has no waves."

I point to the surfboard. It's evidence. "What's that?"

"Optimism." He shifts upright and folds his arms on the side of the bed. He rests his chin on my leg. "It belongs to the waiter's kid."

"I need my laptop back." I hold my hands out.

"You shouldn't work. You're still recovering. I think we should—"

I cut him off. "I'm going to play a game. There will be zero productivity."

He groans but pulls my laptop out. I make a note of where

he stashed it. He watches suspiciously while I boot it up and launch Crystal Cluster Cosmos. The opening screens flash by: the space port, my ship, the hundreds of galaxies to explore. I've logged thousands of hours. In no time at all, I'm maneuvering my spaceship out of the docking bay and into space.

Free. Free, free, free, free.

I investigate an asteroid belt. Find some purple stones. Ozzy finishes his repairs and pads outside to lean the refurbished surfboard against the van. Miguel Ángel Junior will collect it later.

When Ozzy returns, the van seems three sizes smaller, a minefield of accidental touches, leg brushes, hip checks. His things are scattered everywhere. A hair tie. One of his leather bracelets. A flip-flop that has run away from home. He makes himself comfortable, curling up beside me on the bed.

"What are you playing?"

"A game."

I find a diamond. Corundum. A green stone that sparkles in the starlight. I've forgotten its name, but it's lovely.

"Tell me more."

We look at each other. I find the courage to look at him. "You don't think it's childish?"

He shakes his head. "Don't apologize for doing what you love."

I share another secret with him. "I was playing this game the night we met."

"We met in outer space?" He's delighted.

"We did. Should I have asked you out for a romantic date? A plate of spaghetti, red wine, an Italian trattoria with wailing violins?"

He's behind me on the bed. We melt together. Our hips touch, our legs brush. His shoulders are an Ozzy-shaped armchair built just for me. I can see his smile out of the corner of my eye.

"Tell me about the game."

I haven't explained it to anyone in years. It lives online, a ghost ship that only a few people know about. I maintain its code, keep it on life support.

"You get a spaceship." I don't know where to start. "You fly it around outer space, exploring for space gems. The easy ones are on the surface, but some of them are hidden. You have to look in the crevasses, dig deep. Each one's unique. I programmed millions into this universe, but sometimes I put them back after I find them so someone else can find them, too. I wrote it when I was a teenager. There's no winner or loser." I have undressed completely in front of Ozzy. I'm naked. I'm not sure I like it. "No points. Probably no point."

He squeezes me gently. "You love it."

"I do."

I might love you, too. The thought drifts through my head. A solar burst. A molecular cloud, gasses and dust, that has the potential to become a new star.

His eyes are the color of topaz. "Can we play together? Can I be in charge of mapmaking?"

"Maybe." I'd like to try this.

I angle the laptop so he can see the screen. The sound of the waves is filling the van, and cuddly Ozzy is here again.

He rests his chin on my shoulder. If my space trips usually take only minutes, tonight I want to drag it out. Slow down time. When we discover a sparkling blue gem in the crevasse of an unfamiliar asteroid, he crows. He high-fives me when we add an emerald to our cache. Smacks a kiss on my cheek because the universe is just so beautiful. It seems so easy to turn my face into that kiss. Take it deeper.

I can see his mouth forming the words. They whisper

against my skin. "Ask me, Pandora. Ask me for what you want."

I am such a chicken.

I maneuver the spaceship through an asteroid belt. "You really think I'm beautiful?"

His *yes* is slurred, barely a whisper. He's asleep when I look down.

I don't want to hate him.

I don't hate him at all.

Eighteen

Berta is a sex-free zone, but I wake up in Ozzy's arms anyhow.

We're tangled together on the too-small bed. Van life, I've discovered, is an exercise in synchronized swimming. Its favorite game is Twister. I move here, so you move there, and then we both fit. There is no extra space. We both spread to fit the available room.

Last night, after he fell asleep, I landed my rocket ship and lay down next to him. We were side by side, lined up like two crayons in a box. Now my head is on his chest, his leg over mine. We curl into each other, fingers twining, breath mixing.

It's early enough that the light that filters through the half-shut curtains is only pleasantly warm. When I lift my head, I see blue sky. A crescent of waves hitting the beach. A frigate bird screams shrilly and another one answers it back.

Ozzy is awake, too. "You should have kicked me out."

I shift so I can see his face. "Who knew you were such a space-mining lightweight?"

"I blame space gravity."

I mock-glare at him. "That's not a thing."

You know what? I give up, at least for today. I can't compete with him right now, and maybe I won't tomorrow, either. I liked space-gem hunting with him, but I'd also like to own a rocket ship for real, even if finding on-street parking would be a bitch in San Francisco. I should get up, plan out my social media posts for the remainder of our trip, but all I can think of is tying Ozzy to the bed.

He's playing with my hair. He's looking at me. I'm the opposite of put together. When I looked in the mirror yesterday, my sunburn was peeling. Where I'm not vampirically white, I am cherry red with patches of golden brown. The reality of van life is sandy feet, a layer of dust and sweat, and no privacy or hot water to wash. I'm always rumpled now.

And yet he likes me like this. His interest is all around me. It's in the colorful pillows he brought for the bed. The glass bottle of aloe on the table. The funny, quirky photos he's filled my socials with while I've been sick. *And have you said thank you? No. No you have not. You* are *the asshole.*

His mouth twitches. He watches me closely, in a sleepy, pleased way. "We're such a cliché."

I scowl just a little. "I'm going to need more words. Write me an essay. Five pages on why we're overused and need retiring."

"So many possibilities…" Another mouth twitch. He's trying not to laugh.

"Your problem is an overabundance of choices."

He nods. He arranges his face with the seriousness of a mourner at a funeral. "Office rivals. Fake dating for work. Enemies stuck on a business trip."

"So true. I hear your competitor's super scary. She's going to win the promotion face-off."

He's unbothered by the possibility. "Plus she hates me."

"You deserve it."

"I do." He sounds pleased with himself. "And now we've braved the dreaded one-bed scenario."

"A total cliché."

"We're trapped." I stare into his eyes. Fuck the door. The windows. The escape hatch in the roof.

"Forced proximity." He says it with all the joy of *Look! Free cookies!* "Doomed. Doomed, I tell you."

He shakes with laughter, because my fingers are dancing over his rib cage. I slide them up under his T-shirt, stroke over the muscles and grooves, down the line of his ribs. We wrestle playfully, and he lets me win. The sheets are a puff of sad, wrinkled cotton. The blanket has relocated to another continent.

"Why didn't you kick me out?" The hot, thick length of him kicks against my cotton panties like an exclamation point. This is the best game ever.

My body loves him. It's singing a happy song, rolling out the Welcome Wagon. "I'm trying to be a better person. More likeable. Less—"

He leans up, his abs crunching, to kiss me gently. "You do do the best hedgehog imitation ever."

"What can I say?" I grin down at him. "I have *so* much practice. Can I make it up to you?"

I rub myself against him. Use him, ever so slightly. He's my own personal pleasure device.

"Yes, please," he says. He runs his hands down my back to cup my butt. His fingers curl inward, teasing.

"Plus, we have a legion of internet stalkers who claim we're already doing it."

Neither of us is in any rush. I lean into him, kissing him, in charge for the moment, and it's exactly perfect. He lets me lead. I explore his mouth with mine. *This here is my favorite spot*, I think, *and this spot here. And this one, too.* We use our teeth and our tongues. It is messy and imperfect, and I love it.

When we come up for oxygen, we're both panting. I skim my fingers up and down his ribs, tracing the bones and muscles that hold Ozzy's heart. I'm learning him inch by inch.

My panties are soaked when he slides a finger underneath the lacy edge. He strokes me gently, making a place for himself. I make a sound. And then another.

"Are we making out?" His voice is husky, rough.

"Someone's stolen third base." I'm greedy. I push my hand between us, palming him through his shorts. "He should steal home."

He groans. "So we're—"

"Yes." I squeeze the heavy length of him. "How about you? Is that a yes?"

He's gripping my hip with the hand that's not inside my panties. "God, yes. Let's prove our internet detractors right. *Yes*, let's do that right now. I have an idea."

I don't realize what he intends. Maybe because Ozzy is always unexpected. Maybe because I'm pulling off my clothes and the bed really is too small and all we can do is laugh about it and help each other out. And then I'm on top of him again. It does feel so much better naked. *He's so beautiful*, I think. *He's so everything*. I don't care about the world outside or the stupid, stupid digital world. Everyone that matters is right here, and I'm riding him like a horse or a motorcycle or some sexy, wonderful beast. I love how he sees me, his eyes darkening as he looks at my breasts which are *right there* because, again, the bed is small and forced proximity is the *best*. I love how my thighs straddle his hips and he pushes them wider, making space for his monster dick. He's the perfect amount of too much, and I want all of him right now. I need to have sex with him. I so do.

He wraps his hands around my waist, and I giggle because,

God, I'm ticklish, and there's just a moment where I think about showers and prep time and maybe sucking in my stomach and then he's lifting me up and over him and he makes a sound that says *I love you like this and you're perfect and you don't need to hide because I love what I see.* My knees dig into one of the throw pillows he bought for me and I'm off balance. I slap a hand against the wall. He wraps a big hand around my thigh, the other anchoring my hip. This is not—

This is something—

"Yes?"

"It's a definite maybe," I whisper back. I think so. Oh my God. Yes.

He licks my pussy, his tongue parting me. I consent enthusiastically, embarrassingly loudly. There are noises coming from my mouth, the wet sounds from down lower that testify to just how much I like this idea. *Yes, do that. Like* THAT. *Please don't stop, don't stop please.* I have my fingers in his hair, and his mouth plays with my flesh, tasting, learning. His thumb finds my clit and circles. My body goes supernova. The heat in me explodes, lighting me on fire. I grip his head, riding his mouth as I come. I chant his name.

He groans something filthy against my spasming pussy and eases me lower. He presses his face against my stomach, breathing me in.

"Your turn." I scoot down, reaching for his dick. My heart's pounding, my breathing is marathon-worthy. This is already the best sex of my life.

Someone pounds on the door.

"Stop sacrificing yourself for the sake of verisimilitude," Roz bellows. "Also, I'm coming in. Cover up anything you don't want plastered all over the internet."

I toss the crumpled sheet over Ozzy's head. He's mine for a few more seconds.

★ ★ ★

The morning sunlight bounces off the ocean as we drive. I ignore it because nothing can compete with Ozzy.

He drives, I think, like he surfs, with a sure confidence, an utter belief in his body and his ability to make it do what he needs it to do. Berta is just another surfboard, the road another wave. His arm on the windowsill is relaxed, his hair still tousled from my fingers earlier. Today's T-shirt announces Bodysurfing You All Night Long. I pretend I haven't read it.

Mostly, however, I pretend that nothing has changed. I am such a liar.

I sit beside him, rocked by the rhythm of the van. Out the window I spot cactus, cactus, endless ocean. The warmth is hypnotic. Ozzy puts on a playlist from his phone. He sings along under his breath, his hands beating out a percussive rhythm on the wheel as we fly past beach towns with names promising magical adventures that we have no time to take. Punta Estrella. *Star Point*. Playa Hermosa. *Beautiful Beach*. Puertecitos. *Little Doors*.

An idea tickles at the back of my head, and I get out the laptop.

He huffs a breath. "Really?"

I shrug. "I have an idea I need to work out."

Truth is, I think best with my hands on the keyboard. I am not a visual thinker. Or an out-loud thinker. I am at my best when I let the words flow. I write sentence after sentence. If this…then maybe that. Yes that.

I can't let go of the feeling that something isn't right in my algorithm. What if there's a bug and I'm not Ozzy's perfect match? Will I have lured him here under false pretenses, then? If the algorithm comes up with the perfect trip for two perfect people, in what universe would I enjoy camping and heatstroke? That's not algorithmic bliss—it's the code for death.

Ozzy's hand drawing patterns on the back of my neck tugs me back into the present.

I swim up from a haze of code. My laptop is overheating. My upper thighs are striped with red burn marks.

"What?"

"I wrote you a message." His fingers trace lines, swirls, entire letters on my neck.

I arch my eyebrow and save my work. "In invisible ink? Was there paper involved? Actual ink?"

"Luddite." He says this cheerfully. "It's an invitation. Please RSVP."

"Is it better than a Mexican road trip?"

He grins. "This *is* pretty awesome, isn't it?"

"No. Ozzy, we're playing the high-tech version of the *Hunger Games*. It's life-or-death, winner take all. We're battling it out in front of an audience."

"Wasn't there a compromise in that one?"

I frown. "I thought it was a mutual suicide pact."

"Huh." Signs flash past us. We're headed to the next stop on our itinerary where, according to the algorithm, we'll have a blast checking out the two-hundred-year-old shipwreck and getting our pirate on. We might even run around the sand dunes. Grab a fish taco. None of it appeals.

"Let's go that way." He slows the van down, pointing out the window toward the salt flats that stretch away toward the horizon. The salt flats look like the bluest lagoon with crusty white caps.

He's asking, not telling, but his fingers stroke my neck again. *Let's do it my way. Go off script.* Thing is, I'm not sure he realizes that he's asking me to choose him, his way, over my algorithm.

"The algorithm said Playa El Pescador."

"Sure." He shrugs. "We could do that. I forgot how much

you like to stick to your plan." Everything is all mixed up in my head now, the Pro column has jumped the Con column and the cells have merged. It's an orgy and nothing makes sense anymore. The one thing I know for sure, however, is that if Ozzy wins, he'll be my boss. He'll be in charge of the people on my team. He'll call the shots. I can't even remember now why I wanted it so badly, but I can't quite let go of the possibility.

He eases off the gas. "Salt flats—or town?"

The salt flats would be amazing. Maybe. I imagine Ozzy and me hiking through the desert. Parts of it look like a moonscape, littered with huge chunks of salty crystals.

Roz presses her horn. She gestures for us to keep moving.

Ozzy scowls. "She's not the boss of us."

"We should keep going," I say.

Nineteen

When we pull off the road in San Juanico, I sneak into the first bathroom I spot for a bird bath. The town is dry and dusty, but I fill the sink with water nevertheless and wash my pits, my stomach, take care of my southern regions. Do multiple shots of mouthwash. Fish tacos and ceviche are awesome until it's kissing time. And my plans for tonight involve a whole lot of kissing Ozzy.

When I come out, he's leaning against the van staring at the ocean. He must have eyes in the back of his head because he holds out a hand for me, and I take it. He does that thing I can never get enough of, where he pulls me into his side, and I feel wrapped up in him. He's tense, though, his fingers tapping out an anxious message where they rest on my shoulder. My stomach tightens unpleasantly and not because of too much lunchtime ceviche, either. There's trouble brewing in paradise. Ozzy's such a happy guy, but today he's morose. I want his smiles and the delight he radiates back, but he's switched off. We stand and watch the waves come in and go back out again, not saying anything.

I cannot leave him alone. "Everything okay?"

"Great!"

He shrugs, though. He's barefoot, wearing a pair of vibrant blue board shorts and a battered T-shirt. The ocean breeze molds the material to his torso, teasing me with his hard body. The sun is out, the seabirds are dive-bombing someone's picnic on the beach below us, I'm relatively clean, and yet I want more. I have an Ozzy addiction. I'm the newest member of the surf bunny club.

I try again. "Have you surfed here?"

"Yeah." This time, his smile is rueful. "It's a dream spot, you know? Big swells or gentle rollers if you're new to the sport. Water's warm, and you can just ride forever if the swell's good. Once upon a time, not too many people knew about it, either. It used to be harder to get here, the bridge would be out, the potholes in the road would just eat up your ride. It made getting here even more special."

I'm almost positive that he misses it. That he would rewind time if he could.

Not that any of us can. Not yet. That would be a hell of a software app, though. But then I'd spend my time going backward instead of forward. I'd focus on redoing those years when I made everyone around me miserable, and then I'd be missing out on now. The way Ozzy shifts, leaning into the breeze, looking down at the water like a dog that's shut up inside on the best day of summer, I think he might want to go back for some reasons of his own.

And of course, we sort of *have* gone back in time. My stupid algorithm has decided that his perfect trip is one that drives down memory lane in a camper van with a horde of people photographing his every blink. I puff out my cheeks and take stock. There's the ocean. Ozzy.

Me.

"Was there a secret knock to get in? Some kind of map

written in invisible ink that you had to be a member of the tribe to decode?"

He turns his head. I'm wearing a tank top and a pair of patchwork harem pants I bought at a consignment store in San Francisco. The colors are eye-popping, bordering on garish. If I were a bird, my plumage would score me a mate in minutes. It's miles away from the neutral T-shirts, blue jeans, and ballet flats I wear into the office; those clothes are designed to make me blend in and to look like one of the guys. Being a female software engineer is a balancing act between fitting in and not calling attention to the fact that I'm a girl.

"I had a map," he tells me. "You'd have loved it. Very reusable and sustainable. Some guy I met outside of Tijuana drew it on an empty fast-food bag."

"And you just followed it." That sounds like Ozzy. *Here's a freehand drawing that may or may not be topographically accurate, but follow it!* I'm sure he didn't know this Some Guy. He just trusted his instincts and then went on an adventure.

"Of course." His gaze follows a surfer on a peacock-colored longboard on the bay. When the board flips and the guy goes under, he flinches. *He's concerned.* "It was magical. I came down in a beat-to-hell Jeep with my boards strapped to the top. Slept in a tent, rolled out of bed, checked the surf conditions, and then went out. Lived on tacos and beer. And then I won a small local contest. It was the first time that I knew I could really do this."

He doesn't elaborate on what *this* is, but I think I know. When I built a rocket ship out of a text file editor and Java classes and flew it into space, I realized I'd stumbled onto something special. I could *do* this and not everyone could.

"How old were you?" I ask.

"Seventeen." He shrugs. Out in the bay, the fallen surfer

has popped up and is paddling back out to the break. Ozzy breathes a sigh...of relief?

"And your family just let you road-trip on your own in Baja California?" Mine gave me the Stranger Danger talk before I so much as went to the grocery store on my own. Of course, they also reminded me to slow down, check myself, and vent my frustrations on the weight set in the garage.

"They're all athletes. In their minds, you go all in on your chosen sport and do whatever it takes to make it to the top. Point is, I said I wanted to surf, so they expected me to surf."

"You were *seventeen*," I say. "Since when do we let unaccompanied minors run around outside the country? Usually, we limit that shit to shopping malls."

"They saw it differently. And I liked being on my own, going after what I wanted. They weren't forcing me into the water." Okay, so he obviously survived a felonious lack of supervision, but I'm starting to pick up on an uncomfortable suspicion. I want to poke at this, ask a billion and one invasive questions, diagram him on my whiteboard—but I also understand that's a level of interest most people would prefer me to keep to myself.

"And they just thought you'd keep doing that for...what? Forever?" I tuck my hair behind my ears. I need a hair tie. Braids. A pair of scissors. I'm a lurker staring out at the world through a mane of unconditioned hair. Ozzy's eyes follow my fingers, as if I'm more interesting than checking out the surf conditions. There's something about his interest, even if it must be transitory, that makes me feel like I'm the center of the universe, like I'm the sun to his planet and we could keep this up for at least a billion years before one of us goes supernova.

"So you do your thing, you win, and then when you've been hit one too many times or are too badly torn up, you pick out a sports-adjacent career and go do that. That's the next level in your game." The corners of his mouth twitch. "There are big bonus points if that next level comes with trophy opportunities."

"So no charitable work? You're not going to start a nonprofit and toil away in emotionally rewarding but invisible obscurity?"

He gives me a look.

Oh.

"Right," I sigh. "You can give back, but you need to be Mother Teresa 2.0 so you, too, can be canonized by a pope and win a Nobel Prize."

He nods. "Sort of, yeah."

"Wow. Thanksgiving dinner must be fun at your house."

"You can't imagine." He squeezes me a little closer. "You should come this year. You can be my wingwoman."

I scowl at the beach. Unless the world comes to an end and we're trapped in the Sonoran Desert by a ravening horde of zombies, we'll both be back to real life. November is months away. I'll be a blip in his memory by then, *that girl I banged in a camper van in Mexico*. Or *Pandora's brush with celebrity sex*.

"Or not," he says lightly. He turns away from the ocean, tugging lightly on my wrist. "Come on. It's Taco Tuesday."

It's Wednesday, but I don't correct him. Tacos are the best, and I'm in over my head emotionally here. I'll take the fishy lifeline.

We wander up the beach until we come to a taco stand that's part shack, part palapa, and more than part collapsed. I decide it's structurally sound enough for an in-and-out foray and follow Ozzy inside. I'm hoping it's the kind of place with picture-based menus. *Should have paid more attention in Spanish class, huh, Pandora?*

As soon as we set foot inside, however, a middle-aged lady in a blue apron and a ball cap explodes out of the kitchen.

She's hollering, crying, waving her hands. Ozzy hollers and waves right back, sweeping her off her feet and swinging her around in a bear hug. Apparently, he's taken me to his long-lost BFF's taco pop-up.

He introduces me to Daniela, and I smile awkwardly and trot out my baby Spanish. *"Cómo estás? Mi nombre es Pandora."*

How are you? I'm Pandora. I should have planned for this.

It's good enough, though. Daniela doesn't care that I sound like I'm reading Spanish off my phone (badly). She just wants to hug Ozzy and listen to his stories about our van life while she cooks up hot, fried fish and piles it all into plastic baskets along with crema, slices of creamy avocado, and shredded cabbage. Ozzy sneaks behind the counter to pull icy cold Jarritos out of the cooler. They come in flavors I've never seen before: mango, watermelon, a pink one that turns out to be guava. An earthy brown one that is tamarind.

After we've eaten our weight in fish, we return to the beach. The waves that pound against the shore start far out in the bay, blue swells that tower twenty or thirty feet above the ocean's surface before the top curls, foaming, crashing downward. At our back, the scrubby desert stretches away toward the mountains, all barrel cacti and nondescript bushes, but no one looks inland when the ocean is running. The waves sweep in, one after the other, carrying the surfers to the beach.

We walk up it, past palapas and pickup trucks. There are pop-up tents and boards stuck in the sand, a two-story hotel with a red tile roof that rents wetsuits and coolers to the underprepared.

"I wasn't sure you'd go for this." He gestures at the beach with our joined hands. Yes, I'm holding his hand. My palm is glued to his. They'll have to pry him away from my cold, dead fingers. *Poor Pandora, she just couldn't take a hint and held on too long.*

"I like beaches." I sound defensive.

"I wasn't sure you were going to come out of the restroom earlier."

"You thought I'd move into a cantina bathroom? It's an interesting retirement option. I'll add it to my Pinterest board." I squeeze his hand to remind him that I'm teasing.

He squeezes back. "I was more thinking you'd go out the window, head down to Cabo and wait out our trip there."

"I'd hotwire Berta. Drive her recklessly down the highway. It would be the perfect getaway."

In our travels today, we passed an honest-to-God steer with massive horns. It had a baby steer-bovine-thing accompanying it, and I was terrified either mama or baby would sidestep onto the highway and we'd all die in a fiery ball. There is way too much cow action for me to contemplate a mad road race. Plus, the potholes are the size of meteor craters. Anything over thirty miles an hour is risky.

"I know how to move fast." Another hand squeeze. We have our own personal Morse code.

I imagine him cutting across the ocean, the grace it takes, and the balance, his body bending, twisting, ducking inside a barrel and flying toward the beach. Sometimes I think I'd like him to come after me with the same intensity, like I was the biggest thrill, the best challenge he'd ever met. Other times, like now, it scares me. I don't do relationships for a good reason: I don't know how, and it's stupid to color outside the lines of your expertise.

When I don't respond to his teasing, his tone turns coaxing. "Walk with me on the beach. Talk a little. It's a twenty-minute commitment, Panda."

His voice is a husky rumble. *It's a dick, not an engagement ring*, he said the first night I had sex with him. Nothing has changed, I remind myself, and that's a good thing. He's a player. A hot guy. I don't want to be a casualty in his Instagram comments.

I've forgotten how much I love the ocean. Beach trips as a kid were challenging. I had meltdowns when it felt like we'd only just arrived, and then we had to go. I'm better now at transitions and at managing my expectations.

The waves that wash around our ankles are an icy shock. They didn't get Ozzy's memo that the water here is warm. Out in the bay, the surfers wear wetsuits. The sand is brown and not the powder-soft stuff, but it's pleasant.

We dutifully take our TripFriendz pictures. *Look! We're on a beach! We're having* SO MUCH *fun.* I already know what people will see. We lean into each other. His arms are wrapped around me. We look like we belong together, and we do, just a little.

I'm not the only person on the beach watching Ozzy. Not only is he built like a hot lumberjack, but he's likeable. People are drawn to him, some of them because they seem to recognize him, but others just because he's Ozzy. Maybe hanging out at a surf break with a famous surfer isn't my best idea. I'm questioning the algorithmic results again.

We buy *paletas* from a guy selling ice creams out of a pushcart. They're deliciously cold and creamy even if there are zero ingredients listed anywhere and no protective packaging. I guess you have to live a little.

I nibble on mine. There may be inappropriate porn star noises. Beach ice cream is the best, and these are creamy, icy goodness.

He pulls me down onto his lap. I'm happy to sit on him. He'll be the one who ends up with sand in his crack. "I'm jealous."

"Oh?" For an awkward moment, I'm sure he means of me. That he wants me all to himself, just his, no take backs-ies. Then he leans and playfully nips at my ice pop and reality dawns.

"You sound so happy."

I moan deliberately. "Do I?"

"I'm not competing with an ice pop for your attention."

"Mmm-hmm." I lick it just because I can. And also, because I'm feeling just a little bit mean. "What are your plans on that front?"

"Share with me, Panda." He holds his *paleta* up to my mouth so I can taste it. His is strawberry, pink and white goodness with a heart-shaped slice of fruit at the bottom. I lick it from stem to stern and he groans. We pass the *paletas* back and forth like they're sex toys. Someone gives us a look as he wanders by.

"Jealous," I whisper around the *paleta* I'm sucking on. "He's just jealous."

Ozzy nods and clears his throat, examining the leftover bits of frozen dessert with unwarranted scrutiny. He fidgets with the wooden sticks. Inhales. Exhales. He's got this.

"I'm not an indiscriminate dater."

"Quantity and quality are your thing, got it."

He runs a hand over his head. It's the *paleta*-free one, fortunately. "I don't get around anywhere near as much as you seem to think I do. I don't have an open-door dating policy."

Does he expect me to quantify how many ladies and gentlemen are too many? He'll be waiting awhile. And yet...

And yet.

Even as I need this genuine, slightly awkward, sweet Ozzy to be the real man, I'm not sure it can really change things. We're on a road trip. This relationship has an expiration date, and we're chugging down the road toward it.

A group of young twentysomethings in wetsuits skid to a halt in front of us. They're smiling, clutching phones. Unbearably enthused. I want to jettison them out the hatch into outer space. *Moment? Ruined.*

"Hey, bro," the wetsuit-wearing Thing One on the left says. As conversational openers go, it's mediocre at best. "Are you Ozzy Wylder?"

Ozzy jams his *paleta* stick into the sand. I could grab it. Sharpen it into a prison shank and stab Thing One in the knee. He'd go away then. "Yeah."

We're apparently going to be social.

Thing One and Thing Two take turns high-fiving him. "Wow! This is awesome! It's so great to meet you! Are you coming out to the break this afternoon?"

Being rude, inconsiderate, *paleta*-party-crashing nincompoops, they don't even wait for his response. They launch into competing monologues, words like backdoor, bailing, and crest spilling out of them. It's a foreign language. Ozzy speaks it as well as he speaks Spanish.

"You're my inspiration!" Thing Two has tears in his eyes. "I admire your hustle. I'm thinking I should drop out of community college, buy a van, and drive it all the way down the coast here. I could surf Cabo. All the great Baja spots."

Thing One nudges Thing Two in the ribs. "This dude would drive a van to Hawaii or Tahiti if he could."

They hee-haw laugh far more than is warranted.

Ozzy laughs politely. He signs their T-shirts. A ball cap. Someone's suspiciously pristine longboard. I'm not sure black Sharpie is *that* waterproof, but I keep my mouth shut.

More people collect around us, because Thing One and Thing Two are painfully loud in their admiration of Ozzy. There are requests for selfies. I scuttle out of frame. Ozzy looks apologetic.

One of the newcomers watches my crab imitation and puts two and two together. "Is this Pandora? Holy shit!"

Ummm...*what?*

All eyes swivel to me.

"You guys are totally a couple, right? Do you surf? You have to surf!"

I keep it simple. And surprisingly honest. "Nope."

My interrogator looks disappointed but bounces back. He redirects his attention toward Ozzy. He's a resilient one. I'm sure it helps when he's ricocheting off the ocean floor after a bad fall. "So you're teaching her? Are you coming out to the break?"

"Not today," Ozzy says. Then repeats himself again. And again. His answer is an unpopular one.

The ladies in the group crowd around so he can sign the front of their wetsuits. This goes better than the longboard signing, because they're dressed like tropical parrots in lime green, bright pink, blue. The black ink stands out when he scrawls his name across their clavicles.

Sorry, he mouths to me. Uh-huh. I feel the need to autograph him later tonight. Let him sign his name on his favorite portions of my anatomy in return.

"Let's move it along," I tell them. "Give the man some space."

They blink. Thing One looks taken aback. Perhaps he's already mentally sharing the Maui house with Ozzy and they're best bros. Too bad.

"Chop-chop," I prompt when they don't immediately move off.

Hedgehog superpowers activated! It takes me another ten seconds to run his stalker-fans off, but even so, he still gets handed a number.

It doesn't hurt that the ocean-water-swell-huge-waves thing happening out in the bay is apparently truly amazing and only a surf-hating idiot would stand on the beach rather than hop on a wooden board in shark-infested waters. Ozzy and I are left in sole possession of the beach and a phone number scrawled on a paper napkin.

"I thought they might stoop to kidnapping," I tell him when it's just us and the seabirds. "Maybe they'd tie you to a board and take you for a forcible paddle."

"Yeah. Good thing you were here."

To his credit, he crumples up the napkin and impales it with the *paleta* stick. Boom. Game over.

"Does that happen often?" I'm still feeling grumpy. "Do they have some reason to believe that you'd be up for a big sex orgy out there in the bay?"

Ozzy flushes adorably. "I had a little too much fun when I was seventeen. And also when I was eighteen. Then when I won my first big competition at nineteen—"

"Too much fun," I finish for him.

He nods sheepishly. "I had some money, people were paying attention to me, and winning is potent shit."

I think about the surf stars on Instagram. The endorsements. The fact that it was an Olympic sport in freaking Tahiti. It's got all the glamor of water polo, but with sexy Australian accents and laid-back, shirtless sex gods. And goddesses (although they mostly keep their shirts on). It seems crazy-good, but it's not my life.

My phone buzzes in my back pocket.

Ozzy's goes off.

The TripFriendz mothership is calling.

Twenty

Good news: our internet fandom *loves* our road trip fake dates. They eat it up, come back for more. The TripFriendz server crashed twice last night because so many people signed up for memberships. There are almost a million rows of questionnaire data in the database.

But there's bad news.

The TripFriendz mothership is a discontented bitch. It demands more. Specifically: surf dates.

San Juanico seems like an ideal spot for Ozzy to hop on a board, but I think I missed an important clue. We all did. He didn't bring a board with him. No longboard, shortboard, fish board, funboard, or any kind of board, in fact. And while he could rent gear or borrow what he needs from his legion of adoring fans, he doesn't want to.

Ozzy Wylder has sworn off surfing.

He's retired.

Beached.

We run around San Juanico eating tacos and shooting content that does not involve being in the water. It's not that he has a water phobia so much as he's adamant that he's not getting on a board. Not paddling out. And definitely not riding any of the impressive waves that roll in to shore. Honestly, I'm not sure it matters as much as our evil corporate overlords think. Ozzy looks as fabulous as always, lounging on the sand in board shorts. People eye him, covertly and overtly. His collection of phone numbers grows exponentially.

After I emerge from Berta in my swimsuit, Rosie stages an intervention.

She gives my blue one-piece the evil eye. "You need something Insta worthy."

I scan my outfit. I'm covered. My suit is aerodynamic, should I decide to take up professional swimming. The straps stay put (which is a miracle, as any woman knows). Even better, it has yet to give me camel toe.

Rosie is unimpressed. As soon as I've tossed a dress over my boring swimsuit, she hauls me off to a "cute little beach boutique" that she apparently spotted yesterday from the back of Roz's motorcycle.

She tows me around the store. I'm the inner tube tied to her motorboat. It's easier to just give in and hold my arms out to take the swimsuits she pulls off the racks. She is disturbingly fond of Brazilian thongs and colors that are cherry red and could put a fire engine to shame. I don't try to stop her, but those are never, ever going on my body.

I wonder what Ozzy's doing. He had a phone call to take, some kind of meeting with Roz's boss and other TripFriendz people. I wasn't invited. He says it's because they want to yell at him about the lack of surf action. When I suggested that it might be easier to give them what they want and that he was handing me the competition, he shut down, so I let the topic die.

When the mountain of teeny-tiny apparel in my arms

achieves the same size as the monster waves in the bay outside, I decide it's time to protest.

"I don't need a new swimsuit! I have one."

Facts do not sway Rosie. She scans the nearest rack one last time in case she's missed something. "Work with me. Do you trust me?"

I hold my fingers millimeters apart. "This much."

It's a definite maybe.

Rosie points me toward the dressing room. "I can work with that. Get in there and make sure you send Ozzy pictures."

On my way to the dressing room, I spot a two-piece swimsuit. Rosie may have rejected it, but I love it. High-waisted and navy blue, it's covered with a sea of shooting stars and white moons. There's a constellation on the butt and a swirling galaxy on the cups, which are shaped like crescent moons. I am ready to marry it and have its babies.

Rosie trails along behind me. She's less impressed with the space suit, and instead waves some butt floss at me. For added fun, the coordinating top is made of white cotton and has red cherries on the nipples.

I'm not sure it's legal to wear that in public, but I go for the obvious question instead. "Is it lined?"

"Imagine this." Rosie makes jazz hands, undeterred by simple logic. "You strut out of the water and Ozzy can see your nipples. Your cooter. They're gift wrapped in this."

She waves the swimsuit scrap at me like a matador waving his cape at a bull.

I frown. "I feel like this is not a work-appropriate conversation."

Rosie rolls her eyes. "What's up with Ozzy, anyhow? Roz was muttering about a 'Come to Jesus' meeting today."

I know the answer to this. "Roz wants him to shoot some surfing content, but he doesn't want to."

Rosie is baffled by Ozzy's reluctance. "He's in Mexico, doing a victory lap of places where he won competitions. He looks like a swimsuit model. Sticking him on a board is a win-win for TripFriendz. He looks good and people will tune in to our channels to see him surf. Why *wouldn't* he film that content?"

"He says he's done with all that." I dump most of the suits on a chair in front of the dressing room. I'm not wasting my time with those.

Rosie nods. "Because of the wipeout?"

"That's what he said. Was it that bad?"

"Don't you google-stalk people?" She's aghast.

Am I human? Am I an *engineer*? "Of course I do. Did I miss something?"

Rosie rolls her eyes. They're pointed firmly at her parietal lobe. "Yeah. My *Star Trek* porn fetish. What's *wrong* with you? The first thing you do is check the internet for all the details. Look at this."

She flips the phone around to show me her results. I learn:

1. Ozzy is the face of a pineapple-flavored lip balm, an energy bar, a board shorts brand, *and* an eco car.
2. There is an entire Tumblr devoted to shirtless Ozzy pics.
3. The last time he lost a surf competition was his last competition.
4. It's a miracle Ozzy isn't dead.

The video of his wipeout at some international, big-deal, don't-care-what-the-name-of-it-is surf competition is epic. One minute, he's balanced on his board inside the barrel of a monster wave, and the next, he's popping off, somersaulting, a wall of white crashing down over him. The sportscaster is initially gleeful (*Ozzy Wylder just got DRILLED, folks!*) and then progressively more concerned as Ozzy fails to pop up.

Even surf gods have to breathe, and despite having super lungs, there is a time limit before oxygen deprivation kills you. Rescue craft buzz around the scene. There are platitudes. Ostentatious concern for his friends and family watching back home in Hawaii. Even knowing that he's walking and talking and breathing air, I'm still terrified.

I wouldn't so much as get in a bathtub again if I were Ozzy. He's under for almost a minute.

His board pops up. It's been chopped in half. The sportscaster correctly interprets this as a bad sign for Ozzy's chances.

Thirty seconds pass. Forty.

Ozzy's head breaks the surface. He sucks in a breath. The crowd roars—and then another monster wave pounds him under. It takes two rescue craft to pull him out and back to shore. I'm not sure he's conscious from the loose-limbed, awkward way he's draped across the rescue sled. It's the first time I've ever seen him not in control of his body.

I chew on it while I go into the dressing room to try on the suit I liked. Fortunately, I did some preventative laser maintenance before the trip, so at least I don't have to worry about an emergency wax or battling the bush with a plastic razor in a roadside bathroom. Do van life ladies just go hairy? Are they Nair women? Spring for laser treatments?

There's definitely not a whole lot of coverage happening here. If you add up the square footage of these swimsuits, you might have enough fabric for a very small quilt. Most of them are auto-rejects, but I set one aside for Rosie. It's covered with tiny purple daisies and reminds me of her nail polish art. I'm pretty sure she doesn't have the cash to buy it, so I'll just put it in my heap and get it for her.

After ten minutes spent trying to work out which way the bikini top goes, it's still unclear to me which part goes on top and which on the bottom. The triangles are interchangeable.

When Rosie bangs on the door to ask if I need help, I react like I'm peeing and someone just banged on the door. My stress dreams tonight will be epic.

"Just a moment!" The view in the mirror isn't promising. My right boob's hanging out the bottom, and I've got major side boob happening, too. Despite the vampiric white of my stomach, I'm rocking a farmer's tan from the van time. My legs are brown, but my feet are white, and my star-print underpants squeeze out from underneath the swimsuit. There's a lot to take in.

Eventually, I give up, take everything off (including my underpants—don't judge me), put the bottoms back on, and yelp for Rosie to come and tie me up.

She awards me a wolf whistle. "Pandora Fyffe, you look good in a swimsuit!"

I'll take it. "Can you help me with the top?"

I cup my boobs in their new home while Rosie fusses around with the ties. She cinches, pinches, loosens a strap here, tightens one there. NASA rocket launches take less time. I'm starting to get bored, so I take a photo. It looks like we're either doing some weird version of *shibari* or she's feeling me up. I send it to Ozzy anyhow with the comment: Could use a hand here.

Rosie finishes tying me up before Ozzy manages to respond. He's definitely trying though because I can see his texting bubbles.

"Wow." Rosie takes a step back. "Ta-da!"

I confront myself in the mirror. "It could be worse."

Rosie isn't having it. "You look awesome. Say it back to me."

"I look awesome," I dutifully parrot. Rosie won't give up until I do it, so it's better to give in so we can move on.

"And now with some feeling, oki doki?" She folds her arms

over her chest and runs her eyes up and down me. "Take a picture and send it to Ozzy."

I look at her. "Really?"

"Really," she says firmly. "Pro tip—if you want to keep your sex life a secret, don't do it in a van. Everyone knows what that motion in the ocean means."

I shoo her out so I can try on the other suits because I'm being a good sport, but before I can undress, my phone buzzes.

Ozzy's clearly a fan: Holy shit. Can I come over?

Heh. Girl time is done, I text back.

I google "how to take a swimsuit selfie" and follow the directions. They mostly consist of holding my phone up high overhead, smiling, and snapping. My thumb's over the camera with my first attempt, so I try again. It's not a sexy smile, but whatever. I send it. My boobs look good. I try to ignore the flush of heat between my thighs.

Should I try one of the others? There's a black terry cloth vintage-looking number, but the bottom seems a lot like a diaper cover. It claims to have amazing smoothing properties, though, and the top will perk up my girls.

I'm still debating when my phone buzzes with a picture from Ozzy. He has his hand down the front of his board shorts. They're my favorite pair, hot pink with a pod of blue whales. They're ridiculously cute even if I do give him shit for having the taste of a preppy five-year-old. Unlike any kindergartner, he's sporting a massive erection.

He provides a caption for his photo in case I've missed the point: Mission accomplished?

I fire back: Is that you jerking off to my selfie?

The answer is an affirmative: Ten out of ten recommend!

I try to figure out from the photo where he is. Ur not on the beach, r u?

His response is a text asking, **What kind of show-off do u think I am?**

I point out that our ratings would go up and that we could probably get away with posting it "on accident." There's plausible deniability here.

Ozzy is not convinced. This text chain is now evidence.

Unfortunately, he makes a good point.

I switch tactics.

Okay. No NSFW content on the corporate Instagram. Although they totally deserve it.

I don't like how they're pressuring Ozzy to deliver content he doesn't want to make.

I cup myself inside the swimsuit bottom, mimicking his pose. It's nowhere near as impressive because I'm at a natural disadvantage—clits are smaller than dicks—but the contrast between my wrist and the darker color of the swimsuit is nice, plus I push my wrist out to make the bulge bigger. I'm almost laughing too hard to press Send.

This whole text chain is out of character for me. Instead of flying off all alone into an uncharted galaxy, I'm voluntarily landing at a space station and hanging out at the cantina with a friendly alien. Getting my freak on is *fun*. I decide to chalk it up as research for my new role as chief play officer. Also, I'm sweaty and sticky inside this boutique, which just reminds me of other times I've been this…wet. I snort-giggle. OMG. I'm telling myself dirty jokes in my head.

Ozzy sends me a picture of praying hands. **Follow-up picture PLZ.**

I opt to call him instead. Committing this kind of folly to the cloud would be folly. Hackers are everywhere.

"Panda." He picks up immediately. It's flattering. If he doesn't go back to surfing or something sports-adjacent (to quote his fuckwitted family), he could have an amazing career as a phone sex operator. Or recording those security messages I hear in the airport: *the train is stopping—please hold on.*

"Are you jerking off to my swimsuit picture?"

He exhales roughly. His breath sounds like a stick swinging through the air. I giggle. Maybe a dick-stick? I amuse myself by thinking about Ozzy Wylder strolling naked down the beach, swinging his dick like a big club. It's a fiesta in my brain.

"Maybe." I can imagine his sexy smirk.

"How come you didn't wait for me?"

More heavy breathing. Ozzy's thinking about it, and now I'm thinking about him thinking about it, and we *really* need some private time tonight.

"I should have, huh?"

"Rude," I agree. I can hear Rosie chatting up the salesgirl outside. They're having a VIP conversation about triangle cups versus a push-up top. I'm guessing the salesgirl didn't learn that in English class. It's super impressive.

"I'm switching to video."

I'm mostly on board with this plan, but: "Are you going to screenshot me and ruin my professional life at a later date?"

He groans and fumbles the phone. "I won't do anything you don't want me to do."

I'm not sure trusting him is a smart move. Not only is the internet forever, but he could also run for president of the United States someday (everyone under ninety would vote for him), and then they'd dig up all his old phone records and my dinosaur self would be all over the internet. I wouldn't even get paid for it. Plus, this is the kind of thing that *totally* comes back to bite you in a job interview, which is what this road trip is. And we're work colleagues. Neighbors. So many reasons.

Nevertheless, I turn the video on.

This time the whooshing sound is my good intentions flying out the window.

"Model for me," Ozzy says in his husky voice that makes my nerve endings demand an immediate end to celibacy. "Show me what you're doing, Panda Bear."

I realize I'm holding the phone up in front of my face. The screen's practically touching my nose, so instead of a sultry shot, he's just getting a close-up of my nostrils.

I pan it downward, trying to pretend the extreme facial close-up was all a part of my plan. Despite my lack of directorial experience, I manage a boobs close-up before going lower. I may toy with the waistband of the swimsuit.

"I'm going to have to buy this suit."

"You totally should," he groans. "You look amazing."

"I've made it wet." That's not the sexiest way of phrasing what's happening in regions south of my waistband, but it clearly works for him. He makes an appreciative noise, and his hand moves down. He's inside our van, defiling the bed.

"You should come home." He looks straight into the phone, but he's running his hand down his hot body. I'm about to complain about the lack of follow-up action shot when he pans the phone down. There's an impressive bulge in his board shorts that he palms. "We could help each other out."

"Orgasm buddies." I sound a little breathless, but I blame that on him. He slides his hand inside his shorts and wraps it around what he finds in there. I know firsthand that he feels amazing, so I'm jealous that he's there and I'm here.

"Your turn," he says huskily.

I give a microsecond's worth of thought to the proximity of Rosie and the saleslady. There's some music playing on the store's sound system that will cover up some sins on my part, but otherwise I'll just have to be quiet. Can do. Then I'm sliding my hand inside my swimsuit bottom and shifting the phone so Ozzy can watch.

"Pandora Fyffe," he growls. "What are you doing?"

"You know what I'm doing."

I infer from the rhythmic movement of his hand and the rocking of the bed that he's doing it, too.

There's only one possible response.

"Race you," I dare.

I move my fingers farther down. In my head I'm remembering that night in San Francisco. I think this is where I should dirty talk him, but I haven't planned for that. I'd need to figure out my lines before I'm distracted by the way his pupils blow wide, his lips part. He fists his dick, stroking fast. He's totally winning, and I don't even mind.

I watch him work himself hard as I stroke a softer, gentler counterpoint that's no less quick.

"Panda," he groans.

"Ozzy." I know his name, too. I know who I'm doing this with.

We get ourselves off to each other. It's fast, so I stop worrying about our audience and I just feel good. I'm not sure I do a good job keeping the phone on my business while viewing his, but it's my first time. There's bound to be room for enhancements. I come, squeezing my hand between my thighs, and I don't know who's first.

Rosie knocks on the door, and I have to put myself back together and go purchase the swimsuit I just defiled.

And then a few minutes later, he texts: **Can't wait to see you. Rematch?**

I text back: **Always.**

Twenty-One

"Pozzy."

"What?"

"We're Pozzy. That's our ship name. I'm having T-shirts made."

Ozzy sets his phone in my hand. In the ten minutes it's taken me to cover the distance from the swimsuit boutique to our van (and our video sex has put some pep in my step), he's put himself back together and…

"You're surfing the internet?"

Mortification is a bright, hot beacon inside me. I came, he came, and promises were made for more hot sexing, or so I thought. One or both of us needs to look up the definition of *rematch*. My vag has barely begun to come down from her high, but he's moved on.

I scan the screen, feeling raw as I read. I'm not sure what I expected, but it's not Ozzy's eagerness to show me a set of bookmarks in his browser. Playing the dressing room game with him was stupid.

Ozzy frowns, his fingers curling around my wrist. "What's wrong?"

"Nothing." I scroll and hope he didn't record me. I don't think he's that kind of asshole, though. Maybe.

His thumb rubs over my pulse point. "No, look! People *love* our fake travel dating. They've given us a cute couple name."

Pozzy.

I've never been celebrity adjacent before, so I can't say if this happens to all the women he bangs or just the ones he's obvious about. Even knowing better than to read crap about myself on the internet, I do. And he's right. There's all this weird Pozzy fan fiction, which is…

"People write about us having sex?"

He nods. "It's inspirational. In this one I've got to go to an awards banquet and convince you to come along as my fake ride or die, and then we get into it in the elevator."

I skim-read. Fake Ozzy is super, super creative. "And on the hood of your Lamborghini, which you've stupidly risked in the parking garage, in the hotel's rooftop pool, and—"

"While I'm giving my acceptance speech." He nods proudly. "My ability to multitask is unparalleled."

"And here's sex on the beach. More sex on the beach." I scroll down. "Wow. We defile a *lot* of sand."

"Apparently I tutor you in sex before you go out on a big date with some other girl." I look up. "Please be aware that real-life me is nowhere near that unselfish. Any sex tutoring will be strictly selfish and me-centric."

"Tell me exactly how to pleasure you."

He looks adorably earnest. Who am I to discourage a man from asking for directions?

Since I have some idea about what he could do for me, it's necessary to do something about the gating factor. We're parked in an ocean-side campground surrounded by tent sites and RVs. I've heard people getting their freak on, and I'd rather not add to their number.

I snatch the keys off the table and hold them up. "Let's move Berta."

"C'mere." He pats the bed beside him.

He's not so great with directions after all. Plus, if I go near him, I'll jump him, so I stay put. I don't want to have to be mindful of my volume control when we have sex.

"Privacy would be awesome. Consider it foreplay." I can give him road head or just pet his trouser snake.

He jackknifes off the bed. "Your wish is my command."

We race to the driver's seat. It's our thing. I have no intention of winning, but I let him think I do. We tussle playfully, and then he picks me up in a bridal carry and strides around Berta to deposit me in the passenger's seat. It's a win-win situation.

It also means we're both breathing hard by the time we're on the road. Flirting is great cardio. It's also motivational, because Ozzy gets us out of the campground and onto the road in record time. He keeps sneaking sideways peeks at me, so I make sure to do some hopefully sexy lounging in my seat. I put my legs up on the dashboard and run my hands up my thighs. I arch my back.

I could swear he's distracted, which I take as a good sign. Hopefully, he remembers the area enough to pick a safe spot. Baja can be dicey, and no amount of privacy is worth dying for.

I think it's going well, but I'm not sure.

Sticking to hookup sex means that I don't get much feedback. There are requests and the occasional comment, but if my date's disappointed, I don't have to hear about it. I can't say I'm a sex expert, either. I think about this nervously as Ozzy veers off the road, down a dirt track, and barrels right up to the edge of a huge sand dune. As the tires sink into the soft sand, I hope he's going to be able to get us out later. I hope I'm not making a mistake. I've got sweat dampening my under-boob area and some seriously slick palms. It's gross, so I wipe my hands on my butt as I get out. I'm a competitive bitch, so of course I want to be Ozzy's best sex ever.

Maybe he doesn't mind that I'm not a Marilyn Monroe kind of gal. I'm not curvy or chic. I spend more time on coding than personal grooming, and no matter how much I like sex, I'll always be an engineer who knows more about physics and differential calculus than G-spots and orgasms. It doesn't help my confidence levels that my previous experiences fall more along the lines of fast food than Michelin-starred cuisine.

I'll just have to fake it until I make it. It's certainly worked for me so far.

Ozzy is around the van before I can move my ass fast enough to meet him on the other side. He's quick for someone so big.

"Hey you." He laces his fingers through mine and pulls me into a hug instead of going straight for my panties. It's strangely nice. He presses his other hand against the small of my back. That hand slips up underneath my tank top and strokes.

"What's your plan?" I tilt my head back so I can see his face clearly. I should make sure we're on the same page of the sexy book here. Plus, you know, *directions*.

"I was hoping for some quality alone time with you." He does that thing where he presses his forehead against mine and somehow manages to look down at me without going all cross-eyed. It's a gift he's got.

"I'm on board with that plan. Where would you like to start?"

I take a quick inventory of our surroundings just in case he's thinking outdoor sex tops his fantasy to-do list for today. We don't seem to have company, but the beach is only about fifteen feet below us and the van is kind of out in the open. Getting arrested in Mexico for public indecency will not help my career any.

"We could take this inside?"

"Okay."

He opens the sliding door but doesn't immediately toss me inside on the bed or bend me over the table. Honestly, that last might be difficult because he can't quite stand up inside. Vans only have so much headroom and he's tall. Instead, he turns us both around so that we can admire the ocean. Which is, objectively speaking, a pretty great sight, but it's also not why we're here.

"I feel like we might not be speaking the same language here," I tell him.

"Maybe I'd like to take my time with you," he suggests.

"I can work with that." I sound breathless.

He presses his mouth against my throat and the rest of him against my back. As though this is what he's been waiting for all day and now he's soaking me up, running his hands down my sides, nuzzling my ear. It feels so good, and then his hands settle on my hips and tug me closer still, and my brain goes offline. I'm all the feelings, possibly due to the electric current running between his mouth and my nerve endings.

Ozzy is nothing like the guys I've hooked up with before. He's hotter, for one, but he's also much more aware. He's here for both of us, not just to get his dick off. From my ill-advised Google searching, it seems like he's had really creative sex with some super gorgeous women. I'm the opposite of that, and yet I want to be his partner in every way. As an engineer, I'm wired to hate failure—and to iterate until I get it right.

I mourn when he lets go of my hip, but then he fists my hair with his hand and tilts my head so he can kiss my throat some more. His teeth mark me.

"Can we go inside now?" I don't know what the script is, but I do know that I need to have him alone. I don't want to share him with the world.

"Sure, Panda." His mouth moves closer to mine. I grind back against him. "We can do whatever you want."

I make a noise of agreement—*super*—just in case that was a question. *That sounds like a great plan. Let's go inside. Please be naked with me. I'm going to come so fast.*

"You're so beautiful." His hands dance over my body. He's lifting me, cradling me in his arms with his beautiful biceps, his inked-up forearms effortlessly handling the problem of getting us inside. I'm happy to let him do all the work.

He's a rock star at heavy lifting. His long legs devour the distance to the bed in two steps. There's a brief moment where I think his head may connect ever so slightly with the van's ceiling, but he doesn't seem to notice. He sets me down on the bed.

"Don't go anywhere, beautiful."

He slides the door shut and pops the top, so we don't roast. Seeing as how he's busy, I helpfully reach over and pull the curtains shut. We need to get a hotel room next time. I throw myself backward, laughing. God, sex in a van is work. His eyes crinkle up at the corner, and he comes down over me, caging me between his arms. There is inked skin on either side of me. This is a thousand times better than any ocean view. I turn my head and lick a line up his forearm. It's silly, but I want to taste him. I want to get inside his head and learn him from the inside out.

He pushes his big hand up under my tank top. He wraps his fingers around my ribs, cupping my boob and teasing my nipple with his thumb. He's...

Kissing me. His mouth covers mine, and he's not holding back. And—

So good.

He groans. "I've been imagining this. Ever since I kissed you under that pier, I've thought about doing it again. I thought

I'd lost my shot at you. You were so sure you hated me. You looked pretty certain about that, but…"

"And then you let me think you didn't remember me!" I bite his ear in retaliation, and he grunts.

He moves. He's lifting me up, stripping off my clothes. His hands are angling me, bending me here. Opening me there. It's… Yes—

"I don't want to blow my second chance," he whispers gruffly. "So tell me if this isn't okay?"

"Yeah."

One word and he's on me everywhere. Somehow, he's stripped himself down, too, and now we're naked together. His body is still fuck-hot, all chiseled and cut like a Greek statue with his XXL-sized dick out and proud. He's my dearest enemy. Someone I love to hate. Someone I—

"Is this okay?" He's between my legs and he's utterly, completely in control. This letting someone else take charge—that's not my jam. This isn't how I have sex. We should negotiate. Take turns. *I'll do this and then you'll do that,* and *I go down on you and then…* He's not asking me to do anything other than be here, and my fingers are curling into his shoulders and my legs wrapping around his hips. I want to let him all the way inside.

"Pandora." His fingers skim my stomach. "I need you to tell me that this is okay."

"Uh-huh," I manage.

"I can touch you?"

"Yes."

"Thank fuck." His hand moves down, sliding over me. The other one is squeezing my butt. We kiss and grind on each other, my hands twisting in his hair before going lower. He's got his dick lined up perfectly with my southern regions now and is applying the best kind of friction. I am deeply grateful for his washboard abs as he flexes, twists, and moves over me. I press my lips against his ink. Grip his hair when he goes to move down me. I'm not in the mood for an appetizer when I know what the main course is.

"You...in me." *Please.*

Ozzy rolls a condom on and kisses me. His lips are soft and careful. He pushes slowly inside, and he might be trying to kill me, because he refuses to rush. He just goes and goes and goes until I'm whimpering and moaning.

"You—" he shifts forward, and now he's seating himself all the way "—are the best."

I'd like to preen but I'm too full of him and, God, he makes me *feel* the best.

He braces himself on one arm, watching my face. "Eyes on me."

"Okay."

"Pandora." The way he says my name is everything.

I wrap my legs around his waist and hold on. I'm not sure what could make this better, but he's taking charge now, moving harder, faster. He's an athlete and he's got stamina, sure, but he's also listening. When my breath catches as he finds the angle I love best. When it comes quicker, when I make a small sound in the back of my throat, when my fingers clutch at him and, fuck breathing, because I'm chasing the sensations. He remembers it all. I'm on fire, my body going supernova as I come.

He mutters a rough curse, his lashes drifting down. He buries his face against my throat, and then he's pounding into me, pumping hard as he finds his happy ending. We're a panting, breathless mess.

I run my hands down his back. I've left marks there, red lines from my nails, my own brand of ink. We sound like we've just paddled to shore while being chased by a monster wave or a hungry shark. We're wiped. It's been amazing and I want to do it again. Now.

I like him... I *love* this.

"I want to like you so hard," I tell his chest. I'm drifting off. There are weights attached to my eyelids, and I'm not interested in resisting.

I think he says, "Me, too, Panda," but I'm already asleep.

Twenty-Two

We drive two more days down the Mexican coast. Santo Domingo. Las Pocitas. La Paz. Todos Santos. We fake travel date our way from Highway 1 to Highway 19. We spend lazy nights curled up in the van together in hidden campsites.

By unspoken agreement, neither of us checks social media stats. Ignorance is bliss. Instead, our new game is dodging Roz. We both pretend that the road won't end. Our Mexico stretches on forever.

Fittingly, we run out of road on Day Thirteen. Los Cabos rises up out of the desert in front of us. Planes crisscross the sky; the international airport is close by. There are more people, more cars, less time. We're behind schedule, so everything is a rush now. I stare out the window, pretending to take pictures. When Ozzy points to a sign for the route back up to Tijuana, my heart is stupidly hopeful.

"We could turn around," he says. "We could be there in under a day."

"We should." I kid even though I want to beg him to do it.

When we pull up in front of the swanky hotel TripFriendz has reserved, the valet does a double take at the van. Poor

Berta is dusty and road worn, completely unlike the flock of dark-tinted SUVs and white tourist vans that flock the wide driveway.

I don't know what to do with myself when the valet takes Berta away. Can I hold Ozzy's hand? Wrap an arm around his waist? Is he off-limits now that we're here? I inventory his beautiful face. The warm light in his hazel eyes. The throat I've kissed and the shadowed, salty hollow of his shoulder. He's so freaking gorgeous. The laugh lines by his eyes. The broad shoulders that say *lean on me*. The hands that hold me up when I let him. I spent so much time hating him that I haven't *seen* him. He's beautiful underneath his pretty skin.

"I feel like we just dropped our firstborn off at school." I wring my hands like a Georgette Heyer heroine. I should meditate. Dig out my relaxing pants. Fire up my rocket ship.

Ozzy doesn't miss a beat. "She'll do great. Funniest kid in the class. She'll make a dozen friends in the parking lot and will never eat alone at the gas pump."

A van disgorges a bunch of tourists who swarm the steps, pushing past us as Ozzy pulls me out of their way. He sets his hand on my back, steering me toward the lobby. The bellboy disappears with our things, either to fumigate them or sell them to Ozzy's fandom. We are grubby, dusty, and rumpled. When I catch sight of myself in the millions of mirrors in the lobby, I look like a goblin. I have sex hair because we made an unscheduled pit stop twenty miles ago.

"We fit in so well," Ozzy says to me. "I'm so glad there's a dress code here."

"I should have brought my handbag collection." I sigh. "And the Louboutins."

From behind the check-in desk, the hotel manager shoots us looks. Although he's been told to expect us, our disheveled state poses a conundrum. The lobby is full of well-dressed vacationers. We're scarecrows in a field of Gucci and Tuckernuck.

The manager is still deciding whether he should approach or disavow all knowledge of us when Roz bounds toward us. She looks relieved to see us and promptly shoves a daunting stack of paper into our hands. She's got itineraries for tomorrow. An events schedule. Details for the airport pickup that's scheduled for the day after tomorrow. We have separate return flights for reasons unknown to me. She hands out keys for our hotel rooms. We're neighbors once again.

"Tomorrow is the surfing exhibition." Roz gives Ozzy the stare.

"Surfing? You didn't tell me I was giving a demo! Maybe I should practice."

Roz ignores me. "Ozzy? Tell me you're going to be there."

"I said I wasn't doing that." Ozzy looks at her. She glares back. I want to tell her that when it comes to anger and outrage, he's a duck. It rolls right off him like water.

Roz tries a different approach. "Marketing set it up. Fans are coming. You can't disappoint them."

I'll bet he can.

"I am not surfing." A shadow crosses his face. He heads for the elevator like the conversation is over. He's put up an invisible Do Not Disturb sign.

Roz ignores this and barges after him. I do, too. We both want time with Ozzy, although my reasons are far less business oriented. Ozzy stabs the button for our floor. I don't think it's enough to work out his frustrations.

"I can't cancel." There is worry and outrage in Roz's voice, and she sounds so put out that I want to laugh. I slide my hand under Ozzy's T-shirt, press it against his back. *I'm here.* Roz doesn't comment. She knows what we've been getting up to, and she's picking her battles. Maybe it works, because he still holds the elevator door for us, and I know he wants to let it fly shut in our faces.

When she follows him into his suite, still arguing, I reluctantly give up on my plan to get Ozzy Wylder alone in a hotel room.

Instead, I check out my room, which is very much not a suite. I have a double bed and a tiny balcony that's separated from its neighbors by tall walls. If I squint, I can see the ocean.

I eat all the M&M's in the minibar to compensate myself for this injustice and take the world's longest shower. It's glorious. I wallow in the fancy shampoo. I unwrap all the tiny bars of soap and cover myself with free lotion. I will never, ever take indoor plumbing for granted again.

When I come out, swathed in towels, Ozzy's on my balcony. He knocks on my door, and I open it.

"Wow. They let just anyone in here," I tell him. He laughs as I pull him into my room.

After breakfast the next morning, we're bundled into an air-conditioned car and driven to a surf break whose name I promptly forget.

The beach is a strip of sand at the bottom of a steep hill. Waves break on the rocks at the western end, and the water is a darker blue than I've seen before. Surfers bob out beyond the break on their boards, waiting for waves. Condos dot the nearby cliffs, and there's a restaurant serving up fish tacos and beer. It's nice, but I wouldn't bet money on Ozzy getting in the water. He's playing nice right now, but I recognize the mulish look on his face.

There's a crowd of people waiting for us down on the beach. Ozzy flinches when we reach the sand and see the sign: Surf With Ozzy Wylder!

People converge on him, waving cameras, and he's carried

away. It's exactly like the night I first met him except it's daylight and we're no longer strangers. We're—

Lovers, definitely.

And friends.

I think I mean that last one.

On the other hand, I'm standing on the beach alone, exactly like that night. The giant redundancy axe hovers over my neck. The executioner swings it up and up. Any minute now, it will be game over for me. Except that there's a hot, huge man who could be a stand-in for a lumberjack headed up the beach. The ocean breeze tugs his hair from its man bun. His broad shoulders can't be contained by the stupid, silly, so fun T-shirt he wears—Nacho Average Engineer!

This time, though, he looks back. Is he—

He mouths something.

Hi? Or: *see you at the bar.* Maybe: *it's been real.*

I look back. From his hazel eyes to his bare feet. Somewhere between the car and here, he's shed his shoes because he's allergic to footwear. And wandering around fully dressed. *Ask me to come with you*, I hope desperately. *You're so—*

Fun.

Present.

Real.

I'm not ready to let you go.

I squint, trying to read the word on his lips. It could be *tacos!*

But I don't care. I bound across the beach—the wind whips away my family-unfriendly "Fuck it"—and catch up. Who says I have to stay where I'm put? I'm choosing to follow.

Help, I think.

Maybe that's the word he's trying to say.

Rescue me.

"What's the plan?" I hold out my hand.

When he takes it without answering, I know I'm right. I wrap my fingers around his wrist and tug him to a standstill.

"Talk to me," I say.

He concedes defeat. "They want a surf demonstration. Apparently, everyone standing over there—" he waves a hand at the sizable group of people clumped together on the sand with longboards and shortboards and even a SUP board or two "—has come out here to see Ozzy Wylder surf."

The expression on his face says they're about to be disappointed.

"So you're running a surf school." I tap a finger against my lips, running scenarios in my head. If we do this, then that. "Okay. Let's do it. Teach me how to surf."

"What?"

I point to the surf shack at the base of the cliff. "Gear me up. Show me how to do this."

"You want to learn how to surf."

I shrug. "Are there sharks in the bay?"

"Not right now."

"And there aren't any of your monster waves, right?"

We both look at the ocean. The impressive waves, the ones the surfers are riding, require paddling *way* out. That bus stop is blocks and blocks away from me. Ozzy shakes his head.

"So teach me." I tug him toward the surf shack. "Teach *them*. We'll do the surfing for you, and you can just boss us around. It'll be good practice for you."

We go into the surf shack and pick out gear. I'm squeezed into a wetsuit tighter than anything worn at the Latex Ball. I want to grab a towel, wrap myself up like a mummy, and ditch the photographers. As quickly as I think that, I abandon the idea. I'm the decoy duck. My first attempt to put the wetsuit on fails because I assume the zipper goes in the front where I can reach it without contortions. Ozzy sorts me out, although he's still wrestling with the ramifications of my plan.

"You sure you want to do this? If you want a diversion, we could just run off and get married. Get caught having sex in the elevator."

Such great ideas. I give him big eyes. "I could use a diamond ring…"

He snorts. "You'd run so fast if I came near you with a ring. You want that even less than I want to surf."

He picks out the longest, thickest, widest board I've seen. It's at least a foot taller than I am and is—wait for it—a *fun*-board. Apparently, it floats better and is easier to manage than an actual longboard. It's slightly yellowed and a whole lot dinged up, but Ozzy carries it down to the water for me. I don't think he wants to hand me a weapon.

"Last chance to back out," he warns. "Oh right. You don't back down."

He smiles at me, though, and I grin back at him. It's us against them now.

"Am I going to die out there? Is this your last-ditch strategy to land the TripFriendz job?" I hold on to his shoulders while he slips the tether around my ankle. For a sport that's all about flying free over the water, this feels remarkably like a ball and chain. I'm forced to shuffle walk to the water's edge.

He nods. *You got me!* "My evil plan is working."

"Chief Play Officer Wylder, reporting for duty?"

"Maybe we can be co-chiefs," he offers, looking out over the ocean. He hands me a sweet sentiment, a platitude. *Here are the wildflowers I picked for you!* It's a nice thought, but it's never going to happen.

I distract myself with other thoughts. Thought number one: neoprene makes him look like a million bucks. Outlines his big, hard form. Frames his muscles. I'd peel him out of it, but that may be beyond my abilities. It's glued to him, and I blatantly ogle the bulge in his crotch. It's my last chance. We fly home tomorrow.

"Are you naked under there?"

"Inappropriate, Pandora Fyffe."

I'm not naked. I'm wearing my stars-and-moons swimsuit. Nudity was suggested, but given the group effort it took to get me suited up, I'm risking the swimsuit chafe. I'm keeping my dignity as long as possible.

"Do you think this counts as our job interview?"

It's going to happen. One of us will win, while the other loses.

"Fuck the interview," he growls. Growls! "Fuck the whole thing. TripFriendz can pick whoever they want, and we'll get on with our lives."

"I can't just walk away."

He nods. Waits for me to explain it to him. I love his patience.

"I've lost other jobs. I need to prove I can hang on to one. That I'm not expendable or replaceable."

He mutters a curse. "You are one of a kind."

"Look, maybe we should revisit the night we met at Miles to Go. After we kissed, my boss texted and terminated me. He got my name wrong. My superpower is invisibility. If only I wanted a career in bank robbing or secret shopping, I'd be all set."

He cups the side of my face with his hand. On the beach behind us, our audience is getting restless.

"You're never invisible to me." He hesitates, then he does the most Ozzy thing of all and throws himself into the fray. He doesn't hold back at all. "Maybe surfing won't be so bad if you're there. Maybe it will be okay. Will you do this with me?"

My spine melts and runs down my legs. I probably have stars

in my eyes. Pitter-pats in my rib cage. Ozzy Wylder needs me, so I get in the ocean and prepare to surf.

Before my close encounter with neoprene, I'd told Roz to choose five lucky people. They'll be the ones to get a private surfing lesson with the one and only Ozzy Wylder. It's a compromise, and it'll make for good media.

Six seems like enough to be inclusive without dooming us to failure. Roz has picked out two kids, a middle-aged couple, and a twentysomething who looks halfway to being in love with Ozzy. That makes two of us.

Ozzy checks their gear, making recommendations, and then we all head out like a brood of ducklings following the very sexy mama duck.

The ocean is cold even though it's June. The baby waves that slap at my knees, then my thighs, and finally my poor vag in her neoprene castle, are cold. I have no idea how Mexico in the summer can be cold, but there you have it. With each step we take, the surf slaps at us, at our boards. It slaps me in the face, and I shake like a dog. I can't believe Ozzy chose this as a career path.

I lie belly down on my board and listen intently as he goes over paddling—fortunately for me, it's doggy style—and then he promises that we're going to ride the baby waves in to shore on our bellies. The middle-aged couple looks skeptical, but the others are totally on board with this plan. I turn my head—getting a mouthful of ocean water in the process, which is probably full of fish poop and marine semen—to look at Ozzy. He moves between the boards, offering advice and rearranging limbs. It's not quite as easy as it sounds. Even these small waves roll and crest. It takes three attempts to get my chest and head up.

He runs through how to pop up on the board (which is fancy surfer-speak for jump up on top of it with my nonexistent ab muscles and then glide to shore without falling over). The kids get the hang of it in no time.

A surfer rides up beside me. He's straddling his board, legs hugging it kind of like a seahorse. "Nothing better, right?"

Apparently random strangers will make idle chitchat with you when you're both stuck at sea.

"It's not bad." I have a death grip on my foamie. There are living *things* lurking in the water below me and Jaws will be along any moment to bite a chunk out of my board.

"It's even better out at the break. The view of the beach is incredible." He points off into the distance. "I can tow you?"

"Not today." Ozzy materializes by my side. He slaps a proprietary hand on my board. I think he's considering tattooing PROPERTY OF on my boobs.

The other surfer paddles off with a laugh. He's headed back out to the break, and I'm forgotten.

"Ready to surf?" He swings onto my board behind me. I have no idea how we don't capsize. Or sink. This board can't be meant to handle so much weight.

"I tried to get out of it, but my boss-to-be is a tyrant." I lean back against him. My fellow students are paddling like rabid dogs, trying to put some distance between themselves and the shore.

"Don't give up yet." Ozzy laughs and sends us shooting after them.

We don't go far, and we certainly don't go anywhere near the break where the waves crest and curl. But he's behind me on the board all the way, and then he pulls me up, bracing me against his body. The first time, I knock us both off. I slip through Ozzy's hands and underwater. The world goes green and blue. My eyes sting from the salt, and then there's sand against my face, the bottom. I fight the gentle pressure that rolls me, shoving me down. Ozzy pulls me up.

The Code for Love

"You okay?"

I am. I really, really am. "Let's try it again."

The second time, it sticks. We're stuck together, arms out, skimming over the surface, the beach coming closer and closer.

It's magical.

Twenty-Three

I plot to sneak into Ozzy's hotel room while he's out schmoozing with our bosses in the aftermath of our surf school shenanigans. He broke into mine, after all. It's theoretically possible. After hanging dangerously far out my balcony, however, I determine that Ozzy has the climbing skills of a mountain goat. I, on the other hand, am more of a sloth. There's no way I'll attempt the perilous crossing from my balcony to his.

Instead, I play dirty and convince the housekeeper to let me in. She's been following our road trip and is Team Pozzy. All I have to do is tip her and I'm in.

Ozzy's suite turns out to be twice as big as mine, which is probably an indication of how TripFriendz's executive team is leaning. It's fine. I knew it would be an uphill battle, and it's not over yet. *Don't give up yet.* I hear Ozzy's words in my head as I admire his marble bathroom (the tub will hold both of us) and steal the snacks from his minibar. I also steal his hoodie. I flop—sloth-like—on his enormous bed. I burrow under his puffy white duvet and roll around in his sheets.

The way he comes in tells me his meeting with our evil overlords did not go well. He shuts the door hard and tosses his key card onto the credenza with a muttered curse. He angry-rips his shirt off. Now might not be the time to pop my head out and yell *Surprise!* He's already at greater risk of a heart attack because of his rage fit.

The person-shaped blob in his bed gives it away, however. He stops cursing and pads toward the bed. His bare feet slap against the tile floor.

He is a hunter. "Are we playing hide-and-seek?"

"Sure." My voice is muffled by the covers.

He tugs them down. *Resistance is futile.* "I win."

"I think you cheated. You didn't count to a hundred." I consider sticking out my lower lip, but duck face is not my strong suit. His eyes spark with glee as I roll onto my side.

"You're such a poor loser."

"You're worse."

He nods his head. It's true.

I lace my arms around his neck and pull him down onto the bed with me. We're nose to nose, mano a mano. My hair's a giant cloud of snarls around my head. It's my anti-halo. Ozzy doesn't seem to mind. He likes me angry, prickly, sick, cranky, singing along off-key to his playlist. I'm just myself around him, and if there's a side of me he hasn't seen yet, he's always pleased to meet her.

I press a kiss against his jaw where it's five o-clock stubbly. Pull the hair tie out of his man bun so his hair can enjoy some free time. "How'd it go?"

It's his turn to make a face. "They'd like to turn me into their surfing Ken doll. Also, they're self-serving assholes."

It's cute he sounds surprised. "Bob is pretty bad. He could be worse, though."

"How?" Ozzy is outraged on my behalf.

"Is now the appropriate time to discuss our middle-aged director of engineering?"

He makes a humming sound. He's considering it. "There are other people we could talk about. Roz. Rosie. The venture capitalists who think TripFriendz will make them gazillionaires."

"Because they're going to trade on your enormous stardom and my brain."

"They must have a better plan that that." Being the supportive person that I am, I kiss his ear to show him how much I'm listening to him.

"A photo shoot of me in swim trunks." He kisses me back. Ear, cheek, the corner of my mouth.

"Pffft. They should at least make it a Speedo. A leopard-print one would be good. You could shoot across the water beating your chest. It would be Tarzan surfing. When was the last time you really surfed?" I pull his arm out into what I pretend is a surfing pose. Kiss the piece of him I've captured. Trace the dark lines of ink on his forearms with my tongue. It's all swirls and ocean waves. I'm sure there's a coded message in there.

"Fishing?"

"Don't you want to tell me? Maybe I could help."

"I wish you could." He rolls onto his back, pulling me on top of him. My legs hug his hips. His hands grip mine. We're Pozzy for real now, all mashed together.

"Why can't I?"

"Because the yips are just one of those things. There's no magic cure. You can't work through them or talk through them or make them go away."

"Did you see it coming?" I don't think this is coming out the way I want. Feelings aren't my area of expertise at all, but someone needs to hear him, and I want that someone to be me. "I bet the timing was awful."

"Yeah, I'm sure you've seen the video of my wipeout." His fingers trace my spine.

"The longest five minutes ever."

He closes his eyes. "Eternity."

I close my eyes in solidarity. Breathe in with him. Out. He's not underwater.

"I was in the barrel." I imagine what that must look like, the wall of water rising and rising overhead, the curve and the curl of something that isn't solid but you're on it anyhow. "And then I overcorrected. I was just a little off, but I knew I was about to wipe out. Some mistakes can't be fixed, and you just wait them out, start over. I had time for one breath. No more."

We both breathe in. My lungs are balloons, inflating and inflating. I have enough oxygen in there for two Pandoras.

"And then I was under. It happened so fast that I didn't have time to control my body position or even finish that breath. I mistimed my cut and the wave won."

My lungs are burning. I have to take a breath.

"It was a huge wave."

"Forty feet." He shrugs. "I've ridden bigger. Other surfers have ridden bigger. I wasn't going for a record. It wasn't even close. Other people ride fifty-footers all the time, and someday soon someone's going to surf a hundred-foot wave. It'll happen."

He sighs, pining for his monster wave. He loves it as much as he hates it.

"And that wasn't the worst of it," he continues. "Because that was just the first wave. There was a second one right behind it, and then a third."

"It brought friends." I think I need to laugh about this, or I might cry. The concern in the sportscaster's voice makes all the sense in the world now. *Look! Ozzy has a building's worth of water on him! And then two* MORE *buildings! He's been buried under a skyscraper, folks.*

"I hated it."

"I hate that it happened to you."

"I've had bad rides before. It was nothing new." He's all studied nonchalance. *No big deal!*

"But—" I start the sentence for him.

"But then I couldn't do it anymore. I couldn't ride the big waves, couldn't pop up. My fingers wouldn't let go of the board. I tried a lot. Went to my favorite secret surf spots where no one would be up in my face about it or watching to see if I could handle it. I'd paddle out. I demoted myself to a foamie, just in case it was a stability issue. Maybe I had an ear infection or a brain tumor."

"But you couldn't."

"I'd freeze every time. My brain would think and think, visualizing the ride in my head, running through the steps I needed to take. I can't figure out what's wrong, but then once I'm back on shore, I'm replaying the waves over and over in my head and I'm sure I can do it the next time. Except I can't. The yoga and the working out should help, because I can hold my breath long enough now. I'm not gonna drown under there. But—"

"But," I agree.

"My parents want to know when I'm going back on the circuit."

"Because they know you love it?"

He also hates it.

He shakes his head. "No. My mom keeps sending me business cards for sports therapists. She worries I'll lose my endorsements. My dad—"

I stroke the side of his face with my fingers. This is not the Ozzy who flew across the water on his board the night we first met. He's not the man who scaled my wall and gave me shit and laughed with me. His face is tight, and he's misplaced his smile. I want to fix this for him and then rage at all the people who haven't told him that he's so much more than what his body does.

"He doesn't see what the point is of all the sacrifices, of the money invested, of the time we spent living in Hawaii to get me the right exposure when I was still young enough to benefit from it. It's all wasted if I quit now."

"Sometimes—" God, I need my whiteboard and an hour of alone time to plot this out. I'm making choices, and I have no idea where they'll lead. "Sometimes when I'm in my rocket ship, I go out and I explore. I get all the space gems. I fly everywhere and I'm the first one there, the best."

"I love your space gems," he says roughly. "So pink and sparkly."

"Sometimes. Other times, they're kinda plain on the outside. Lumpy. You have to really look to spot them even if they're important rocks. NASA found one once that wasn't anything special at first glance. It looked like a lump of coal. Black. Boring. But it contained all these tiny amino acids. It was full of the building blocks of life, and it came from a really ancient meteorite that crashed in Antarctica when there was no one around to notice."

"Someone noticed," he says.

"Yeah. But even that scientist who was all, 'Oh, I'll just pick this random rock up because I want to, and not because I think it's anything extraordinary,' didn't need it to be an antediluvian clue. He just liked it because it was a rock and it was interesting and there it was, right in his path. So he took it home with him."

My metaphor is going off the rails.

"He liked it, and that was enough. I like you and you're enough just as you are. You don't have to be a space meteor."

He's staring up at me. I can't tell if my TED Talk has helped or if he's finally decided that I'm deranged.

"You are a rock." *Solid, present, my hidden joy, and someone I think I would like to take home with me.*

"Thank you for picking me up," he whispers against my throat. *Thank you for playing the game of Life with me. Let's not compete anymore.* "It helps, talking with you."

He sounds surprised. I think this over while he rolls me beneath him. Ozzy and I have something in common. Same song, different verse. Neither of us knows how to be second-best. People can't see past his pretty face and ripped body. No one sees *him*.

If he can't stand up on his board, if he's not the fastest, the best on the water, then he's no one. That's what he thinks.

I know he's wrong.

Twenty-Four

Ozzy and I tackle one last event before we head to the airport. It's an awards ceremony for a second-tier surfing competition that wrapped the day we arrived in Cabo. Roz explained our presence as two hours of mingling and eating free canapés. Various TripFriendz executives and their venture capital buddies are also supposed to put in an appearance, but I don't pay much attention to that guest list. She asks us to play nicely with others, which means I smile with grim determination while Ozzy's pretty jaw imitates granite. He's so tense that I'm afraid his mechanical clapping may crack him.

When we enter the ballroom, he's hailed by dozens of people, all of whom want to have a conversation that iterates on the following:

1. Ozzy looks awesome for someone who had a near-death experience five months ago and had to be dragged out of the water and resuscitated.
2. When is Ozzy "getting back out there"?
3. Does he plan to surf at contests X, Y, and Z?

His response is to imitate a caveman. He grunts. He fists his hands. He strides around the ballroom like he'd like to kill something. I try to mitigate his crankiness, but Roz is not going to be happy with us.

Mostly he keeps a protective hand on the small of my back. He fetches me champagne and snacks. When he spots yet another surfer that he knows, I promise to meet him at our table and steal away to the restroom. My inner hermit needs emergency alone time.

After longer than anyone should spend hiding in a bathroom stall, I wash my hands, give myself a pep talk in the mirror, and start over.

In the seven eternities it takes me to find our table, I learn three important facts. Fact number one: the competition isn't well-known. If it's even televised at all, it's on an obscure channel that has maybe a dozen regular viewers. TripFriendz has brought us to a middle school musical and not to a Broadway production.

Fact number two: I stick out like a sore thumb. The dress code is cocktail attire, and the room is full of lean, built men and toned women. I guess that's to be expected when most of the people here work out for hours a day.

Fact number three: these are my people. It takes five minutes to figure out that they all have one thing in common: they're hungry, and not for the weird canapés that are being passed around. They want to win.

When I came to TripFriendz I was determined to make a name for myself. I was going to do whatever it took to be the best, and I don't think I considered what I would do after I won my dream job. Step one was becoming the new chief play officer, but step two was vague.

But now that I've gone for it—and gone on this road trip—I don't know what I want to happen next. Mostly, I just want to keep spending time with Ozzy. I want him, and not as my boss or a sexy workplace romance. Ozzy is the best of prizes.

I want him all to myself. I want to toss him into the van and drive off into the horizon with him. We'll have van-rocking sex at sunset in the desert. We'll live happily ever after. I'll ride on his board like a surf dog, adoring him with my eyes, tongue out, little life jacket firmly affixed.

The room is full of round tables that seat six, like fancy polka dots or craters on the moon. Naturally, ours is right up front where everyone can see us. We might as well be seated on the stage.

I'm the first one here, so I collapse onto my assigned chair and whip out my phone. Ozzy's been waylaid across the room by a toned brunette in a black cocktail dress. She's talking animatedly at him, waving her hands like a pissed-off octopus.

As I don't know anyone and don't feel like making friends, I code. The phone is not my favorite development environment, but it beats staring off into space.

It's been ages since I did dev work on Crystal Cluster Cosmos, but it doesn't take long to get back in the rhythm. I code a few fixes and then decide to make a new planet for Ozzy. It's nice to be God in my world. Plus, I think he'll like it—planets are just really big rocks, and rocks are now kind of our thing. I add an ocean made of gas so he can surf if and when he decides he wants to. For good measure, I pepper the planet's surface with rocks. Big ones, small ones, sparkly, non-sparkly, and in all the colors of the rainbow.

Other people turn up eventually, although not Ozzy. Ozzy gives me head tips, smiles, and warm eyes from across the room, and I try to communicate telepathically with him. *Can you believe we have to do this? This is the* WORST. *You look superhot in your suit, though, so there are compensations.*

I meet a few TripFriendz executives and their venture capital buddies. I'm unclear as to why they'd bother to fly down to Cabo just to witness the end of our road trip, but maybe they really like Cabo. Or getting to take a road trip of their own.

Someone sits down in the seat to my left, a big, broad-shouldered man who's probably in his fifties. He introduces himself as Benji. He's wearing an expensive dark-colored suit with a baby blue tie, and his graying hair has been clipped ruthlessly short. His eyes crinkle up as he takes me in, and I hastily slip my phone in my purse.

"You're the gal who wrote the algorithm for fun. TripFriendz's secret weapon!"

It takes me longer than it should to figure out he means that probably I'm the girl who turned having fun into a software project.

He moves the conversation along.

"How was your trip?"

I give the only acceptable answer. "Great."

In the ten thousand variations of this conversation that I've had today, the other person either asks me to find them *their* perfect trip buddy or monologues extensively about their most recent Mexican vacation while I stand there awkwardly.

Ozzy saunters up to our table and glowers at Benji. Apparently, they've met because they greet each other by name before Ozzy throws himself into the empty chair on my right. He picks up my phone and, when I nod, launches his starship into the galaxy.

"Which sports do you play?" Benji asks me. "Do you surf?"

"No."

Ozzy's mouth curls upward. He's amused.

"Ozzy here has two brothers and a sister." He nods toward Ozzy, who is flying over an asteroid belt with grim determination. "A football player, a golfer, and a surfer. She won this week's tournament. He's second-string on the family sports team!"

He laughs jovially—hur, hur, hur. His voice belongs on TV.

"I didn't know Ozzy's sister surfed." I also didn't know he had a sister, but details. Rosie would be disappointed in me. This is Stalking 101.

"She's very good," Ozzy says. He directs his rocket ship a few degrees to the north. "She hasn't fallen off her board in forever."

Benji's mouth purses up. "My baby boy is such a kidder."

My eyes are cartoonishly wide. "Excuse me?"

"Ozzy likes a good joke," Benji clarifies. "He's the jokester in our family."

The floor falls out from underneath me. He told me his family was sports-adjacent. *You pick out a sports-adjacent career and go do that. That's the next level in your game.*

"I'm pleased that Ozzy's taking an interested in his post-surf career. He's an asset to the family business."

"Benji," Ozzy warns. "I don't think we need to discuss that now." He sets my phone back down on the table with a click. He's shutting down this conversation.

"What is the family business?" I'm a cruise ship, not rocket ship. I'm sailing through a nice, peaceful lagoon with pretty, turquoise water. I am the calm.

"Venture capital," Benji says like it's no big deal. *Oh, yeah, we have so much cash that we invest it in other places—like your workplace. We own your asses.* "We mostly fund sports and adventure lifestyle start-ups. When Ozzy brought TripFriendz to my attention, I knew it had potential. Sending people out to explore the world. Rock climbing, surfing, paragliding…" He lists off a phone book's worth of sports. "Ozzy needed a new direction after his last competition, so I convinced him to come in with me. Put up some cash. It was great the way the two of you met. Real serendipity."

Ozzy is a *backer's* son. I'm fuzzy on exactly how venture capital works, but a case could be made that he's a part owner. He certainly has a financial stake. No wonder the executive team was so willing to bring him on board. I'm sure they've been wondering when I'd figure out that I was banging an investor. It will 10,000 percent look like I slept my way into a job.

"Ozzy?" I can give him a chance, I decide. Maybe he can explain this.

"Benji is my dad," he says.

Benji frowns. "Didn't he tell you? He had a lot of fun with you on the road. You're such a good sport to go along with this. He's so excited about the idea of adventure travel. He's been working like crazy to identify prospects, get our feet in the door. TripFriendz was perfect. I shouldn't have left so much of the heavy lifting to him, but he's the best at charming folks. He's game for anything. He's such a fighter."

Benji laughs a good-natured laugh. This is my cue to declare him charming, too.

"He's something," I mutter.

"Panda." Ozzy sets a hand on my arm.

It weighs a billion pounds. Ozzy stares at me with concern.

It was never real between us, was it? I was stupid to think that I was his choice. That what we felt was real. It was just computer code, lines of text that tell a machine what to do and how.

My phone screen blinks.

Game Over.

You can't code love.

Twenty-Five

The Mexican desert falls away beneath the plane. I'm glued to the window, reliving the trip. There's the highway we drove down. The ocean we surfed in. I pretend that I see every pit stop in the handful of minutes I have as the plane climbs and Cabo drops away beneath us. I even try to pick out Berta. She's the one thing I know for sure is down there somewhere, but then we're up above the clouds and Cabo is just a memory.

I wallow in my misery as the stewardess offers drinks and pretzels, and by the time we're back in US airspace, I'm a rage monster. I cry when we touch down in San Francisco. Six hours after takeoff, when I open my front door, I've shifted into failure analysis. I poured my heart into my algorithm, and then I made the choice to stop hating Ozzy and love him instead.

I'm one part stupid, one part sad, and all parts mad, but my ire is directed mostly at myself for believing Ozzy was different. That I was different when I was with him. And so I feed my feelings with Whole Foods deliveries and hide in my loft, wearing my oldest sweatpants and the T-shirt with the spaghetti stain on my boob. I fail to shower, refuse to adult. I should have stuck to hating Ozzy.

On day three Rosie comes over to help me look for a new place. Somewhere between San Francisco and Cabo, we became friends, and staying put is not an option. I love my loft, but I have to move on. For twenty delusional minutes, I debate converting my life savings into a van and driving across the US and into Canada. The boho chic of Instagram van life is soothing. There are *pillows*.

It's Rosie who points out that van life means interacting with strangers on an almost daily basis. Peeing in Walmart bathrooms. Downsizing my things. She suggests I consider remote work instead. I don't want to live in a van permanently, but maybe I'm not quite so stuck in a rut as I was before.

In the end, I do move, but only across the Bay. We find me a tiny chocolate box of an urban farmhouse in Berkeley. It looks like it belongs in France and not in California. The second floor is reached from a set of stairs so steep they make the Mayan pyramids look flat. When I stand at the kitchen sink, I can stretch out my arms and the touch the French doors that lead outside. The front yard is a riotous jungle of flowers. Best yet, I can (just barely) afford it, and the neighborhood's safe, if colorful. People in Berkeley have plenty of room for another quirky neighbor.

Two weeks after my ignominious return from Cabo, I start over. I hire a moving service to pack me up and move me out while I hit up a home goods store for more pillows, because you can never have too many. I don't look to my right when I close the door to my loft for the last time. That's no man's land. Taboo. I've nuked that neighbor from my memories. Rosie, being more practical, has blocked Ozzy's number on my phone and subscribed me to a pricey service that promises to scrub all traces of me from the internet. She's as optimistic as ever.

After my first night back in San Francisco, I temporarily

relocated to an Airbnb. An old Victorian not too far from my old condo so I could send Rosie to pick up more clothes or to water my succulents when my phone revealed that Ozzy was safely away. Once Rosie defaces his dry cleaning with hospital-grade antiseptic when his delivery service makes the mistake of hanging it on his door handle.

"An Armani suit!" She is gleeful. "Take that, cocksucker!"

Ozzy. In a suit?

Who is this stranger?

In the past, I've shrugged off breakups. Since I mostly just hook up, the ends weren't particularly notable. I'd stop texting or he would, and then we'd mutually ghost each other. I have no frame of reference for what I'm feeling, other than the certainty that it sucks. The moping is seemingly endless, and then I angrily tear up when I find the jar of seashells we gathered in a moment of environmental carelessness or the panda bear *alebrije* that he bought outside Tijuana. Each time I accidentally spot them, I reset the Ozzy clock. *It has been zero days since I last thought about him.*

Rosie, who has invited herself to live on my sofa as my "personal honor guard," suggests we bury my "intimate souvenirs" in a giant time capsule in the redwood forest north of San Francisco. When I point out that this is a national park and digging is highly discouraged, she proposes the municipal dump as an alternate site. I promise to think on it.

Fifteen days after I return, I officially find out that I did not, in fact, get the job of chief play officer. The email is polite but brief: Bob thanks me for my service but they've decided to go in another direction! He wishes me the best in my endeavors! The enthusiastic punctuation makes it seem unlikely that he wrote the message himself. I am not shocked, although his sheepish follow-up message the next day is a surprise.

TripFriendz, he messages, would like to offer me a consolation prize: would I care to return in an engineer role? Since they have a happiness engineer-in-training, an innovation engineer, and a chief fantasy engineer (Enzo's new job title and a reflection of his highly aspirational sales targets), they suggest I join them as their new intergalactic engineer. I'm immediately sure that Ozzy made them say this, and I angry-cry some more.

I turn them down.

I move into the new house, which comes with a bonus feral mama cat. Rosie paints flowers on my nails to match the ones in my new garden, and we watch *Stargate*. We both applaud so loudly that mama cat startles when the hero chooses to spend the rest of his life on an alien planet with his hookup, because when it's true love, it's true love.

"You are not going to believe this." Rosie hands me a flower that looks like an orange pom-pom stuck on top of some salad greens. According to the app I just downloaded onto my phone, it's a marigold, and if the world comes to an end, I can eat it.

My social skills may be rusty, but even I know that's my cue to say, "What?"

Rosie pops another baby flower out of its black nursery pot. She's stopped by to say hello and has brought "flowers with roots because otherwise I'm just delivering corpses." I appreciate the thought, although her estimation of my gardening skills is wildly overinflated.

"So you know how TripFriendz launched yesterday?"

"Yes." I was sent a complimentary T-shirt, a bumper sticker, and a matchbox van that did not look the slightest bit like Berta, who is one and only.

Rosie takes a minute to pat me on the shoulder. Apparently, the expression on my face is dire.

"They found a bug!"

From *her* expression, I deduce that the bug was not of the cockroach-tarantula-insect variety. "Bugs are not uncommon, Rosie."

She should know. She's introduced more than her fair share of them to TripFriendz's product.

"Yeah, but they found this one when eight hundred people got matched to the same trip with the same person."

Ouch. That *is* bad.

"Look, I know you don't want to talk about Ozzy and your road trip, but I thought you should know that it wasn't exactly a match made in heaven. Also, it wasn't your fault. Or mine. Noah, however, would like me to pass on his résumé in case you know of any openings."

"Ouch."

"Yeah." Rosie shakes her head. "His database query skills need remedial work. He *literally* wrote a query that matches everyone to Ozzy."

I debate whether or not I want to ask follow-up questions. I decide I don't. "He'll be a very busy man," I say, and leave it at that.

I don't need to know how TripFriendz's new chief play officer is working out.

We manhandle some very patient marigolds into the ground while Rosie tries to keep her thoughts to herself. She almost makes it to the end of the flat before she caves.

"Ozzy never started, you know."

I do not know.

"Maybe you should talk to him?"

"I don't think that would be wise."

I dig a hole to China and stab the final marigold in. I may water it with my bitterness. It turns out that it's much harder to stop loving someone than it is to stop hating him.

Rosie's not finished, though. "He came by the office, looking for you. He sent fruit baskets. They might have been bribes to whisper his name to you. I'm not sure." She taps her lips with her fingers, redistributing leftover potting soil to her chin. "We ate them and left him hanging."

I guess he thought I'd take the consolation prize. I fooled him. Instead of accepting TripFriendz's offer of gainful employment, I decided to work freelance while I turn Crystal Cluster Cosmos into an app that I can sell online. Rosie's promised to be my first employee. She also offered to drop out of Stanford in order to guarantee our success, but I made her promise to graduate before she comes onboard full-time in nine months or so.

Speaking of Stanford, she has to take off to catch the BART, the train, and the bus back to the apartment she shares with two other software interns.

She narrates her journey back, and I answer each of her texts. That I miss talking with someone scares me, especially since I've done so well in my fortress of solitude. I didn't realize how big an Ozzy-sized hole could be, and I don't know what I'll do if it doesn't fill in with time.

Twenty-Six

Despite working forty hours a week on Crystal Cluster Cosmos (Rosie insists that I need to maintain a healthy life-work balance and threatens to install parental control software if I start pulling ninety-hour weeks again), the first thing I do on Friday night is launch my spaceship and head off into space. I'm not sick of it at all.

I've customized my spaceship since the last time I flew: it's bright yellow now, the color of rudbeckia and bananas, and it sparkles in the starlight. The nose cone looks like it's been plated in gold, just like a real spaceship.

I skip my favorite spots and head out into a corner of the galaxy that is largely unexplored. It's also ever so slightly near the planet I built for Ozzy, but that's completely happenstance.

I float around in space, taking gorgeous pictures. Stars, meteors, a belt of purple gas. I flit from one to the other, picking up a few space gems along the way. It's all super relaxing until I make the mistake of looking over at Ozzy's planet.

There's a rocket ship hanging out in orbit.

Crystal Cluster Cosmos is an online world that supports multiplayers. This means that I'm by no means the only person who flies around collecting space gems, but you do generally have to know where to go to get started. You need to code your spaceship. Not just anyone can play in my world.

The rocket ship is the blue of Sour Patch Kids or toilet bowl cleaner. It's vibrant and totally obnoxious. Not only have I never, ever seen someone else in this part of my galaxy, but this craft is an eyesore. Too bad there's no space homeowners association that can board the offending vessel and lay down the law about acceptable paint colors for ships.

A message flashes across my console. *Incoming Message. Accept?*

This is new. I dither for a moment but I'm curious (and nosy), so I smash the Accept button and wait to meet my new neighbor.

When Ozzy's picture flashes across my screen, I suck in a breath. My ribs squeeze my heart. I have *puncture* wounds. No one warned me that love would be so bad for my physical health. I haven't seen Ozzy in weeks, other than furtive, guilt-ridden forays onto YouTube where I've illegally downloaded his shirtless surfing videos. That's historical Ozzy, though, someone who once was and who is no longer. He's frozen in time, always smiling and wearing his happy face, although now I know he's not a one-note song. Ozzy is a rainbow of emotions, even when some of them leave me feeling raw.

My heart flutters disturbingly. I'd like to dismiss it as a panic attack, but experience says it might be love.

Ozzy is not looking his best. His man bun has come apart and his hair fills the screen. His jaw has more grit than sandpaper; I'm not sure he's shaved since Mexico. He's haggard, his edges rougher than they used to be.

"Panda Bear." His smile still lights up his eyes, though. It tugs at the corner of his mouth, rueful and hesitant, as if he's (rightly) afraid that I'll terminate this call right now and ban him from the galaxy forever.

I should do it.

Instead, I snap, "What?"

"I love you."

He puts it right out there. His hazel eyes meet mine, because he always sees me. They hold hope, anxiety, and a whole lot of heat as he looks at me. I'm suddenly reminded that since I've been working from home and moping, I haven't put a whole lot of thought into showers or hairbrushes. He doesn't look as if he cares about that.

"I'm sorry."

He cares about *me*.

I let that sink in for a moment before he launches into a speech. I suspect he may have practiced or written out talking points. I would have. And as he talks on and on about how he's sorry, and for what—not telling me about the VC stake, about making me feel less than and invisible, for not making it clear that the only reason he had for going on that road trip from hell was me—I think about the lede.

Ozzy Wylder loves me.

And he's here.

I don't know what to say, which isn't a first, but it is a problem because I'm staring, mouth open, and it's not a good look. I should be responding or asking questions. *Engaging.* But my brain is entirely disconnected from my heart, which has taken over absolutely every inch of my body and is beating so hard that this time I'm definitely having a heart attack. Or a love attack. Or something equally, horribly, wonderfully cheesy.

"I love you," Ozzy says again. I think I need him to repeat that every morning for a century or two if it turns out that's where we're headed.

"Permission to dock? Pandora, can I come over?"

"We can try?" I don't know how this will work. Intergalactic boarding missions are not something I've coded into this game.

Ozzy's rocket ship hovers over the planet I built.

There's a knock on my front door, and when I look out, he's standing there. I open the door.

He looks uncharacteristically solemn, his body tense. I stand there in the open door, wondering if I look the same. If my road trip tan has faded. Whether we'll go somewhere together ever again. If I really want to play this game again, and if he'll let me.

My stomach pinches. No one smiles forever, not really, but an unsmiling Ozzy makes me worried. Sad. A whole lot concerned because, when he smiles, he is the most beautiful person I've ever known, and I can't not think that. He starts to relax, lounging toward my door frame, then catches himself and stiffens. "Hi again."

My stupid heart leaps. It tries to escape my rib cage and launch itself toward Ozzy. It recognizes him. It's hopeful.

Ozzy is just a person, I remind that stupidly optimistic organ. And he's not *my* person. There are a thousand reasons he could be here IRL.

To drop off something I left in the van. Maybe Benji wants to buy a gaming start-up.

He does none of those things, though. Instead, he extends his closed hand. His eyes search my face. Not for something so much as taking inventory. As if he's really, totally glad to see me and wants to remind himself of everything he's missed. He's wearing a flannel shirt over a T-shirt that's the hunter green shade of pine trees.

I stretch my own hands out automatically, and his fingers unfurl like a sea anemone. Something lands in my palm.

A gold spider carved out of topaz, the rock still warm from his grasp.

"You didn't take the job."

Yes, I lost.

No, I no longer care.

I'm silent for a moment, turning that over in my head.

And then I give him the truth. "TripFriendz didn't offer it to me."

"Didn't offer it?" He frowns, shoving a hand through his hair. The lion's mane is tousled on end. "You earned it."

"Did I? I tried, but—" It was a job, a really good one, but that was all it was. I poke at my feelings again, and decide I mean it. The wound stings, but it's feeling better. It *will* be better. "Actually, I've moved on. I started my own thing. Company."

I almost demur, undersell what I've done, what I've decided to do, but my galactic mining game is good, and it deserves to be acknowledged. I've accomplished things, and I'm owning them. I won't sell myself short. Not to Ozzy, at any rate.

"It'll be the best, although I can't recommend a VC to you." His lips tighten, his jaw all tension beneath its layer of stubble. "Benji and I are not currently on speaking terms."

My stomach drops. My mind turns into a time travel machine, whisking me back and back some more to that stupid hotel ballroom. I can't forget the confidence with which Benji dropped down into the chair beside me. He'd been so sure he was top dog, that he could call the shots. I'm not surprised that Ozzy's pushed back. He likes to pick his own path, after all.

We're headed somewhere better... We don't need that map.

"Can we talk about my dad?" he asks. "And then we need to talk about what I did."

"All right." I watch him shove his hand through his hair

again. Scratch his jaw. Shift his weight. I think he just planted his feet, but I could be wrong. "If you think it will help."

If you think it will help is something you say, right?

Just words and not a commitment.

"Please." He's bold, as fearless as always, and yet, underneath the calm expression, the resigned amusement I see on his face, I discover new strata. Discomfort. Embarrassment. *Fear.* This conversation matters to him. "What happened in Mexico was not okay. I told him that. I told the TripFriendz board that. I resigned, of course. It wasn't a fair competition, and they took advantage of you." He is nodding now, agreeing with himself, rushing his words a little because he really wants to get them out even if neither of us knows what comes next. "I think *I* took advantage of you. I should have told you about Benji, about him being my dad and my having an inside track."

He's right. "You should have."

A car drives past. An owl calls.

"I should have," he agrees. "But I didn't. I made the wrong choice."

He did. But so did I. Maybe.

"What about your start-up funds?"

His hands tighten by his sides. "They don't matter. I'll find another project. There will be something else to do. But I'm not working for my dad, and he's not going to play any role in my future."

Ozzy taught me about the importance of following my passions, of allowing myself to—not color outside the lines, but maybe to daydream ever so slightly near the edge? He plays hard, competes hard, but he does it the right way. Benji might not have broken any laws, but it wasn't fair what he did, and I'm not surprised Ozzy wants nothing to do with him. "I'm sorry I got between the two of you. He's your dad—"

"Yeah." Ozzy inhales. Exhales. It's his Pilates breathing, the one he swears by when things are hurting. I hope it helps. I hope there's a cure for the way he feels right now. "He's my dad, and sometimes he's a good one. Right now, however, he's the one who's screwed up, and I don't know how to handle it. That's my job. I'm the one who messes things up."

He says *things* and I think…

It's code.

For *you* and *us* and *Pandora Fyffe*.

I inhale. I'm a rocket on a launchpad. I may not have gone anywhere. There have been some high winds. Fueling issues. Unexpected cloud cover. I've been grounded—or have grounded myself—but now…

"Why didn't you tell me that your dad was one of TripFriendz's backers? He found out about the company from you. You must have told him all about it."

He nods, owning it. "I did. I went to dinner with him, and I went on and on about this amazing girl and the work she was doing at this travel start-up. It was groundbreaking, really original. She was so smart and so undervalued, and I knew that, someday soon, people would recognize her for what she was. Benji agreed she sounded amazing, and it took me a while to realize—weeks, really—that he'd been pumping me for information. He saw a business opportunity, while I saw—"

"What did you see?"

"You," he says. "I saw *you*."

I think it's a true story. He won't look away and I look right back. Our eyes are locked in a staring game. I don't have to compete for his attention or demand he look or play stupid pick-me games. He's just here, waiting for me to choose him back.

"I thought… I thought you picked TripFriendz. And that you'd be mad at me for ruining your shot at chief play officer. And maybe your relationship with Benji, and…it won't be as easy to…"

"I can always be a wildlife photographer, Pandora. All I have to do is pick up a camera." He mimes framing the squirrel running through my new yard with the lens of his fingers. The moth that's come to check out the porch light. "That's just a choice I make, the same way you can choose to fly a spaceship through the cosmos. If you want to do it, you'll do it." He tosses aside his imaginary camera, hazel eyes holding mine. "Will I make money? I don't know. Will I shoot the cover of *National Geographic*? Don't know. I can't control that—and it's not what matters, anyhow."

"What matters?"

"You," he says. "Me."

I take a step closer, wanting to reach out, needing this. "Us."

"Yes." He nods. "Us."

My fingers close around the spider. I'm keeping it.

"I feel," he continues, "like I should either climb up your wall in the spirit of starting over or fall on my knees and grovel. Rosie urges the grovel, but I know how you feel about drama."

"To be strictly accurate, we met on a beach."

He points to the patch of dirt where my newborn marigolds are incubating. "Sand."

"Close enough. And maybe it's my turn, anyhow. To climb up your wall and invade your space and make it absolutely, completely impossible to ignore me."

The smile that spreads across his face is beautiful. It moves up his face like a sunrise. "Yeah?"

I cup his face between my hands and gently tug his face down to mine. "Hi. Remember me?"

"Always. I missed you." He whispers the words against my skin. "Fuck, I missed you, Pandora."

"Permission granted," I say. My lips brush his.

I throw my caution overboard. There's no *if* statement to test this condition. I'm in or I'm out. He's in or he's out. We either love each other or we don't. The man bun doesn't survive my fingers threading through his hair. We're leaning into each other and then we're kissing. *Hello, how are you, I've missed you, let me make it better, I'm sorry, I love you so much.* His lips say these things with warm touches, tender nips, the soft stroke of his tongue. Mine say them back. *I love you and you're home. Please come in.*

When we come up for air, I'm pretty sure my neighbors are aware that I am no longer single, solo Pandora, and that Ozzy Wylder is mine.

I fist the front of his T-shirt and tug. "You better come in."

He does.

And then he stays.

★ ★ ★ ★ ★

afterglow BOOKS

Afterglow Books is a trend-led, trope-filled list of books with diverse, authentic and relatable characters, a wide array of voices and representations, plus real world trials and tribulations. Featuring all the tropes you could possibly want (think small-town settings, fake relationships, grumpy vs sunshine, enemies to lovers) and all with a generous dose of spice in every story.

♪ @millsandboonuk
◉ @millsandboonuk
afterglowbooks.co.uk
#AfterglowBooks

For all the latest book news, exclusive content and giveaways scan the QR code below to sign up to the Afterglow newsletter:

SCAN ME

afterglow BOOKS

The place to come for your next romance fix, Afterglow Books features authentic and relatable stories, character you can't help but fall in love with and plenty of spice!

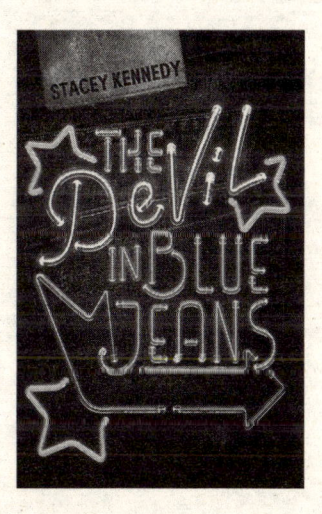

OUT NOW

New stories published every month, find them at:

millsandboon.co.uk

LET'S TALK
Romance

For exclusive extracts, competitions and special offers, find us online:

- **f** MillsandBoon
- **X** @MillsandBoon
- **○** @MillsandBoonUK
- **♪** @MillsandBoonUK

Get in touch on 01413 063 232

For all the latest titles coming soon, visit
millsandboon.co.uk/nextmonth